The Moon-God's Bride

First there were the eyes. A dozen, circular, burning and unblinking, big as plates, staring out in all directions from a dark, half-seen, half-suspected bulk.

Then—tentacles! Tentacles like nests of fat pink worms . . . tiny feet to carry the larger, heavier, true tentacles. And out from the pit, out from beneath the luminous eyes, those true tentacles now uncoiled, pink and translucent but pulsing with a green fluid. Thicker than a man's body, one, two, three—ten in all. Like the suckered arms of some sentient squid, but huge beyond belief!

The tips of the hovering tentacles opened like mouths as they descended on David Hero and his companions where they lay against the pit's wall. An open tentacle tip touched Hero's thigh.

Hero screamed then—more in agony than horror. Green juices flowed from the open mouth of the pseudopod and dissolved away a patch of his tough leather trousers—dissolved, too, the skin beneath. And now that mouth became a sucker, slurping back the *solution* which the green juice had become.

David Hero cried out again—this time in true horror—for now he knew how Oorn fed!

BRIAN LUMLEY

MAD MOON OF DREAMS

A TOM DOHERTY ASSOCIATES BOOK
NEW YORK

MAD MOON OF DREAMS

Copyright © 1987 by Brian Lumley

Cover art by Tim Jacobus

A Tor Book
Published by Tom Doherty Associates, Inc.
175 Fifth Avenue
New York, N.Y. 10010

Tor® is a registered trademark of Tom Doherty Associates, Inc.

ISBN: 0-812-52421-7

First Tor mass market printing: February 1994

Printed in the United States of America

0 9 8 7 6 5 4 3 2 1

Contents

PART THREE: *MOON MADNESS*

The Quest

PART 1

Mad Moon Rising

"In the waking world," said David Hero that weird night (Hero of Dreams, as he was sometimes known) to his friend and constant companion Eldin the Wanderer, "—if indeed the waking world truly exists—"

"Oh, it does, it does," Eldin rumblingly cut in. "I lived there once, and so did you; but I can't remember much about it, and you seem to remember even less."

"Well, then," Hero continued, a little miffed at being interrupted, "since your memory is so superior to mine, perhaps you'll recall the waking world's moon?"

"Its moon?"

"I mean, did it really *have* a moon?" Hero fumbled the question out, frustration plain in his tone as he struggled to plumb the murky deeps of memory. "*Was* there such a thing as a moon—in the waking world, I mean?"

They sat with their backs to the trunk of a massive cedar on the banks of the Skai, embers of a small fire glowing at their feet and sputtering acridly on the bones of a pair of trout tickled to death by Eldin's practiced fingers some hours earlier in the perfumed twilight. Hero's question, for all that it may have sounded trivial, naive and hardly typical of his usual patter (though certainly he was a romantic in his own way), was pertinent indeed in this particular place and on this particular night. Why, the pair had walked down the riverbank from

Ulthar just to be out in the open night air for the moon's rising; which must say *something* for its pertinence! That two such as these should be out here to witness a moonrise when they could easily be boozing or wenching or both . . . ?

"Was there a moon?" Eldin musingly repeated, frowning up into cloudless indigo heavens aglow with all the stars of night. "Why, of course there was! I remember it well, because . . ."

"Because?"

Eldin stirred himself reluctantly and shrugged. "Because it rhymes with June and spoon," he answered, however vaguely.

"Spoon?" Hero too sat up straighter. "Are you pulling my leg, old lad?"

"Of course not," the other sighed. "It's just that I remember how the moon featured in almost every love song. Moon over this or that—moonlight bay—silvery moon and blue moon—and so on." He shrugged again, somewhat self-consciously. "All very mushy, I know, but that's how I remember it."

After a little while Hero said: "Perhaps I do remember it. Blue moon and silvery moon, yes. But how about bloated moon!"

"What?" Eldin cried, aghast. "In a love song?"

"No, I suppose not," Hero was forced to agree; and his eyes suddenly narrowed as they stared across the star-strewn river. "After all, how in all the dreamlands could anyone write a love song around a monster like *that*, eh?" And he pointed toward a spine of distant mountains where even now a scabby, silvery-yellow rim floated up into view.

Spectral light flooded the valley of the Skai, paling the scattered lights of lanthorns in the towers of near-distant Ulthar and driving some of the lesser stars from the heavens. The moon rose higher, like the pitted pate of some luminous monster peering over the edge of the world, with shadowed craters for eyes. The dreamers climbed to their feet and absently dusted themselves down, then stood silently, in a sort of lunar awe, gleamingly illumined by the vastness rising up into the night sky of dreamland.

"Why, the damn thing's bigger than ever!" said Eldin, and Hero detected a shuddering note in the unusually hushed voice of his companion. "No," the Wanderer continued, steady once more. "No, I certainly wouldn't consider writing *that* moon into a love song! What do you make of it, lad? A moon that grows bigger and bigger each night—like a huge balloon, bloated beyond belief. Almost as if—"

"As if it were about to pop and fall in tatters!" Hero muttered, giving substance to Eldin's unspoken thought.

At that very moment, invoked it seemed by Hero's words, something did fall: a fluttering something that stilled the voices of the river frogs with its clapping and thrumming as it dropped to Hero's shoulder and clung there, rubbing its downy head against his cheek. Momentarily frozen in shock, he quickly recovered and put up a still trembling hand to carefully catch the bird about its slender body, drawing it down unprotestingly.

"A pink pigeon!" cried Eldin.

"A bird from the Temple of the Elder Ones in Ulthar," added Hero in a quieter tone, frowning as he took from the aerial messenger's leg a tiny cylinder, unscrewing its end and drawing out a tight wad of extremely thin paper. Eldin took a brand from the fire, holding it up to the paper which Hero now spread against the cedar's rough trunk. Written in the clean, clear glyphs of dream, they could read a message. It said simply this:

> "Hero, Eldin—
> Come at once to Ilek-Vad. Waste no time—there is none to waste. The dreamlands are threatened, and in your hands the power to save us all. A sky-floating ship awaits you in Ulthar, to bring you to Ilek-Vad. If you want a sign, only look at the moon!
>
> All speed—
> Randolph Carter."

As if satisfied with a job well done, the pigeon now flapped aloft and drew the eyes of the adventurers skyward. Moonlight streamed across the land, but not the healthy moonlight that Hero and Eldin were used to. No, it was a diseased, creeping moonlight, undulating down from a bulging monster moon which already filled slightly less than a third of the entire horizon. Sickly that moon, its evil power oppressive—and not alone over human beings. From far away came the baying howl of a wolf, a sound seldom heard in the dreamlands and a powerful omen, which was answered by a vicious and concerted feline spitting and yowling along the riverbank.

"The cats of Ulthar are restless tonight," said Hero, his own voice ashiver.

"Little wonder," answered Eldin, and added a low curse as the guttering firebrand burned his fingers. "This moonlight clings like a film of yellow sweat! What does it all mean, d'you think? What trouble brews?"

Hero shook his head. "At this rate we'll never know," he said. "But there's a quest in it for sure, on that you can bet. And the note said to hasten."

"Then let's hasten," grunted Eldin. "We've been idle for too long, lad, since our last adventure. We could use a little exercise."

"Oh?" answered Hero as he stepped out beside his friend along the river path. "A little exercise, you say? Well, if it's exercise you're after, I can feel it in my water that we're in for a lot!" And with that the pair grew silent as their pace quickened and their ill-lit strides stretched out . . .

Beneath that glowering, diseased moon, along the river to Ulthar, the shadows of the pair were long and inky when they emerged from the trees and strode the pebble path. Now, in that sickly moonlight, the men took on solid shapes and became more than the gray ghosts they had been beneath the cover of the cedars. And had there been an observer—a man or woman born of these lands of Earth's dreams, say—then certainly he or she would have recognized in these two a certain ... outsideness?

Outsiders, yes, for they did come from outside—from the waking world. There David Hero had been an artist of the weird and fantastic, and Eldin had been an erudite if somewhat eccentric professor specializing in psychology and anthropology. And both of them had been dreamers. Now late of the waking world ("waking-worlders," in the terminology of all true dreamlanders, those races indigenous to dreams which Eldin had dubbed *Homo ephemerans*), they had become questers—sellswords, thieves, adventurers for gain, rogues, call them what you will—in the land of Earth's dreams.

And dreams had been kind to them. Oh, they had not had an easy time of it, on the contrary, but so far they had come through all of their many adventures with flying colors. And in the process they had gained something of reputations. Some good ... some not so good.

Hero was tall, rangily muscled, blond as his waking self had been, good humored—generally—and slow to anger. Blue of eye and fast on his feet he was, bursting with easy laughter and yet, in a tight corner, wizard-master of his curved blade of jungled Kled; the dreamlands were fortunate that Hero was a force for good—generally. He loved a good fight, yes, but he loved songs and poems too. And girls quite a lot.

Eldin, on the other hand, was very different. He was older by a good fifteen years than his companion (though he didn't much like admitting it) and clad in night black as compared with the other's bark-brown; but the lands of dream have often known stranger companions. Perhaps it was their differences which made them so mutually attractive. Scarfaced, black-browed and a little apish in his movements—but exceedingly quick-minded for all that, and quick to anger on occasion, too—Eldin did have several things in common with the younger man. He shared the same wanderlust, for one, and the same sometimes acid sense of humor for another.

No room for humor tonight, however, not in David Hero and Eldin the Wanderer. Neither in them nor in all Ulthar; not with that giant moon of ill-omen hanging huge and heavy in the sky over the Skai. The cats of Ulthar, for which that venerable city was famous, were especially out of sorts, as witness their rooftop yowlings and increasingly malicious (if strangely sexless) caterwaulings; which carried clearly on the tingly air to the two where they left the river to come through the steep and winding streets of Ulthar's suburbs toward the city's tallest hill.

Crowning that hill, the vast and circular stone tower of the Temple of the Elder Ones stood ivied and ancient, and tonight its windows were aglow with numerous lanthorns; a singular circumstance in itself, in that half-fabulous and centuried fane of peace, quiet and changeless charm. Indeed, Ulthar would normally share these restful qualities with the great stone tower, but very little seemed normal in the dreamlands these days. For as the moon had waxed so it had become swollen and angry, and when it should have waned it had not done so but continued to bloat in dreamland's night skies, and for a fortnight now an unspoken madness had taken root in Ulthar as in all of dreamland's saner places. There was an unaccustomed bustle to the city's inhabitants and a half-hysterical babble to their voices.

So that even now, when by rights Ulthar should be sleeping, small parties of people hurried to and fro in the crooked streets, with numerous lanthorns bobbing in the darker districts, where even the whispers of lovers in garden bowers were hoarse and nervously shrill. And all of this silvered (or rather yellowed) by that sick lunar glare, whose touch was physical and left one feeling damp and filled with nausea; and the muted question on lips grown grotesquely pallid, seeming to echo to the adventurers from all quarters: "What is it? What is happening? What is wrong with the moon?"

What indeed?

. . . So Hero and Eldin climbed steeply in a street leading to the Temple of the Elder Ones, and as they turned a corner the tower came back into view and they saw the many lights that moved within. Above the tower and moored to its topmost turret, rocking slowly and majestically in the night breeze, the familiar shape of a ship of the sky was likewise illumined with moving lights; and even as they watched, spidery figures went up and down the rope ladders which fell from ship's side to ivied aerie.

"Surely that's *Gnorri II*!" cried Eldin, his bearded face inclined toward the aerial man-o'-war. "It's Limnar's ship."

"Aye," Hero answered, "I believe you're right. And a welcome sight, too!" He took the other's arm in steely grip and quickened his pace to a trot. "Come on, let's find out what Captain (or is it Admiral?) Limnar Dass can tell us about all this. Since he's been sent to fetch us, he must know something."

And in another minute they were entering in through the temple's oaken doors . . .

In the Temple of the Elder Ones

Inside the temple, young, shaven-pated acolytes identified the pair and took them to a room with a table bearing bread, meat and wine. Having already eaten, the adventurers merely picked at the food until Captain Limnar Dass (he had reverted to Captain in order to volunteer for the present job) was fetched from on high where he was supervising the provisioning of *Gnorri II*. Although Dass was *Homo ephemerans*, his ways were so like those of waking-worlders that he had been "adopted" by Hero and Eldin almost from first acquaintance. Now he grinned as he entered the room, greeting the pair in the gentle manner of the dreamlands and suffering their less than gentle clouts and buffets as they punched his shoulders and slapped him on the back.

Dass wore a trim beard, the loose-fitting blue uniform of a sky-Captain with the trousers tucked into the tops of wide-cuffed boots, and the aforementioned grin. He was tall for a man of the dreamlands, but his fine bones were light as those of birds, and his features—solid enough now—occasionally wore that blurred look which instantly gave him away for one born of dreams. Perhaps, somewhere in his family tree, there had been a man or a woman of the waking world; which might possibly account for the bond which existed between him and the adventurers.

The broad grin on the Captain's face quickly turned to a

frown, however, when his friends asked him to tell them what he knew of the mission. "But what more do I need to know?" he answered with a question of his own. "Isn't it obvious? The moon is—"

"—Is falling?" Hero finished it for him.

"I believe that's what they think, yes," Limnar answered.

"They?" growled Eldin.

"Kuranes of Serannian, King Carter of Ilek-Vad, Governor Dymnai of Dylath-Leen," Limnar shrugged. "All of the upper echelon," he finished.

"And do they know why the moon is falling?" Hero asked.

"Again, I believe so ... Let me tell you what I know of this thing so far—how come I'm involved—and by the time I'm done *Gnorri*," (he refrained from using the "II"—the loss of the original *Gnorri* would be a bitter taste in Limnar's mouth for a long, long time to come) "will be ready to sail." He cleared his throat, then took up his story proper:

"It started for me in Serannian—" he began.

"Of course!" Eldin gruffly cut in, as was his wont and a habit which never failed to annoy Hero considerably. "The sky-floating City of the Clouds! Naturally Serannian would be first to feel the influence of the mad moon, and her citizens first to suspect and fear the dread possibility of its falling!"

"Eldin, old lad," sighed Hero, "you become more expert each day at stating the obvious. Now do let Limnar tell it in his own way, else we'll be here all night."

The other merely grunted, then sat back and gnawed idly at a leg of chicken as finally Dass continued:

"King Carter was there at the time, during those first few days of the moon's monstrous swelling, on a state visit. Actually, I suspect he visits simply to spend some time with Kuranes, his old friend. Certainly he's not much for pomp and ceremony. Anyway, after the third night of the moon's unnatural bloating—when it became clear that this was something far more serious than mere atmospherics, that in actuality the moon *was* descending toward the dreamlands—then the King of Ilek-Vad cut short his visit and prepared to leave for home.

"Since his royal sky-yacht had returned to Ilek-Vad and was not due back in Serannian for a week, a ship was required to carry Carter home. Kuranes would not trust his care to any other," (Limnar shrugged, as if in apology for having been so honored) "—and so *Gnorri* was made ready and I got the pick of the finest crewmen in all Serannian.

"Now then, having already met you two—when you returned Aminza Anz to Ilek-Vad—"

"Please, don't!" Eldin groaned, holding up one huge hand flutteringly, protestingly, and putting the other dramatically to his forehead over lowered eyes. But in fact he had loved Aminza Anz dearly—right up to the moment of her return to the waking world! For Aminza had been a dreamer who eventually woke up. "Don't remind me," Eldin groaned again.

"Uh!—Sorry," said Limnar. "Anyway, King Carter and I had that much in common—knowing you two, I mean. And for all that the voyage back to Ilek-Vad was a short one, well, we got to know each other fairly well."

"Well enough for him to tell you what caused him to cut and run?" asked Hero.

"Hey!" said Eldin. "Whoa, boy! Randolph Carter's no ordinary man. Why, he's dreamed dreams you couldn't even begin to imagine!"

"Eldin's right," Limnar nodded. "King Carter is a master dreamer. Be careful how you speak of him."

"No offense," Hero held up his hands. "I'll rephrase it: why was he in such a hurry?"

"Two reasons. First, if the moon really is falling, there's a device King Carter can use to save at least Ilek-Vad. The city's master scientists and white mages long ago created a machine which, when it's used, throws a near-impenetrable screen—like a great dome of invisible force—over the whole city. The machine was last used during the Bad Days, but King Carter has the power to bring it back into use. Thus he

could perhaps save Ilek-Vad, even if the rest of the dreamlands were to be destroyed. That was his prime reason for returning home: to reactivate the great force dome. You see, his
first loyalty is to Ilek-Vad."

"What of his second loyalty?" Eldin grunted. "What was
this other reason you mentioned?"

"Why, to serve the dreamlands as a whole, what else?"

Hero nodded. "And just how does he intend to do that?"

Limnar shrugged. "We didn't get around to talking about
that—not at any great depth—but you can be sure he has
something up his sleeve. You have to remember, King Carter
is one of a very few dreamers ever to visit the moon and return unharmed! No mean feat, that."

"Aye," Eldin nodded his agreement. "The one sure sign of
a really powerful dreamer: to do what no man ever did before, to dream dreams beyond the mundane imagination."

"Oh?" Hero raised an eyebrow. "I don't find it so very
difficult to imagine. I would gladly undertake just such a
journey myself—for a good cause. Why, I've heard it whispered that the horned ones of Leng do the trip regularly in
those vile black galleys of theirs!"

"Right!" Eldin nodded. "That's how Carter got there,
shanghaied aboard one of those double-damned ships of the
horned ones. What's remarkable, though, is in the way he returned."

"Oh?" Hero still looked a trifle skeptical.

"Yes," said Limnar, "for he returned—"

"Don't tell him!" Eldin snarled.

"Eh?" said Limnar, astonished at the other's outburst.
"Why in the dreamlands not?"

Lowering his voice a little, Eldin turned just a shade pink
as he answered: "Because he—he'll scoff, that's why. He's
like that, is Hero."

"So don't tell me," Hero shrugged and pretended to pick at
his fingernails. "Let's face it, most of dreamland's legends
are a pack of damned lies anyway," he deliberately goaded
them. "Dreams and fancies, that's all."

"Dreams, yes," Limnar Dass had stiffened a little, "for dreams are the essence of existence. Lies—no!"

"A strong dreamer may direct his own dreams, guide his own destiny," Eldin growled. "Haven't you learned that much, lad? Is there still so much of the waking world left over in you? I mean, if you don't believe in dreams, then what the hell are you doing here in Earth's dreamland?"

"All right, all *right*!" Hero snapped at last. "Give me a chance, can't you? You said I would scoff. How do you know? Maybe I will believe! So just how *did* Randolph Carter get back from the moon to the dreamlands?"

"In a great leap of cats," said Limnar before the Wanderer could stop him. "He was rescued by the cats of Ulthar, who leapt down with him from the moon. That's one of the reasons why the felines have such special privileges in Ulthar. Like that old Tom there," and he pointed to a huge sleek cat which lay curled on a blanket in the corner of the room. "He's a temple cat, and that's an honor which was probably bestowed upon him for just such a deed as—"

"Cats!" said Hero, who had seemed momentarily stupefied. "A leap of cats? . . . Oh, my!"

"Huh!" Eldin snorted. "I told you he'd scoff."

"Now you have to admit—" Hero started, but paused and frowned when the temple cat sprang lithely atop the table and marched to a position central between the three where they sat. The great cat looked at Hero through half-shuttered eyes—disapprovingly, he thought.

"I've warned you to watch what you say," Limnar grinned. "Why, it's possible that this old boy is one of the very cats who rescued King Carter!"

While Limnar spoke, Eldin scratched the great cat behind its ears. In return the cat purred throbbingly and fondly arched its back against the Wanderer's brawny arm. Hero stretched out a hand to do the same—and the animal hissed, struck with a heavy paw, left crimson dew welling on the back of Hero's hand. Then even as he snatched back that wounded member, the cat was gone, leaping to the floor and

walking haughtily out of the room with never a backward
glance.

While Hero cursed, Eldin and Limnar laughed out loud and
thumped the table; but in another moment one of the Captain's crewmen entered the room to report *Gnorri II*'s air-
readiness.

"We'll be up immediately," said Limnar, still chuckling a
little, sending the man about his duties. Then the Captain
turned back to his friends. "Well, gentlemen, shall we go?"

"What?" cried Eldin. "And what of the preliminaries?
Why, we haven't agreed to the quest yet. Damn me—we
don't even know what the quest is!—Or, what's more to the
point, what's in it for us."

"That's all very true," Hero agreed, peering at his
scratches. "I mean, we didn't get much out of our last little
venture, did we? We are *professional* questers, after all. What
about payment?"

"Ah, but you *have* accepted!" Limnar contradicted. "Just a
few minutes ago. As for payment: didn't you say you'd do it
for a good cause?"

"What?" said Hero, beginning to feel a bit lost. "What's
that you say I said?"

"That you'd gladly journey to the moon," Limnar reminded him, "for a good cause."

"Now hold on there, Cap'n Dass—" Eldin blustered, but
this time it was the sky-Captain's turn to interrupt him:

"He said it, Eldin," Limnar repeated, "and he may very
well be held to it. Both of you, in fact, since it's well known
that you speak for each other. But that will have to be King
Carter's decision."

"I said it, yes," Hero began to protest, "but—"

"It was your boast," Limnar reminded.

"But—" Hero and Eldin started together.

"But why not look at it on the bright side?" Limnar interrupted again. "I mean, you may not be required to go
aquesting to the moon. I'm merely guessing, that's all . . ."

After a moment's silence, the Wanderer gave a derisive

snort and headed for the door. There he paused, turned, bowed and inclined his head toward the corkscrew stairwell. "Well?" he growled. "The ship's waiting. Shall we go?"

And as Limnar and Hero brushed past him he grated in the latter's ear: "You and that damned *mouth* of yours!"

In the Mad Moon's Glare

"What I find," said Hero when they were under way, "is that I'm restless. And not just because I've been on the run lately. I mean, I can't settle to anything. Not once the moon's up. Not in the sick glare of the mad moon."

"We're all the same," Limnar agreed. "There's a fever loose in the dreamlands once the moon has risen. Men and beasts alike, we all feel it, a madness blown on the night winds—blown down from that bloated moon."

Eldin shivered and said, "And we talk in whispers. Everyone talks in whispers, as if the blasted moon were listening! Me: I'm not used to it. I've roared in the faces of kings and lords, monsters, magicians and metal men—and yet, beneath this made moon, even my voice is muted."

"Hmm," said Hero thoughtfully. "It seems there's a bright side to everything!"

They stood on the smooth pine planking of the bridge and leant on the rail, gazing out over the nighted dreamlands where they lay below, all yellow and queasy in the near-liquid moonlight. And high overhead (and yet seeming so close that you might reach out a hand and touch it) the mad moon sailed in a sort of gloating glory through the sky, her mountains and craters clearly defined and etched with inky shadows.

"Even on this ship," said Limnar under his breath, his

whisper breaking what threatened to become a sort of hypnotic strangulation. "Look at the crew, all abustle—and half of them ought really to be in their hammocks by now. Do you feel the breeze? It feels damp, but if you put your hand up to your face it's dry. What kind of moonlight is it that flows like dry slime?"

"Enough!" muttered Eldin with an involuntary shudder. "Let's go inside Captain, and crack a bottle of your fine wine. My throat's parched as a witch's tit, and my eyes would much prefer lamplight to the leering illumination of old Luna there!" And all being in agreement, they made their way to the Captain's cabin.

There, comfortable about Limnar's table and enjoying sips of his clean, clear wine, listening to the slow creak of timbers and relaxing a little as the lamplight glowed in their faces and shifted with the gentle roll of the ship, the waking-worlders soon began to feel more themselves. Then it was that Limnar bade them relate their doings since last he had seen them. That had been in the seaport of Baharna on the Isle of Oriab in the Southern Sea, where he had dropped them following the destruction of Zura's fleet of black galleys in the sky off Serannian.

"And while you're about it," he added, "you might also like to tell me what you've been up to that's so upset the twin Dukes of Isharra."

"You know about that?" Hero questioned in return.

"Only that they're after your blood," said Limnar with a nod. "And something about two girls, also twins, who you're supposed to have abducted and seduced?"

"Huh!" grunted the Wanderer. "How the truth gets twisted, eh, Hero? Listen," he turned to Limnar, "and I'll tell you how it really was." For a while Eldin was silent as he poured himself more wine, and then he began:

"Ula and Una were beauties," he said with feeling, "and they threw themselves at us. Seduction? I hate to admit it but you're right—except *they* seduced *us*! Their reason? Simple. Their daddy had arranged for them to marry these ugly buggers, the so-called Dukes of Isharra, and to qualify they had to be virgins. The girls had minds of their own; they ran off to Baharna and found themselves a pair of likely lads; us, Hero and me."

"And I," said Hero.

"I said you," Eldin grunted. "Be quiet!"

"Go on," Limnar pressed. "Let's have the rest of it."

"The rest you've already guessed," Eldin shrugged. "Ham Gidduf, Ula and Una's daddy, put a big price on our small heads—bounty-hunters came after us in force—we had to flee Baharna in a hurry. We stole a boat—"

"Again," said Limnar, knowing that this was nothing new to the pair.

"—And with a lot of luck and fair winds we made it to olden Dylath-Leen on the mainland," Eldin continued. "There we laid low for a couple of weeks—"

"Until a certain ship sailed in and disgorged a gang of cut-throats on Isharra's business," Hero put in.

"—And so we left town under cover of darkness (of which there wasn't too much due to the size of the blasted moon), crossed the desert until we hit the green banks of the Skai, and followed the river up into Ulthar. We were planning to move on when the temple pigeon found us."

"A neat trick, that," said Hero as Eldin finished. "Those birds: how do they do that? Find people like that, I mean, and at night too?"

"The priests of the temple could probably tell you," said Limnar, "but they wouldn't. A little magic, one would presume."

"And would one presume that these people who are tailing us also have magic on their side?" the Wanderer asked. "Or is it simply killer instinct that enables them to track us so surely? They were in Ulthar less than a day behind us, which is why we were planning to move on."

"Magic, no," Limnar answered. "Instinct, yes, probably. The Dukes of Isharra are not only ugly, they're evil. And rich. They can afford to hire the best in bounty-hunters. Oh,

I suppose they might have suborned a magician, but it's doubtful. Magic men usually manage to keep themselves out of that sort of trouble."

"White magic men, sure," said Hero, frowning, "but what about a sorcerer? A black magician? To my knowledge they're not so funny about who they work for."

Limnar shook his head. "Not many of that sort in the dreamlands," he said. "And they're usually loners. They do their plotting or whatever far from the haunts of common men."

"Right enough," agreed Eldin. "Old Thinistor Udd was just such a one—until we put a stop to his little game."

"Well, if magic's not involved," mused Hero, "this time we really ought to have lost them. They'll surely not track us through the night skies of dreamland!"

"Which leads me to my next question," said Limnar. "Did you two plan to run forever? It's not like you . . ."

"Listen," said Eldin gruffly. "We were hoping they'd tire of the chase. If they didn't—" He shrugged.

"Then we'd choose our times and places," Hero continued Eldin's explanation, "and we'd pick them off one by one. And they pretty soon *would* tire of that sort of chase!"

"Murder?" said Limnar.

"Self-defense, surely?" the Wanderer half-snorted.

"We're not murderers," Hero added, "but we don't skulk either. Not for the Dukes of Isharra or anyone else."

At that precise moment, as if to fill an awkward silence, there came a loud banging on the door of the Captain's cabin. Murmurs of awe and amazement reached the three even through stout wooden walls, then hoarse exclamations as the crew reacted to some unseen wonder. As the banging on the door resounded, more urgently than at first, Limnar barked, "Enter!"

The door crashed open and a crewman stood silhouetted against a deep yellow glare, as if limned against a sky of flaring saffron. "Captain," the man croaked. "The sky . . . the moon . . . !"

"What in all the hells—" Limnar hissed. And in the next moment the three men were springing to their feet, sending tankards and stools flying as they raced for the door.

Hero was first out onto the bridge, then Limnar followed by Eldin. They made for the rail, their eyes staring skyward and following the gaze of those crew members who gathered there. Limnar knocked several of the latter aside and ordered them down onto the deck proper to tend to their duties. They went . . . but they could not take their eyes from the moon, that mad moon whose sick yellow gleam was now a blinding glare, a'pulsating, throbbing brightness like bile vomited up by some great, golden, alien idiot!

Hero shielded his eyes against the ever-brightening glare. "That crater there," he gasped. "What in all the dreamlands . . . ? Is it volcanic? Something is spewing out—a beam of brilliant yellow light—and yet more than a beam. Look!"

Limnar and Eldin were looking, hands to their eyes as the great globe of the moon seemed to loom momentarily over the ship, as a giant looms before his foot comes crashing down. Then—

The heavens seemed rent asunder! A great wind blew downward from the moon, blasting the clouds outwards and leaving a clear path in the heavens. *Gnorri II* felt that mighty rush of air and reeled as her sails were filled and her masts bent before the sudden onslaught of frenzied air. And blown off course as she was—tossed aside like a cork in a flooding river—it was that very moon-spawned maelstrom of wind which saved the ship and her passengers.

For now that mighty moonbeam was reaching down like a solid yellow shaft, and through all the tumult of air there rang a long, humming, continuous *sound* like an unending note struck from some great golden anvil or cosmic tuning fork. Down swept that titan moonbeam, expanding, rushing past *Gnorri II* and striking earthward, striking at the surface of the dreamlands.

Still at the rail, where they clung for their lives as the ship tossed like a leaf in a gale, the three friends gazed down along the path of the great moonbeam to see where it struck. Down there, lit by the evil glare, a hamlet nestled in a bay on the coast of the Southern Sea.

Yellow roofs and paths and fields and gardens—and the vast moonbeam falling to earth and engulfing all! For a moment the beam glared brighter yet, until its liquid fire threatened to burn out the eyes of the three where they stood frozen at the rail, but then—

The golden note rose higher, became a whine—the near hypnotic, faithless song of a siren—and the moonbeam began to retreat, to flow *backward* along its own path! Not rushing in retreat, no, for this was no rout; almost languorously, writhingly, with a seductive swirling and twining of golden streamers, the beam drew back. And the single note became an almost animal sound, a vast exhalation, the concerted sigh of a million lovers falling back from a scented night's excesses.

Struck dumb the three could merely listen and look: listen to that slowly changing sigh of sound as it became a massed moan, long-drawn-out, low, pitiful and seeming to signify all hope lost; look as the long golden funnel of light flowed upwards, a tube of irresistible force, the honeyed tongue of a sated siren. Sated, yes, for within that hideous haze of yellow fire—

"By all that's merciful—" Eldin hoarsely cried.

"Nothing of mercy here!" was Hero's gasped denial.

"Monstrous!" whispered Limnar. And again: "Monstrous!"

For that beam of light was no longer empty, no longer a mere shaft of golden fire and mindless allure. No, it was filled now. Filled with writhing humanity: the twisting, twining forms of the moon-blasted hamlet's inhabitants! Men, women and children all—the entire population of that doomed village—their faces staring blindly, in petrified terror, staring up the path of the beam, along which they were drawn like thistledown, resistlessly and inexorably toward some horror as yet unknown. . . .

Through the Dome

CHAPTER IV

From then on the winds were fair, filling *Gnorri II's* sails and blowing her on a course straight as the path of an arrow. All through the rest of that night they sailed, through the sunrise and morning and into the afternoon. Then, ahead, the Cerenerian Sea was sighted and the mighty promontory of volcanic glass where towered the splendid city of Ilek-Vad.

Approaching from the west, Limnar's ship began a gentle descent as her flotation chambers were vented and gravity began to exert its natural pull; and then, on the desert sands below, in the shade of a tiny oasis, a nomad encampment was sighted and the Captain took his crystal-lensed glasses to the rail. This was little more than curiosity on Limnar's part, but after peering for a moment through the long-barreled glasses he stiffened and turned to Hero and Eldin where they lay sunning themselves on the bridge.

"Hero," he called. "Eldin, what do you make of this?"

Feeling inordinately weary after a night of muted discussion about the mad moon and its terrible beam, Hero sighed and stifled a yawn as he got to his feet. He moved to the rail where Limnar handed him the glasses, and yawning again he idly focused the instrument on the small encampment far below. Then he too stiffened. "Horned ones?" he grunted, surprise and sourness in his voice. "Camped here so close to Ilek-Vad? They're a long way from home."

"Eh?" Eldin now stirred himself. "What's that you say? Lengites? Camped here? What are they up to?" He got to his feet.

"Nothing," Hero grunted. "They're just camped—and there are too few of them to pose any sort of threat to Ilek-Vad."

"Hero's right," said Limnar with a nod. "Ever since the Bad Days people have shunned the horned ones as if they were rabid dogs, but they're not much without leaders. During the Bad Days they were working for Cthulhu's minions in dreams, and those were rough times for the gentle folk of the dreamlands. But that's just so much history now. The horned ones backed a loser, and they paid for it."

"I've heard about that," Eldin grunted. "It was a couple of waking-worlders stopped 'em, right?"

"That's right," Limnar nodded again. "Titus Crow and Henri-Laurent de Marigny, but they didn't stay here very long . . ."

Hero became interested. He gave back the glasses to Limnar and said, "You mean they woke up?"

The sky-Captain shook his head. "No, not really. You see, they had a machine. A wonderful machine which enabled them to go . . . anywhere! To most men in the waking world the dreamlands are places which exist only in the deepest reaches of the subconscious mind; places a man might now and then visit when he sleeps and dreams, which are forgotten when he wakes up. But with their wonderful machine—which they called a 'time-clock'—Crow and de Marigny could come here any time. Or go anywhere else for that matter. When their work was done here—" He shrugged. "They left."

"Now why can't we do that?" Hero slapped his thigh. For all that he should know by now that he and the Wanderer no longer existed in the waking world, still he hungered for that part of himself which must remain forever lost.

"We are dead men," Eldin answered with a sigh, "late of the waking world, which proved fatal to us. How many times do I have to explain? To anyone who ever knew us, we are long dead and gone and buried. Do you know what we are in the waking world? A couple of markers over unvisited graves, that's what we are. But here in the dreamlands—we live on!"

For a moment there was agony in Hero's eyes, but then it passed. He relaxed and said, "You're right, old lad, and I'm a fool." He managed a grin. "Damn me, but I'd rather be a quester in the land of Earth's dreams than a corpse in the waking world! It's just that . . . I wish I could remember more of how it was. But every day it slips farther away."

"Better forgotten," Eldin rumbled, but his face too showed that he had felt those same bitter pangs—if only for a moment . . .

". . . Ship *ahoy*!" came the sudden cry from the crow's nest, and all eyes followed the pointing arm of the lookout where he leaned from his station on high. There between *Gnorri II* and Ilek-Vad's fabulous towers and minarets, proudly riding the sky and flying the colors of King Carter himself, the Royal Yacht of Ilek-Vad sailed under billowing purple.

In a little while the two ships closed with each other and Limnar hailed his counterpart aboard the Royal Yacht. "Ahoy there, Captain E'tan. Is something wrong? We're expected, surely?"

"Aye, Captain Dass," the other called back, "that you are. You and your passengers, David Hero and Eldin the Wanderer. I'm only here to lead you in—to ensure your safe arrival."

Limnar immediately bristled. He was sensitive in the area of his aerial ability (though in fact he had no need to be, for he was a very fine Captain indeed). Perhaps it was because he had lost two of his ships in the war against Zura, though that had been through no fault of Limnar's. "You're what?" he yelled. "Now I know you captain the Royal Yacht of Randolph Carter, E'tan, but I really don't think I need anyone to see me safely berthed. I'm pretty well experienced myself, you know."

"I'm sure you are," the other hurriedly agreed, "but you

need me for all that. Since you've been gone from Ilek-Vad
they've activated the force-dome. You won't get through
without me. If you'll just follow on behind, however—"

Limnar reddened. "Captain E'tan, I—"

"I fully understand," the other cut him off. "If I had stated
my business with a little more diplomacy, you would not be
embarrassed. My fault entirely. And certainly I did not mean
to belittle your skill, of that you may rest assured."

"My thanks," said Limnar gratefully, "—but I still don't
understand. Surely the dome is only effective against outside
manifestations? That is to say, inimical forces or beings not
truly of the dreamlands?"

"True in the case of the old dome, aye," Captain E'tan
agreed, "which was more magical than material. But this new
dome is far more powerful. It admits nothing!"

Limnar nodded across the gap. "I'll follow you," he said,
and he shouted the necessary orders to his crew. A few minutes later, as they approached the city single-file at a height
of some five hundred feet, the Royal Yacht's bow cannon
roared and a single shot rocketed from its muzzle. It might
seem to any observer that the ship fired on the city, but this
was not so. In the next instant the shot fragmented against an
invisible wall and released a scarlet stain which spattered
here and there and ran in streamlets toward the earth below.
It did not fall in droplets but *ran*, as down a solid surface;
and in other places the stain remained, hanging (or so it
seemed) upon a curtain of the very air itself.

Still sailing forward with no reduction of canvas, now the
Royal Yacht fired off a pair of signal rockets which burst
high on the dome in twin showers of crimson stars. For a few
seconds these fireballs cascaded and jumped and sputtered
down the curve of the dome—but in the next moment all the
sky over Ilek-Vad seemed to shimmer and blur to the gaze,
and the smoking firework fragments fell straight to earth. The
dome had been momentarily switched off.

The ships passed through, and then behind them the air
once more shimmered momentarily as the dome was reacti-

vated from somewhere within the city. Hero took Limnar's elbow and said: "Seems to me we really did need E'tan's help, eh?"

"Aye," the other nodded, shrinking inwardly as he envisioned a wrecked *Gnorri II* sliding down the invisible wall to her doom.

Eldin, who had been looking thoughtful for some little time, now spoke up. "Captain E'tan said that this dome admits nothing?"

"True enough," answered Limnar. "Look over there. Now that we know the dome is here, why, you can see how the clouds are piling up against it and sliding around it!"

"The Royal Yacht's marker-shot certainly shattered on something," Hero added. "Surely you see that, Eldin?"

"Oh, I see all right," the Wanderer answered, and he fell musingly silent.

Hero sighed. "Go on then," he prompted after a little while. "Let's have it. Say what's on your mind."

"I think," said Eldin, squinting skyward, "—I think that for a wall which admits nothing—well, that there's an awful lot of sunlight shining down on Ilek-Vad! Also, the air is as fresh in here as it is out there . . . Also—"

"Also?" Hero and Limnar pressed together.

"If a ray of simple sunshine may pass through the dome," Eldin continued, his voice falling to an uneven mutter as he vexedly chewed his lip, "why not a beam of mad moonlight?"

Which left the others with nothing to say in return. Nothing at all . . .

When *Gnorri II* was safely anchored and floating on air only a few feet above the gardens of the central palace, then the two sky-Captains disembarked, greeted each other properly and exchanged a few words. There was little enough time to spend, however, for the Royal Yacht was one of four of King Carter's ships at present on watch in the skies about Ilek-Vad, and she must be under sail and about her duties immediately.

Thus the sky-sailors wished each other luck, following which E'tan returned to his vessel. Shortly thereafter the Royal Yacht climbed toward heavens in which the first star was still to appear, her purple sails filling against the clear evening sky.

Now Hero and Eldin had been here in Ilek-Vad before, though admittedly in happier times and under more auspicious circumstances, and they were not total strangers to the palace and its customs. What did surprise them was that Randolph Carter himself, always the soul of hospitality, was not there to meet them; for after all they were here on the King's business and at his bidding.

Several of the King's ministers were available, however, to escort Limnar and his waking-worlder friends into the palace proper. One of these, an old and valued counsellor named Arra Coppos, explained to them King Carter's absence as he led them through marble halls and mirrored passages to a sumptuous inner sanctum.

"The King considers the present threat to the dreamlands of such a grave nature that he has gone personally in search of a solution," said Arra. "As to when he went——" the old counsellor peered at the three through thick crystal spectacles. "Had you arrived three hours earlier you might have had time for a few words with him. But do not ask me *where* he has gone: that is something I may not presume even to guess."

They had come to a room whose centerpiece was a huge divan or raised dais of marble, covered in rich silks and soft cushions. Candles burned at its four corners, emitting exotic scents. There reclined a pair of silk-robed, motionless forms, wan and breathless as corpses, seemingly frozen in death. Here Arra put a finger to his lips, signifying silence; and he led the visitors to stand at the foot of the huge couch, gazing upon the two where they lay. King Carter was one, the other was unknown to the three, though Limnar Dass suspected that he knew of him.

Then, after a little while, maintaining the silence and without more ado, the long-bearded counsellor led them from that place and toward rooms of their own where food awaited them. As they went he said: "You know King Carter, of course, but de Marigny was probably strange to you."

"De Marigny?" Eldin's ears pricked up. "I thought he had left the dreamlands long ago?"

"That was Henri-Laurent de Marigny," Limnar explained. "This one's son." He turned to Arra. "I take it that the other sleeper upon King Carter's couch is Etienne-Laurent de Marigny?"

"You are correct," Arra answered. "He and Randolph Carter were friends in the waking world long before they renewed that friendship here in the dreamlands. The difference between them is this: that Randolph Carter found his destiny right here, as King of Ilek-Vad, which he loves above all other places. But Etienne—he was always a seeker after mysteries, a wanderer of strange ways, the eternal explorer. The dreamlands could not hope to contain such as him. There his shell lies upon that couch, as it has lain for many a year—but where is he, eh? Not here, I assure you, no! For he has dreams of his own, which have taken him out to the very limits of the cosmos."

"And King Carter?" questioned Hero. "What of him?"

"Why! Is that not obvious? He has gone in search of his old friend, to see if perhaps he knows the answer to the mad moon's monstrous bloating."

"Then King Carter himself did not have such an answer?" Eldin grunted. "But surely he must know something; why else would he send for us?"

Arra shrugged apologetically. "Be sure there was a reason," he answered. "Perhaps his letter will explain. He wrote it in the hour before he sought the Great Sleep, and now it waits for you in your rooms . . ."

King Carter's Letter

When Arra showed them to their rooms they bade him enter with them, and stay while they read Randolph Carter's letter. The letter was sealed in an envelope bearing the royal insignia. It lay on a table which also bore plates of food and several large bottles of wine. Limnar saw the envelope first, picked it up and weighed it thoughtfully, then passed it to Eldin. The Wanderer tore it open, glanced briefly at several fine sheets of crested paper, handed them to Hero. The latter coughed, glanced once into the faces of his companions, and began to read out loud:

> *Hero, Eldin, and whoever else it may concern—*
> *I have gone where few others could ever follow,*
> *to seek out an old friend of mine long departed*
> *from the lands of Earth dreams into the dreams*
> *of alien universes. I may find him, I may not. I may*
> *return, and . . . the guardians of the gates to alien*
> *worlds are strange and terrible and their moods*
> *are often unfathomable. If I do return, it may be*
> *that I shall have an answer to the encroachment*
> *of this demon-ridden moon upon the dreamlands.*
> *If I do not return . . . then at least you shall know*
> *what I know, and may the knowledge guide your*
> *actions accordingly and rightly, to the common good*

*of all the lands of Earth's dreams and the peoples
who dwell therein.*

 First, the threat as I see it:

 *1. An unholy alliance between the horned ones
of Leng and certain **inhabitants** of the moon has
been an established fact since my own younger days.
Indeed, the toad-like, tentacled moonbeasts are the
true masters of those horned almost-humans from
Leng. Some of my contemporaries, however, have
seen fit to believe that since the Bad Days the Lengites
have mended their ways; that they are now honest
traders in gold and jewels. This is not beyond
the bounds of possibility, since Leng is vast and
largely unknown and may well harbor huge mineral
deposits of precious stones and metals.*

 *Personally, I believe that the horned ones are
inherently evil, that they do not belong in any
corner of the sane dreams of Man, and that they
have not given up their allegiance to the moonbeasts
at all but, if anything, that they yet pursue their
old and utterly despicable ways with more vigour
than ever! And I further believe that the raw materials
of their trade are not found on Leng's nighted plateau
but brought to the dreamlands from the moon.
If I am right, what, pray, do the moonbeasts get
in return? What nameless services do the horned
ones perform for their polypous masters?*

 *Nor are my attitudes and suspicions too harsh
in this matter, I assure you: my own experiences
with the almost-humans were such that I could not
be mistaken; and I have always warned the sane
inhabitants of dream against any dealings with
them. Now I say this: that unless an end—a **total**
end—is put to them, they will bring down a doom
on the dreamlands quite beyond conjecture and
certainly beyond my limited powers of
description.*

2. *The twin Dukes of Isharra (Byharrid-Imon Isharra
and his brother, Gathnod-Natz'ill Isharra, of whom I
believe you may have heard?) are a pestilential pair
whose record is a veritable register of greed, treachery
and brutality, and a mire of seamy criminal activities in
general. Only their wealth has so far prevented punitive
retaliation; they have purchased themselves an army of
thugs (to protect their assumed "nobility") and have
always managed, through graft or intimidation, to buy
off any suits or actions brought against them by those
they have wronged.*

*I am given to believe that they were gangsters
in the waking world, whose activities in the stews
and gambling dens of a large and largely corrupt
city earned them "concrete wellingtons"? And
yet they were dreamers, too, though I can only imagine
that their dreams were both vicious and avaricious
as they themselves. However, I do not govern
access to these dreamlands (nor could I desire
that responsibility) and who am I to say who should
or should not dwell here once he becomes defunct
in the waking world? But I do know that we
would all be far better off without them.*

*Now it is a known fact that the goldmine which
supplied Isharra's wealth has recently become played
out. The vein has dried up; there is no more gold
in Isharran earth. The business of the Dukes
might therefore be expected to decline. This has not
been the case; indeed their trading has expanded
extensively until they have a foothold in the great
majority of dreamland's regions. It has become
noticeable, too, that the quality of their gold is not
what it used to be. A metallurgist friend of mine informs
me that it is quite indistinguishable from Leng's
gold which, as I have said, I do not believe is
mined in Leng at all.*

3. *Let me now go on to mention one or two*

associated facts, or facts which I consider to have associations with the above, before we draw any final conclusions.

Firstly: it appears that the Dukes of Isharra and the horned ones of Leng trade with each other in gold, and then that they **vie with each other** in the sale of that precious metal at ridiculously low prices! Unscrupulous dealers in all corners of the dreamlands are snapping up vast amounts of so-called "Leng" gold as fast as they can. Now I can hardly blame them for that; it is their business after all and they would be fools to miss such advantageous opportunities. But ... How best may I make my point?

If the horned ones have a monopoly on gold, which I believe they have, **why do they bother to deal with Isharra at all?**

Secondly: it is rumored that both Isharra and Leng have recently had dealings with Zura; Zura the land, and Zura the vile Princess of Zombies. To what end? Not to any end beneficial to the dreamlands, you may be sure. Similarly, galleys of the horned ones have been seen sailing into Thalarion, whose hive queendom is ruled over by the Eidolon Lathi. Now I know that you believed you had destroyed that monstrous Queen of termen hordes (and indeed I am sorry you have not!) but she lives still and her termen with her; aye, and they have started to build Thalarion all over again from the ashes you made of that execrable paper city. And the Lengite galleys that sail so readily into the stench of that place—why!—they sail **out** again, which could never have happened in the olden times. If Lathi does not destroy them, what, pray, **does** she do with them? What hideous plots are brewing even now in dreamland's darker places, and how may we deal with them?

4. Finally, and in an attempt to tie all of these

*foregone facts together (even though I am well aware
that I could be wholly mistaken), I will draw my own
conclusions. This is how I see it:*

*For some as yet unknown reason or reasons, the
malignant side of dreamland is recruiting and massing
its forces. We may count Leng, Isharra, Zura and
Thalarion as being the enemy. Something sinister is in
the wind in respect of the massive distribution of
"Leng" gold. Worse than all of this, the moon draws
closer every night, bringing a madness and a terror to
the sane and civilized places of Earth's dreamland.
When it comes (whatever the culmination of all this will
be) I am sure that the push will be massive, its
machinations monstrous, and its effects devastating!*

*Moreover, it may well be that the root of the
problem— the enemy command post—lies within the
moon itself. If I may be permitted to digress for a
moment:*

*In olden Theem'hdra, the waking world's Primal
Continent at the dawn of time, the moongod was known
to some as Gleeth, to others as Mnomquah. It is
interesting to note that there were no cults dedicated to
Gleeth, for he was that smiling, serene god of the full
moon whose round, yellow, changeless face was formed
of craters and mountains. He was a blind god and
deaf—blind to the revels of lovers, mercifully deaf to
the death-screams of warriors—and he had no
favorites. In short, he was an elemental god whose
presence was reassuring to the primitives of a dawn
world.*

*He and Mnomquah, however, were not one and the
same god. No, Mnomquah in no way corresponds to
Gleeth; for where the latter was a half-imagined face
espied on clear nights, the former was very real! He
had his cults, his sacrifices, his dark worship . . . and
he has them still. I suspect that the moon's jelly-like*

toad-things worship him to this day, but of course I can't prove it . . .

In that time when Cthulhu and the Great Old Ones oozed down from alien stars and dimensions and built the throne-city of R'lyeh in the waking world, Mnomquah was one who fashioned himself a mighty crypt at moon's heart, there to rest from his billion-year's journey across strange universes. Aye, and when the Elder Gods came and sealed Cthulhu and his ilk in their immemorial prisons, Mnomquah too was sealed in the moon. His mate, Oorn, however, fled before the coming of the Elder Gods. They found her somewhere in the dreamlands—it is not known where— and prisoned her where she was found.

Now this last is lore; it is written in the **Pnakotic Manuscripts,** *which I have read—though often I wish I had not—and it might explain many things which must otherwise remain mysteries. The influence of the moon at its full on dogs in the waking world and cats in the dreamlands—and men in both dimensions. The incidence of lycanthropy. The strange activities of gaunts and ghouls. Aye, and it is of old renown that dreamland's gugs and ghasts became the subterranean things which they now are because they could not bear the moon's glooming upon them.*

Now, I have taken a few moments to read over all I have written here, and I find it jumbled and less than completely coherent. But . . . I am in haste, and it says most of what I desired to say. As to why I called upon you for aid: you have more than once proved yourselves true friends of the dreamlands, while yet you have retained certain instincts and talents of the waking world. If I had ten such as you, then I know the threat could be combatted, contained, conquered . . .

Kuranes has promised aid; three of his vessels are on their way from Serannian even now. Three more ships of my own fleet are standing by at your

*command. Also, I have sent a letter to one
Gytherik of Nir, of whom I have heard many good
things. He is a friend of yours, I believe, who in
some way controls a grim of night- gaunts? That
is something I must see with my own eyes! And
then again, perhaps not . . .*

*And now I must away. If I can find my old friend
Etienne-Laurent de Marigny out there in the lands
of alien dreams—or perhaps Titus Crow and the
marvelous time-clock—I am sure that either one would
make an ally of fantastic strength and amazing ability.
As to the dreamlands, these beloved lands of
Earth's dreams: I leave them in your care. They
are yours to protect as best you can, and so I command
it. How you will do so is your concern, but I am
convinced that you, above all others, have the
necessary skills.*

> *Use those skills wisely, and wish
> me luck as I wish it for you—
> Randolph Carter.*

Hero finished reading and looked up. "He knew nothing of
the moon's magnetic beam," he said.

"Eh?" Arra's eyes peered through the thick lenses of his spectacles, moving from one face to the next. "Beam? Magnetic?"

"Well, perhaps not magnetic," Limnar answered, and he
quickly told what they had seen of that terrible attack from
the moon and how close they had come to being trapped in
the beam's golden, nightmare net. And as the sky-captain
talked, Eldin caught Hero's arm and drew him to one side.

"What Limnar just said," he grunted low in his throat.
"About the moon's 'golden net'—"

"Yes?" Hero pressed, frowning. "Go on."

"Well, you know how a northstone always points north, or
toward any massive concentration of iron?"

"Yes, of course. What are you getting at?"

"King Carter's letter went on about the horned ones and

the Isharrans selling vast amounts of gold at ridiculously low prices," Eldin's voice was growing louder as it picked up momentum, his excitement plainly visible in the bristling of his beard.

"That's true," Hero's frown deepened. "But iron is iron and gold—"

"Is gold!" Eldin cried. "Are you blind? How do you suppose the mad moonbeam finds its targets?"

Meanwhile Limnar and Arra had drawn close, listening to Eldin's reasoning. Now Limnar said: "And that party of horned ones we saw, so close to Ilek-Vad. Do you suppose . . ."

At that moment a palace attendant appeared at the door. He bowed nervously, and to Arra Coppos said: "Arra, Lord, a strange thing—"

The four turned toward the newcomer and Arra answered, "What's that? Something strange? Of what do you speak?"

"One of the King's patrol vessels has just now returned to the city," said the man. "They found something in the desert to westward, and they brought it back with them."

"Found something?" said Arra. "What did they find?"

"A statue, Lord. In the image of King Carter himself, and seated upon a great horse."

Arra sighed. "And you disturbed us to tell me that? There are many statues of the King. Some sculptor has doubtless been at work in the seclusion and privacy of the desert. Is that so strange?"

"No sculptor, Lord," the man replied. "Goldsmith, perhaps!"

Eldin stepped forward and grabbed the attendant by the satin lapels of his jacket. "Are you saying that this—this *statue*—is fashioned of gold?"

"Indeed, Wanderer, that is what I am saying . . ."

Eldin released the man and wheeled to face the others. "The last time something like this happened the horse was of wood," he gasped. "If I remember aright the name of the city was Troy—and she was doomed no less than Ilek-Vad!"

The King in Gold

CHAPTER VI

"This statue, where is it now?" Eldin snarled. His face was a mask of mixed emotions—mainly fear, but not for himself. For the city, for Ilek-Vad.

"In the gardens, Lord Wanderer," the bewildered attendant haltingly answered. "By the great fountain." And he shrank back before the four, unable to understand and unnerved by the tensions he had thrown into them.

"Show us," cried Hero. "Come on, man, quickly—lead the way!" And he thrust the little man out of the room ahead of him into the corridor.

"Arra," said Limnar to the old counsellor, "Do you think you can find this metallurgist friend of yours? I would like him to see this statue before we move it back out of the city."

"I know where he is," Arra nodded, glad to be of service. "I'll bring him at once." He turned on his heel and headed in the opposite direction.

"And what time is moonrise?" Eldin cried after him.

"An hour or so at most," Arra called back. "You'll find it's grown quite dark outside."

"Arra." This time it was Hero calling. "Can you muster the Master of the Dome, whoever he is? The chief technician or magician or whatever, the one who controls the shield about the city?"

"There are several," the answer came back as the counsellor passed around a bend in the corridor and disappeared from view. "I'll send the top man to see you in the gardens," his voice trailed off.

Now the three friends clattered along hot on the heels of the small but fleet-footed attendant; and though they ran for all they were worth, still the way through the great central palace seemed far longer than it had been when they entered. At last they burst into the gardens and headed for a mighty fountain where it jetted water to a height of a hundred feet or more.

Unfortunately *Gnorri II* was moored some hundreds of yards away, her sails furled, crew gone "ashore"; it would take some little time to get the men recalled and the ship ready for the skies. And as Arra Coppos had pointed out, it was now quite dark and the moon would soon be up. The ship which had brought the statue into Ilek-Vad had already left to carry on with its patrol; it stood off in the sky, a dark silhouette that sailed for the invisible wall of the dome where soon it would signal its need to exit.

And now the three saw the statue itself: a massive, crudely structured thing. Obviously the golden figure which sat the golden horse was that of King Carter, but he was in no way flattered. There was something sardonic about the statue: the King's lips displayed a spiteful curl, and the horse's nostrils flared viciously while its ears lay flat along a lumpy, less than elegant head.

"The thing's a mockery!" cried Limnar. "The king is not like that—nor would he sit so mean a beast. No, this work should be destroyed."

"First it must be shifted," Eldin grunted, his eyes keenly scanning the as yet quiescent horizon. "You can destroy it later if you wish, but not until we've moved it. Aye, and if we don't move it right now—why, *it* will very likely destroy *us*!"

Limnar needed no further urging. He was already running toward *Gnorri II*, his voice ringing through the muted lighting of the gardens, calling his skeleton crew to him and ordering that they get into the city at once and return immediately with as many of his men as they could muster. Hero and Eldin were close behind him, offering their help, full of a hideous frustration, a monstrous urgency. And even as they ran, so the mad moon's pitted rim rose like the notched blade of some cosmic scythe behind a distant range of mountains.

"Ropes!" Limnar was shouting. "Hawsers and nets, tackle to lift ten tons of gold!" Then, as a new thought struck him: "No, belay that. I'll have ropes, yes, but get me a dozen of the ship's flotation bags. There are plenty of spares below. Fire the flotation engines and get 'em filled at once." He turned to the waking-worlders to explain, but Hero cut him short:

"By the time the crew gets back we'll have the statue roped up to your flotation bags. We can tow the thing out of the city!"

"Right," Limnar answered, "but not with *Gnorri*. She'd never make it, for the wind has died away. No, we'll have to manhandle it."

"What?" cried Eldin. "Why, it's two or three miles to the wall of the dome!"

"So?" Limnar turned on Eldin with a snarl which would do the Wanderer himself justice. "We tow the damn thing, I said, and so we do. And we start before the crew gets back. When they return they can spell us. It will be a hard job and a slow one—agonizingly slow. So the sooner we get started the better."

By now a small party of men was hurrying out of the palace gardens and into the city proper, and others aboard the ship were dragging balloon-like flotation bags onto the deck, attaching mooring ropes and tossing the loose ends down to the three. Others of the crew came clambering down rope ladders to lend a hand, and soon the first two bags were being hauled across and roped to the statue. Amazingly buoyant (and despite the fact that they were only part-filled), each bag took three men to hold it down, so that in the darkness they looked like massive kites in tow behind frantically toiling, grotesquely bounding children.

Seeing their struggle, many of the city's people came into the palace gardens to offer their help. These were mere passers-by, folk on evening errands eager to be home before the moon was full risen. But the urgency of Hero, Eldin, Limnar and his men was infectious. The common folk of Ilek-Vad could not help, however, but only served to get in the way. They were truly *Homo ephemerans* and now, where physical bulk and muscle were needed, they seemed more insubstantial than ever and all of their efforts less than useless.

But at last members of the crew of *Gnorri II* were returning from their brief excursion in the city, and under orders from their Captain they were soon far more effective. Something of the waking world's vitality had rubbed off on them from Hero and Eldin (particularly onto Limnar Dass), giving them an unaccustomed purpose and direction in the land of Earth's dreams. And so at last the massive golden statue of man and horse began to move, suspended beneath a cluster of flotation bags, dragged along behind a gang of men, through the palace gardens and into the city's streets. And all of this taking place as Limnar had said it would; agonizingly slowly. The great statue kept getting stuck in narrow alleys where the balconies of houses jutted out over cobbled streets; the ropes would make themselves fast to ornate stonework; the flotation bags threatened time and again to burst against the spiny ironwork of balcony rails or wrought iron signs above the many shops. But somehow, after what seemed like several hours, the sweating, swearing, weary gang maneuvered the clumsy aerial thing out through the suburbs and toward the wall of the force dome where it reared invisibly to the west of the city.

Now out in the open, the toilers could see just how high the moon had risen—the vast pitted orb of it, whose lower edge was just clearing the horizon of hills—and the sight renewed their flagging strength and drove them to further excesses of muscle-wrenching labor. A slight breeze had sprung up which caused no end of trouble: being enclosed by the dome, the gusts of air came from no certain direction but tugged the balloon-borne mass of metal this way and that, willy-nilly. And now the gold of that awful work was a sickly yellow to match that of the clammy moonbeams which fell in nauseous waves from on high; and the sardonic face of the golden King of Ilek-Vad seemed demonic in the terrible light, and the eyes of his steed full of moon madness.

"Damn it!" cried Eldin in a rage, putting his massive strength to work and hauling on a rope until the muscles bulged in his back, arms and legs. "We're not going to make it!"

"We *must*!" Hero answered, straining just as hard, his teeth gritted against the night and yellow with sickly moonlight. Then, exhausted for the moment, the pair handed over their ropes to a team of *Gnorri II*'s crewmen and rested a while. Limnar joined them, and a moment later a figure came running from the city where it sprawled behind them on its great glass promontory.

"Lord Hero," gasped the man, struggling to draw air, "Lord Eldin and Limnar Dass. I am Eeril Tu, the Master of the Dome. Arra Coppos sent me . . ."

"Listen, Dome-Master," Hero grabbed hold of the newcomer. "I've a feeling your dome is useless against the mad moon. Its beams come through unaffected, and there's a special moonbeam which might yet suck us all up to hell! Now tell me, how may the dome be strengthened?"

"Strengthened?" The man had his wind back. "It may not be strengthened! All available power is already in the dome, but it will not shut out the light—it will not shut out moonbeams."

Hero gripped him tighter and almost shook him. "There *must* be something else you can do. Think, man!"

"I am thinking, Lord," the other gulped and wriggled in Hero's grasp. "Perhaps—"

"Yes?"

"The city has a battery of ray-projectors, Lord. The batteries store energy—the energy of the sun—during the day, and so may be used at night. They were used in the Bad Days. Their clean light draws the life out of foul and evil things, burns them up, removes them utterly."

"But moonbeams have no life!" Hero cried, his frustration mounting. "Of what use—"

"Fight light with light!" Eldin snapped his fingers. "It might just work."

"What?" Hero and Limnar asked in unison. "What might work?"

"Let the ray-projectors play their beams onto the ceiling of the dome," Eldin grunted, "into the descending moonbeam when it comes. Diffuse the damn thing, scatter its evil rays, destroy its power!"

"You," Hero turned back to the Master of the Dome. "Eeril Tu. Do you follow the Wanderer's reasoning? Good! Now get back to the city. Have the ray-projectors manned and prepared. It's worth a try. Only run now, run!" And he released the Dome Master and propelled him on his errand with a hearty shove, sending him hurrying back in the direction of Ilek-Vad.

By now a second stranger had joined the party. He introduced himself as Jahn Killik, Arra Coppos' metallurgist friend. "I've seen the statue," he told them, peering up at its yellow bulk where it rocked in its cradle of ropes beneath the flotation bags. "Leng gold for certain. You can tell by its sickly sheen. Fine and rich by daylight, but damp and strangely oily in the night. Anything else you'd like to know?"

"No," Limnar shook his heed. "We already guessed as much. Thanks anyway, and no-thanks. For in your confirmation you may just have sealed the doom of Ilek-Vad!"

"Four hundred yards to the dome's wall!" came a cry from somewhere in the darkness ahead. "And look," the crewman's voice continued, "a ship approaches!"

"A patrol ship," said Limnar, his eyes taking in the silhouette of the vessel where it sailed the night sky beyond the invisible dome of force. "One of the King's ships. Look, there go its signal rockets!"

Twin streaks of fire raced up the sky like ascending meteorites, bursting in crimson balls high on the dome and showering sparks down its mighty curve. Deep in the city the signal was seen and the night air seemed momentarily to shiver as the dome went down. The ship came sailing in, and in its wake—

"What?" cried Hero, his hand pointing skyward. "Do you see that?"

For a split second, limned against the moon's ogre face, it had seemed that a flock of great silent birds followed the patrol ship through the de-energised screen. In the next second the air shivered again—and was instantly astir with a throbbing of great wings. But wings fanning the night: a sound that Hero, Eldin and Limnar would recognize anywhere, any time.

"Gytherik!" Hero breathed. "The gaunt-master has arrived in answer to Randolph Carter's summons."

"Aye," Eldin agreed with a similar sigh. "And not a moment too soon!"

The Doom That Came to Ilek-Vad

"Ahoy up there!" shouted Limnar Dass, cupping his hands to his mouth and using his Captain's hailing voice. "Gytherik—we're down here!"

The throb of wings, momentarily receding, immediately resounded. "Is that Limnar Dass?" came a youth's strong but surprised voice above a sudden stir of air and a whirling of dust.

"Aye," now Eldin gruffly called. "And Eldin the Wanderer."

"And David Hero, too," Hero added his voice to the hailing, glaring at his companions for omitting to mention him.

The air became a tumult of small, rushing winds as a grim of gaunts, all horns, barbed tails and leathery wings, landed close by. Leaping down from his saddle on the largest of the faceless beasts, a slim, pale-faced youth—a lad barely out of his teens—stepped forward through the glare and the dust. "Hero?" he queried. "Eldin? Limnar?"

"All present and correct, Gytherik," Hero answered, taking his arm. "Come into the shadow of this rock. Give your eyes a chance to get used to this hellish yellow dazzle. It will only take a moment."

"We may only *have* a moment," said Limnar. "The mad moon rides high—look!"

A few wisps of cloud hurried across the face of the bloated monster in the sky, as if eager to be gone and out of harm's way. Looming in the heavens, the great pitted disk looked like some ancient golden coin, bruised and abused by time, and its "face" of mountains and craters wore a look of pure malevolence as it seemed to gaze down upon Ilek-Vad.

Eldin shivered in spite of the sweat which made his clothing hot, heavy and sticky. "By all that's holy," he said, "—I swear I'll never more cuddle a girl by moonlight. Not so long as I remember this night!"

"Which may not be for very long," Limnar repeated his warning. He turned to Gytherik. "Lad, can you get your gaunts to tow this golden blasphemy out through the force-dome? At once, before it's too late?"

"A dome of force!" cried Gytherik. "So that's what it is! Come to think of it, I've heard of Ilek-Vad's force-dome. It was used in the Bad Days. My gaunts sensed it was there, of course, but it completely baffled me. Fool I may be, but not my gaunts. They followed yonder ship of their own accord, under no instructions of mine! And you wish that statue taken outside the dome, eh?"

"Indeed," Limnar answered, "and urgently!"

"So be it," said Gytherik. He turned to where the grim, eight strong, clustered together in the scrub. The creatures were ill at ease in the mad moon's glare, shuffling uncomfortably and using their membrane wings like vast umbrellas to keep the moonlight off their bodies. Gytherik gestured, no more than that, and at once the gaunts spread their wings and sprang skyward. In a second they had snatched up the ropes from astonished, struggling teams of crewmen, and in the next they were towing the statue straight for the invisible wall.

"But how are they to get out?" Hero asked of no one in particular. "What about the signal?"

"I thought of that back in Ilek-Vad," Limnar answered, drawing out a pair of rockets from his jacket. "*Gnorri* carries signal rockets, too, you know."

He jammed the sticks of the rockets in the crumbly soil, angling them toward the dome. Eldin produced firestones and struck sparks, which soon ignited the touchpapers of the fireworks. And as the rockets sputtered, spewed fire and leaped skyward, so the gaunts reached and were brought up short by the invisible wall; at which very moment—

"Trouble!" Hero saw it first: that heightening of the yellow glare about the crater which formed the mouth of the monstrous moon-face, the throbbing pulse of it, like the vast heart of some alien living thing. And rising (it seemed out of the very night), there came that note struck from some great golden tuning fork, that nerve-scraping single note that went on and on and on.

"*Big* trouble!" roared Eldin, throwing up his hands before his face as the brilliance of the moonlight increased so as to become painful. "Where the hell are those ray-projectors?"

High overhead the rockets burst in crimson splashes, and on the very instant there came that curious trembling of atmosphere which signified the screen's subtraction. The gaunts shot forward, dragging their aerial burden after them across the now open threshold.

"Now tell them to let go the statue," Hero shouted in Gytherik's ear above the brain-numbing whine (which, it suddenly dawned on him, were it colored, would have to be bright yellow!) "—and if you want to keep them, get them back on this side of the line before the screen goes up again!"

Gytherik asked no questions; the near-frenzied urgency so visible in his friends had finally communicated itself to him. Instead he put fingers to mouth and blew a great blast of a whistle, and moments later the gaunts were landing in their ungainly fashion like faceless pterodactyls and cowering once more beneath their own arcing wings.

"Now we'll feel the dome go up," shouted Hero, his voice barely audible over the sudden rush of winds which struck *downwards* from the sky, "and after that—then we should see these much-mentioned ray-projectors in action, and—" He paused uncertainly. Something was wrong ... Desperately wrong.

"No dome!" roared Eldin. "Do you think some fool in the city misinterpreted Limnar's signal? And how could it be misunderstood anyway? What in hell is going on? And by all that's ... *look at the moon!*"

But in fact they could no longer bear to look at the moon. Its sick brilliance was such that the entire sky was a saffron dazzle that seemed to flow like some mighty aerial ocean of steaming bile. And at last there came that sound they had all dreaded—that change in the *tenor* of the dinning single note—that gradually rising whine which they knew was harbinger of the monstrous moonbeam.

"Doomed!" groaned Eldin. "The beam descends!"

Then, through seconds which seemed to last for hours, all was a nightmare of languorous slow-motion, of senses suspended almost to the infinite. A vast sigh went up like a wind rising over a forest; and despite the blinding brilliance of the sky, all eyes turned up to that epicenter of horror, the mad moon. A nameless longing—a hideous fascination—filled every heart; arms were raised to the sky as to a promise of splendors and delights beyond endurance.

Hero knew in his inner being that this was wrong, an utterly unholy adoration, but could do nothing about it. The others were the same, even Gytherik's gaunts, lifting their wings for flight and craning their rubbery necks skyward. In the city, lured by that magnetic beam and unable to still the craving, people erupted from their houses and crowded into the streets; and even the blind gazed into the moon's sick Cycloptic eye, and cripples stumbled in the glare and raised their arms to a deliverance of doom.

Back on the desert in the scrub and rock, Hero and friends were now filled with a peculiar lightness—not only of heads but of bodies, too—and from somewhere deep within himself, fighting the hypnosis which gripped his mind and body in rigid iron (golden?) bands, Hero found the strength to croak: "Eldin—damn, I'm floating! My feet are off the ground!"

"Me too, lad," came an answering groan, "—and all the others. We're in the beam, moon-bound!"

And slowly they floated free of the desert, inches at first, then feet as the stony ground receded—at which point the night seemed to give itself a mighty shake, brilliant beams of white fire sprang upward like dazzling searchlights from the city, and gravity returned in a tumbling of bodies and a thumping of earth as by a shower of mammoth hailstones! The force-dome was up, the ray-projectors in action, the doom averted.

No one had fallen more than six or seven feet, some much less, and casualties would be light. There would be broken bones in the city, especially among the aged; here on the desert it was all bumps and bruises and the occasional groan or moan, but mainly thankful sighs.

Hero, dusting himself down, strode purposefully for the city, his face contorted with rage. Eldin, limping a little from a sprained ankle, hurried to keep up. He understood his young friend's muttered curses and complemented every one of them with a few choice remarks of his own. Limnar Dass, too, where he came running up behind.

"I've a bruised behind, a fat ankle and a lumpy elbow," Eldin growled. "Someone will pay for it!"

"What the hell was the delay?" Hero demanded of no one. "Another second or two and we wouldn't have survived the fall. Ten seconds and we'd have been sucked right up to the moon! I've a few questions for Eeril Tu, you may be sure ..."

Gytherik's slightly shaken voice floated down to them from where he once more rode his great gaunt. "Want a lift, you three?" He spoke a word to the strange creatures he controlled. Gaunts paired off, two apiece to Hero and Eldin, and picked them up. A fifth, second largest of the grim, grabbed up Limnar. Not a man of them was able to suppress the not unnatural shudders they felt at contact with the silent, faceless night-gaunts; despite the fact that they were accustomed to this mode of travel, still there was that about the creatures which repelled and disgusted. Old myths and legends die hard, and Gytherik's gaunts were a living denial of dreamland lore from ages immemorial.

Now the ray-projectors were in repose—their brilliant beams no longer illumined the mighty dome's ceiling—and the night had returned to normal . . . or as normal as might be expected with that bloated moon sailing the sky, its sickly, all-enveloping light coloring the desert, the city and the ocean beyond the promontory a sweaty yellow. Up above, retreating like the snatched-back tentacle of some frustrated, golden god-octopus, the mesmeric moonbeam shrank down into its source in the mouth-like crater and dulled into quiescence. The terror had passed—

—For the moment.

And beneath that moon of madness, the human-burdened grim sped cityward, and jut-jawed men clung tenaciously to prehensile paws which alone kept them from gravity's jealous grasp . . .

A surging, cheering, lanthorn-bearing crowd—a mob of delirious people—greeted the aerial party as it passed overhead and across the rooftops of the suburbs into the city. Plainly the people had connected the golden statue's removal from Ilek-Vad with the barely averted doom; and they knew that they had Hero, Eldin and Limnar to thank for a timely intervention. As for Gytherik Imniss: since Zura's defeat at Serannian, most everyone in the dreamlands had heard of the young man with power over gaunts. And since Gytherik was with the trio he must be that man, for they had all fought for Kuranes in that same war against Zura.

A second, smaller crowd waited in the palace gardens. These were mainly palace staff, but among them Eeril Tu was supported by a pair of hefty guardsmen. As the grim landed Hero saw the Master of the Dome—saw too the blood-stained bandages which swathed his head and the sling which supported his right arm. Close followed by Eldin, Limnar and Gytherik, Hero ran to Eeril's side where he was greeted by the counsellor Arra Coppos.

"A near thing," said Arra. "And indeed I stand amidst heroes this night!"

"What happened?" Hero growled. And to Eeril: "Who bloodied you?"

"They did," the Dome-Master answered, and he pointed painfully to where a pair of shrouded bodies lay upon stretchers in the grass. "I was with one other engineer in the tower which houses the dome's machinery. I saw your signal and switched off the force-field. Then, when I would have switched it on again—"

"These two jumped you, eh?" Eldin bent down and tore aside the sheets which covered the strangely squat bodies of the traitors. The two were quite dead—their slant eyes closed, their faces waxen—but still their too-wide mouths seemed to grin as at some evil secret, and the shapes formed by their peaked turbans were terribly suggestive. Eldin ripped away the turbans and his lips drew back in a snarl of loathing. "Horned ones of Leng!" He spat out the words.

Limnar nodded. "King Carter was right about the Lengites. Well, we can make a safe guess as to how these two got into the city: they must have waited for a patrol ship to enter and slipped through while the screen was down. We know where they came from, too: that party we saw out in the desert as we flew in aboard *Gnorri*."

"Right," Hero growled again. "And by the same token we know where to go to get some answers! But tell me, Eeril—if this pair jumped you, who jumped them?"

"As you can see," Eeril answered, "they didn't quite finish me off. I took a clout on the head and a knife thrust in the back, and they must have thought me done for. The lad I was with got the worst of it, but I'm told he'll recover . . . Anyway, when I came to—it could only have been seconds—the horned ones were peering out of the tower windows and grinning evilly, and I could see that the dome was still down."

"And even injured you managed to take them?" Eldin's voice was full of admiration.

Eeril nodded. "More by good luck than anything else," he

modestly stated. "I snatched a knife from the belt of one of
them, and before they knew what was happening I had managed to stab them both. Then, when I would have switched
on the dome, I suddenly found myself weightless and floating
toward an open window. Outside the glare was awful and a
hideous sound filled the night. I felt half-hypnotised—weak
from loss of blood and yet filled with an awful fascination—
but as I floated over the machinery I stretched down my hand
and at last switched on the dome's power. Then I fell, and—"

"And knew no more until you were found sprawled in your
own blood," Arra Coppos finished it for him. The old counsellor turned to Hero and company. "The ray-gunners had
been similarly affected by the mad moonbeam, but when the
dome came on they were released from the trance and immediately began to fire their weapons. The rest you know . . ."

"Man," said Eldin to Eeril Tu, "you should be abed." He
laid a massive hand gently on Eeril's good shoulder. "Aye,
and a hero's bed at that. Ilek-Vad must care well for you.
Well indeed, for without you the city was surely dead this
night!"

Black Ship of Leng

Through the rest of that night—what little remained of it when the adventurers finally got to bed—they slept a sleep of utter exhaustion in which there was no room at all for dreams within dreams. Up at dawn's first light, they were aboard *Gnorri II* and gone from Ilek-Vad before the city's less exotic citizens were even out of their beds. Westward they headed, out through the invisible force-screen and across the desert and scrublands.

They left behind the three ships sent by Kuranes of Serannian, which had arrived during the night and were now provisioning, and three others of King Carter's fleet which were ready to sail but not required immediately. Limnar had spoken to the commanders of the latter trio, asking that they remain in Ilek-Vad until the newcomers were fully provisioned and rested; then that they lead them out over the desert to an aerial rendezvous in the west. By then *Gnorri II* should have had time to locate and deal with the Lengite party, and from then on the course and actions of the sky-flotilla would be governed by whatever the leaders of the expedition had learned from those treacherous horned ones.

Back in a palace tower, Arra Coppos and several others of Ilek-Vad's dignitaries watched the ship until it was gone from sight, then turned to those tasks which must now commence to ensure the safety of the rest of dreamland's peoples. For word must be sent to all of dreamland's cities, towns and hamlets warning of the peril in so-called "Leng gold," of the dangers inherent in any sort of trading with the horned ones, and of Zura's, Thalarion's and Isharra's complicity in the moon-doom now threatening these lands of Earth's dreams.

The first step would be to get a message to Ulthar, for then the messenger-pigeons of the Temple of the Elder Ones would make light work of the rest of the task. And once word of the terror began to spread, then the work would gain momentum, accelerate, until all regions near and far would know and take steps to combat the danger.

As for Hero, Eldin, Limnar and Gytherik; their task was equally immediate, and they pursued it with an urgency apparent in the way *Gnorri II* forged westward under full sail. And as they sailed, so the adventurers exchanged stories of all that had passed since last they were all together. When it was the gaunt-master's turn he shrugged, pulled a wry face, then set about to explain why the months between had been for him less than happy ones.

"As you know," (he said) "I used the egg of a Shantak-bird to break the spell which kept my father, Mathur Imniss, in the underworld cave where Thinistor Udd had prisoned him. Then I flew him home, back to Nir, where my mother was waiting. Of course, their reunion was wonderful and the first month was sheer bliss for all of us. I had not realized how much our adventures had wearied me, and now I could simply relax and take things easy. But—

"I had to look after my gaunts. Now, you'd think nightgaunts would be simple creatures to tend, wouldn't you?" He shook his head. "Not so. They don't like too much daylight—not any, in fact, though they'll work in sunlight for me—and Nir is a particularly bright spot. They prefer to sleep in caves, of which Nir is particularly lacking; and worst of all they like to fly by moonlight (normal moonlight, that is) and the people of Nir didn't much care for that. Gaunts have a very bad rep, as you probably know . . .

"So what with cooping them up in a stable, and them

frightening the yaks—and their moonlight excursions frightening the townspeople—and the Town Elders forbidding me
to ride with them (which they said was unhealthy and unnatural and a bad example for the village children . . .) well—"

"Pretty miserable, eh?" Limnar commiserated.

Gytherik nodded. "Just so. Miserable for me and worse for
my gaunts. Listen, I want to tell you something. Would you
believe, I actually think I *like* my gaunts?"

Hero frowned. "Oh, I wouldn't go so far—but I can't deny
they've been damn useful creatures in their way."

Again Gytherik nodded. "Anyway, it got so bad for them
they really began to suffer. They grew even thinner; their
bodies lost all their horrid *feel* and became almost dry and
bearable; it was awful! I had the gauntest gaunts in all the
dreamlands, I'm sure. And when word got out that a gaunt-
master dwelled with his grim in Nir . . . why, people flocked
to see us! We were like freaks, my gaunts and I."

"Pretty grim," Eldin said, with never a trace of humour.

"I don't think I could have taken much more of it,"
Gytherik went on. "I planned to return to the mountains, perhaps to Thinistor's complex of caves. I could study magic
there, become a sorcerer—a white one, of course—and generally make something of myself. It seemed to me suddenly
that something was missing from my life, and finally it
dawned on me what it was."

"Adventure!" said Hero with conviction. "Eldin and I are
just the same when things are too quiet for too long. You've
got the bug, Gytherik. Once a quester, always a quester.
You're stuck with it, lad."

"You're right," the youth answered. "So you can imagine
how delighted I was when King Carter's letter reached me—
particularly when I learned I was to be in league again with
you lot . . ."

Hero turned to Eldin and grinned. "Funny how *Homo
ephemerans* grows more like *sapiens* with continued contact,
eh, old lad?"

"It's a two-edged sword," Eldin answered. "I seem to remember my old mother warning me that I should stop being a dreamer or else the day might come when I couldn't wake up. Seems she was right."

"Curious, that," said Hero.

Eldin was pleased. "You think so?"

"Yes. I've never thought of you as having a mother."

Before Eldin could muster a sufficiently blistering answer, a lookout at the rail called out: "We're there, Cap'n Dass. This is where we spotted those Lengites yesterday on our way into Ilek-Vad. You can still see the remains of their camp in and about the oasis."

The four got to their feet around the small table Limnar had had set central on the bridge. "Time to bring on your gaunts, Gytherik," the sky-Captain said. "Let's see how they perform as bloodhounds!"

The gaunt-master went down onto the deck, threw back the covers of a large hatch and called out two of his gaunts. Sniffer and Biffer, he called them, two of the smaller gaunts with certain individual peculiarities of their own. Sniffer could follow scents and trails with deadly accuracy (though how this was accomplished with neither nose nor eyes was hard to say!) and Biffer was endowed with a completely uncharacteristic aggressiveness. Hence Sniffer would track the almost-humans while Biffer flew overhead on the lookout for ambushers and such.

Up onto the deck the two waddled and flopped in their gaunt fashion, uncomfortable in the rays of the morning sun but eager to please their human (at least dream-human) master. He spoke to them, in no language *Gnorri*'s crew could hope to understand, and they shortly flapped overboard, and circled down to the desert floor. At the oasis Sniffer quickly picked up the scent of the horned ones, at which Biffer soared aloft, higher even than *Gnorri II*, to scan ahead with aggressively out-stretched neck.

Soon Sniffer was flapping north-westward, ten feet or so above the sand and scrub, and *Gnorri II* changed course to follow the speeding gaunt. Hours passed in this fashion, with

gaunts and ship following a more or less straight course, and
the day gradually grew toward noon. The sun was high and
hot and Gytherik began to worry about the welfare of his
gaunts. The rest of the grim was safe and cool below decks
in the cargo hold, but Sniffer and Biffer were starting to suffer from the sun's bright rays.

Just as the gaunt-master decided to call back his pets,
Biffer began a frantic swooping and circling overhead, motions which were interspersed with a deliberate and very ag-
gressive pointing forward. At that very moment, as Gytherik
whistled the pair back to the ship, the reason for Biffer's agitation came into view: a squat black galley rising from behind low hills some miles to the north-west.

"A Leng ship!" cried Limnar. "Fat, black and ugly! She
must have picked up our quarry."

"Aye," Hero nodded, "and see how she rides so heavy?
Her cargo is gold, I'll give you odds! Leng gold—moon gold!
That's where your King Carter caricature came from. Well,
we can't just let her run. There are Lengites aboard with answers to our questions. It's battle stations, Limnar—but whatever happens we have to take at least one of the
almost-humans alive!"

"Ahoy, crew!" the sky-Captain called down to his men.
"Get me within hailing distance of yon black galley. We talk
before we attack—and then perhaps we'll not *need* to attack.
But it's battle stations anyway, just to be on the safe side.
Right—let's go!" And he clapped his hands sharply.

There followed a flurry of activity. The crew prepared for
aerial action; Gytherik brought out the rest of his grim onto
the deck, where they clustered in the shade of the sails; Hero
and Eldin donned swordbelts, swords and other small arms,
and *Gnorri II* sank down to the level of the Leng ship and
cautiously approached. Within hailing range at last, Limnar
put hailer to lips and called:

"Ahoy there, ship of Leng. This is Captain Limnar Dass
speaking. Admiral Dass of Kuranes' sky-fleet. I know your
purpose here and my crew is at battle stations. Make no false

move but oblige me by descending to the desert whence you came. We will follow you down."

After a slight pause, back came an answer in the guttural accents of Leng. "Ahoy, Dass of Serannian. This is free airspace. Your actions border on piracy. Leave us in peace and begone!"

"Begone?" Limnar sputtered, his eyes widening in disbelief. "Begone?" He returned his lips to the hailer and roared, "Listen, you lippy Lengite! Land on the desert at once, or by all that's holy I'll—"

A puff of smoke erupted from a cannon's muzzle where it projected from one of the black galley's ports. More puffs followed suit, all along the side of the black ship. An instant later there came the roar of the cannonade, and at the same time *Gnorri II* shuddered as she was hit by two or three of the balls. Part of the stern rail shattered and leaped skyward where a fourth shot struck home.

"Conventional cannon!" roared Eldin, reeling at the rail as the ship rocked.

"Theirs may be," raged Limnar, "but mine are not!" And to the gunners he roared: *"Return fire!"*

Gnorri's cannon opened up on the instant, their balls chewing gaping holes in the black galley's substructure. And out from these holes poured a swirling green gas, a vapor which every man aboard *Gnorri II* remembered from the war against Zura. For this was that gas which neutralized a skyship's flotation essence, denying her aerial buoyancy. *Gnorri II*'s cannon balls were filled with the stuff under pressure; they were designed to fragment within a ship's hull, rupturing the enemy's flotation bags and destroying her essence.

More shots found their mark, until the black ship staggered from their impact. Her hull was now full of green gas, and such was its efficacy that already she was listing badly to port. She fired back, but lying at an angle as she was her gunners were faced with an impossible task. Their shots whistled harmlessly overhead.

"She's going!" Limnar yelled. "One more volley, now . . . *fire!*" And again the black ship shuddered as fresh holes appeared in her flank. Then, suddenly, her stern dipped steeply and she began to spiral down out of the sky. Members of her almost-human crew could be seen sliding down the tilting decks and falling like ants from the rigging. Her altitude was not great, however, and her spiralling descent more a glide than a fall proper. In less than a minute her twisting mass struck the desert in an explosion of planks and a snapping of masts, and the screams of her crew could plainly be heard echoing up on the desert's thermals.

Then, as *Gnorri II* began her own far more leisurely descent, scuttling figures could be seen running (and some limping) from the wreck of the Leng ship and hurrying off into the desert to hide. Seeing these refugees of the wreck, Gytherik turned to *Gnorri*'s captain.

"Hold it, Limnar," he said. "No need to go any lower than this. Sniffer here can seek out a couple of horned ones for us, and the rest of the grim can bring 'em back alive for questioning." He went to the gaunts, grunted and gestured, and in another moment the grim was airborne and falling like a flock of leathery vultures to the floor of the desert. There Sniffer did his work with dispatch, and in a very short time a pair of struggling, fearful almost-humans were deposited none too gently on *Gnorri II*'s deck.

"It's question and answer time," Eldin growled low in his throat. "And if no one objects, I think I'll ask the questions!"

Eldin: Inquisitor

"You know," said Hero in a quiet aside to Limnar and Gytherik, "it's a funny thing, but of all dreamland's unhuman creatures and beings, I reckon these almost-humans are just about the most obnoxious. I mean, I'm even learning to appreciate gaunts—a little. And I've had dealings with Zura's zombies and Lathi's termen. The former can't help themselves and the latter are more termites than men. They have insect instincts—termentalities, so to speak. But *these* buggers—"

"They are something else, I agree," Limnar answered. "And I believe I know why we find them so objectionable. It's because they are what they are: almost-human. Zura's zombies, whatever they are now, were *once* men, poor creatures—and Lathi's termen *never were* men. But the Lengites *could* be men! That is to say they're intelligent, they have emotions (I think), they trade with men—however dubiously—and they share other human traits. They are, literally, *almost*-humans! That's what so disgusts you: the fact that creatures so nearly men should be so, well, *un*-manlike."

Gytherik gave a little shudder. "Me, I prefer gaunts any old time. Even ghouls might be better than horned ones. King Carter, I'm told, has a personal friend in the ghoul-leader, who himself was once a waking-worlder. So ghouls can't be all that bad."

"I never met a ghoul," Hero shrugged, his attention on Eldin, "so I don't know. But just look what the old lad's up to." Half-frowning, half-grinning, he nodded in Eldin's direction. "You can talk about un-humans all you like, but when it comes to devious minds there's nothing to touch the minds of men. And my pal there can be devilish devious when he's of a mind."

The Wanderer had had the Lengites trussed up in small nets, to each of which he had attached a rope. Now, on his instructions, as *Gnorri II* sailed higher, her crew lowered the horned ones over the side and made fast the ropes to the ship's rails. Eldin, grinning, leaned over the rail and peered down at them. He casually picked at his nails with the razor-sharp point of a wicked-looking knife.

"Right, you two," he said at last to the helplessly dangling pair. "Your Captain called us pirates, so I don't see why we shouldn't act the part. That being so, this is my version of walking-the-plank. It's called cutting-the-rope. I'll explain how it works ... Are you listening?"

Their yellow eyes gazed hatefully up at him; but each in his turn, they nodded. "Good," Eldin continued. "Right then, this is how it works: I ask questions and you answer them—truthfully. If you don't answer, or if I suspect you're lying, then I cut through a little strand of rope. There are perhaps ten such strands to each rope. Now you black-hearted sods being what you are, there are bound to be lots of lies, which means that sooner or later one of you goes whistling down to the desert. *Splish!*" Eldin paused a moment to enjoy the low moans of terror which now floated up to him from his squat, until now silent, captives. Finally one of them spoke:

"You could not do it," came the creature's paradoxically oily croak. "Your much-vaunted human compassion would never allow it."

"That voice," said Limnar, frowning. He crossed to the rail and peered over. "Your red sash gives you away, my friend," he said after a moment, speaking to one of Eldin's victims.

"Your sash and your voice. You are—were—the Captain of the wrecked ship!"

"As one Captain to another, then," came the gravelly answer, "I request you put an end to this and set us free. These waking-worlders are marked men. If you side with them you too are marked."

"When I asked you to land your ship you fired on us," Limnar was quick to remind. "You are now paying the price. What the Wanderer does with you is no concern of mine." He moved away from the rail.

"Which leads me to my first question," Eldin continued. "How, exactly, are we marked men? Hero and me, I mean?"

The almost-human Captain clamped his wide mouth firmly shut and glared up at Eldin with a look designed to sear his soul. Slowly he turned in his net entanglement, his cloven hooves projecting, his horns caught in the fine mesh. Eldin waited for a second or two, then sliced at a rope—but *not* the Lengite Captain's rope. Instead, threads parted and unwound in the rope of the crewman.

" 'Ere!" that miserable creature burst out in a guttural gabble. "That's *my* rope you're 'acking at, not 'is!"

"Didn't I mention that?" Eldin innocently asked. "But that's the whole point of the exercise. You see, I know that your Captain will not let any harm befall you—which is to say that he'll be obliged to answer my questions, right?" The Wanderer grinned—but so did the almost-human Captain!

"Now then," Eldin went on, poising his knife over the hapless crewman's taut rope. "First I would like to know your name, Captain . . . ?"

The Captain's mouth was once again tight-clamped, however, his grin gone, slant-eyes glaring as before. Eldin's blade caressed the crewman's rope, at which that unfortunate creature immediately babbled: " 'Ang on, 'ang on! 'Is name is Hrill. Cap'n Hrill, 'e is, an' 'e knows everything you want to—"

"Quiet, fool!" Hrill hissed, glaring venomously at his un-

derling where they swung together alongside *Gnorri*'s substructure. "Can't you see you're falling right into his trap?"

"I'm *in* 'is trap!" the other hotly retorted.

"Just you wait," Hrill threatened. "When we're out of
this—"

"*If* you're ever that lucky," Eldin cut him off. "Let's have
no more arguing now, Cap'n Hrill. Let's have some answers.
We were talking about marked men, if I remember right. How
marked? By whom?"

"Balls!" said Hrill.

"Really!" said Eldin, apparently taken aback. "Rudeness
does not become you." He pursed his lips thoughtfully. "I'm
afraid I must make an example." With that, and without further warning, he sliced through the crewman's rope. Its end
zipped out of sight over the rail. The horned one's thin
scream came echoing up through thinner air, and *Gnorri*'s
crew—Hero and Limnar too—rushed to the rail. Their horri-
fied eyes barely had time to fix upon the hurtling, rope-
trailing net and its wildly thrashing contents before it
disappeared into a bank of clouds.

Hero's mouth, wide open in shock, snapped into a sudden
grimace. "Eldin, I—"

"Quiet, lad!" the Wanderer growled. "This is man's work.
I've always thought you were too soft . . ."

Meanwhile Gytherik had beckoned Hero and Limnar to
one side. Now he whispered: "It is not what it seems. If you
count my gaunts you will see that there are only six. The
other two are beneath the cloudbelt, where they've doubtless
arrested the Lengite's fall by now. Eldin planned the whole
thing—with my assistance. We worked it out while Sniffer
and the grim were down below hunting horned ones."

"And you thought it best that we should remain ignorant?"
Hero could hardly believe his own ears.

"If only you could have seen the look on your face as you
looked over the rail—which doubtless Captain Hrill saw—
you would understand why. Your horror looked so real that it
lent the whole thing a marvelous authenticity."

"My horror *was* real!" Hero answered. But in another moment he was grinning. "Still, I can't complain, can I?" He scratched his chin wonderingly. "Didn't I say Eldin was a devious old dog?" Then his frown deepened. "Gytherik, are you sure you're not descended from a waking-worlder?"

At last the Wanderer had the almost-human Captain's entire attention. There was little doubt now but that Hrill would tell him everything he wished to know, for the Lengite had obviously and very seriously overrated the human capacity for compassion. Eldin had just repeated his last question, in answer to which Hrill was even now babbling a perfectly acceptable answer.

"Marked men, yes," he gibbered. "Both of you, Eldin the Wanderer and Hero of Dreams. The Dukes of Isharra have put a price on your heads—the Eidolon Lathi likewise, aye, and Zura of Zura too, though I fancy they would prefer you living to dead! Doomed you are, for how may you prevail against Zura and her zombies, Lathi and her termen, the Isharran Dukes and the entire nation of Leng?"

"How indeed?" growled Eldin. "But if you don't mind, I'll ask the questions." He paused for a moment before asking, "These Dukes of Isharra: I take it they're against us personally? Because we stole their intended brides away, eh?"

"Of course," the Lengite chuckled obscenely, "that's part of it—though by now they've stolen 'em back again. But mainly—"

"Hold it right there!" said Hero sharply as he moved up quickly beside Eldin. He gripped the rail, leaned over it and frowned down at the netted horned one, his gaze fixing the almost-human Captain like a pin through a butterfly. "What do you mean, they've stolen them back again?"

"They've taken 'em," Hrill repeated. "Snatched 'em off to—" and he stopped abruptly, as if biting his tongue.

"Say on, greaseball," Eldin demanded in his most fearsome growl, knife poised over the rope. "Where have the girls been abducted to?"

"Sarkomand!" the almost-human gasped, his terrified yellow eyes on Eldin's knife.

"Sarkomand?" Hero repeated. "That ill-reputed place? Why there?"

"I ... I don't know. I—" and his voice quavered up to a shriek as Eldin sliced a thread of rope and watched it rapidly unravel.

"The truth!" Eldin roared.

"It ... it is the Place of the Priest," Hrill sobbed. "The Place of Propitiation. The Place of the Pit. There, beneath Sarkomand, at the bottom of a great pit—" He stopped and gave a piteous wail. "If I say any more my life will not be worth a pebble."

"And if you don't you'll fall like a pebble," Eldin grinned mirthlessly. "A big, fat, juicy pebble." His knife parted another strand of rope.

The horned one gave another shriek. "Don't, don't!" he screamed. "I'll talk—I'll talk!"

"Talk, then," commanded Hero.

"At the bottom of the pit in Sarkomand, there is— madness! Madness—and magic! It is a place where the forces of nightmare are strong, where Mnomquah's mate Oorn awaits His fond embrace, as She has waited since the dawn of time. But She need wait no longer."

"Explain," said Eldin, parting yet another strand.

"I will, I will!" Hrill sobbed, a mad gleam beginning to creep into his eyes. "Only please ... the rope!"

"Talk," Eldin remorselessly rumbled.

"When the moon draws closer there will be great waterspouts in all the seas of the dreamlands. Volcanoes will erupt as mighty earthquakes rend the land. Also, there will be madness amongst all of dreamland's peoples. A great madness, brought about through the will of Mnomquah. And then the people will return to His worship. But too late!

"Finally the moon will break up, and in that breaking Mnomquah will be freed! As the moon's pieces rain down and shatter the dreamlands, He will race in a fireball from crumbling moon's heart to Sarkomand and plunge into the pit. Finally, when darkness and terror reign supreme, He and Oorn shall rise up, together, free, to be worshipped in all the lands of Earth's dreams!" And as Hrill finished speaking he broke into a prolonged, nerve-racking cackle of insane glee.

"Stop that!" Eldin commanded, viciously slicing at the now badly frayed rope. When Hrill had calmed down a little, the Wanderer asked: "And why would the Dukes of Isharra abduct a pair of lovely girls to that awful place?"

"What?" Hrill burst out hysterically. "Would you deny Mnomquah's mate Her sacrifice?" And again there came that hideous cackling. Hero and the rest looked at each other, their faces drawn, nerves all atingle. Finally, in what was little more than a whisper, Eldin asked:

"What of you Lengites? What do you get out of all this?"

"We?" the horned one madly chortled. "We are Mnomquah's chosen ones. We serve the moonbeasts, who in turn serve Him. We shall be saved."

"And Zura?"

"Is it not obvious? Her army of zombies shall swell, her demesnes increase. She will be Queen of the Dead! As for Lathi: her hives shall spread across all the ravished land— Mnomquah permitting—and all of us, all the chosen ones shall live in wonder and glory forever!"

"The Isharrans, too?"

In his net, Hrill contrived to shrug and his eyes fixed on those of his tormentor. His wide mouth gave a mad grin, and when his voice came it was like stirred mud. "The Isharrans are human," he gurgled. "They served a purpose, at present, but in the end—"

"Yes?" said Hero.

"Fodder! All of you—all the dreams of Man—fodder for the moonbeasts, for Zura and Lathi, for Mnomquah and Oorn—*and for their myriad nestlings!*"

Gritting his teeth, Eldin gave a great slash with his knife. The rope parted and Hrill went cackling away down a funnel of air, finally disappearing in fluffy clouds. There was silence, disturbed only by the moan of the wind in the rigging ...

Long moments later Hero said: "Gytherik, I've just now counted your gaunts again. There are eight of them."

"I know," the gaunt-master nodded, his face deathly pale. "The two came back a moment ago, silently, over the other side of the ship—too late for me to send them after the Lengite Captain." He spoke to his creatures. Two of them shuffled a little, which seemed to suffice for an answer. Gytherik turned back to his friends. "The crewman's rope was round his neck. When the gaunts caught it—" He paused. "At least, that's what they tell me."

"And Hrill?" Eldin asked, his normally bull-voice barely audible. "Not that he didn't deserve to die—but are you saying that I've just murdered him?" Gytherik turned away.

"Fool I may be," the youth muttered, shaking his head. "Faint-hearted, compassionate fools all of us. But not my gaunts. No sir, not them ..."

Destination Sarkomand

They spent the rest of the afternoon cruising to and fro above the wrecked ship searching for more horned-one survivors, without success. Even Sniffer was unable to locate the rest of the runaways; though when Gytherik ordered the gaunt back to the ship, he seemed loath to give up the search. Then, toward evening, sails were sighted in the east and six men-o'-war came sweeping in to rendezvous. All seven ships made moorings against the fall of night in the desert some miles westward of the wreck, following which the six subordinate Captains were called aboard *Gnorri II* for Limnar's briefing.

The outcome was that the flotilla would remain here for the night and in the morning sail for Sarkomand, there to attempt the rescue of Ula and Una (the abducted girls) and do whatever else was feasible toward thwarting the enemy's plans. With the talking done the six sky-Captains returned to their vessels, leaving the four friends to sit at their ease in Limnar's cabin and sip wine by the light of a ship's lantern.

The afternoon had been awkward, with very little conversation and a sort of moving apart taking place between the friends; but now that night was upon them and the moon all set to put in its hideous appearance, they were drawn together again. Yet even now there were barriers, however tenuous.

"Those gaunts of yours," said Eldin to Gytherik after a

while. "I wasn't aware that they had minds of their own—if you know what I mean."

"In the wild," the gaunt-master answered, "they do appear to be pretty mindless, I'll agree. But once they have a purpose—" He shrugged. "Perhaps something rubs off on them. You see, they don't just obey me, they *care* for me—for you too, now. Take my word for it: they will protect you with their own lives."

"And the way they dealt with Hrill and his underling," said Hero, joining the conversation, "that was them protecting us, eh?"

"In their way, yes. From ourselves."

"Against your instructions?"

"Perhaps they thought my orders invalid. Maybe they were invalid! I mean, our purpose is to kill horned ones, surely?"

"Um," Eldin thoughtfully rumbled. "See, I like to think that when you tell 'em to do something, they'll do it. Not go taking matters into their own hands—or paws. I mean, two of those little pets of yours carried me into Ilek-Vad last night—over some very high rooftops!"

"They also carried you over Serannian!" Gytherik hotly retorted. "Over the sky-city itself! They snatched you from thin air when you were blown out through the sky-island's flotation vent; and when Zura made you walk the plank—all three of you—who was it saved you but my gaunts? They also flew you to the roof of the Museum, and they waited to rescue you if the Curator made you jump from that miles-high place! How can you doubt my gaunts?"

"How indeed," said Limnar, but quietly. And Eldin was plainly unconvinced.

"Listen," said Gytherik, exasperated. "King Carter has warned about the horned ones. They've been a source of trouble in the dreamlands since time immemorial. They've brought the dreamlands close to ruin more than once. They serve the moonbeasts who serve Mnomquah. Closer to home: they brought that terrible statue to Ilek-Vad. They sent saboteurs into the city. But for our intervention, Ilek-Vad's peoples—ourselves included—would all now be dead or worse somewhere in the moon, and all through the activities of Lengites. They have sided with Lathi, whom you tried to burn, and Zura, whose zombie fleet we destroyed, *and* the Isharrans, who have taken captive your ex-girlfriends to sacrifice to Oorn! Need I go on listing their crimes?" His voice had gradually risen to a ringing shout and now he sprang to his feet.

"Yes, do," Hero grinned in his most disarming way. "Why, I was really working up a hate for them then!"

Gytherik sank back into his chair. "My gaunts," he finally said, "were right. It was bad of them to disobey me, but their motives were good." He turned angrily to Limnar Dass. "And how can *you* complain? You wrecked their ship and killed a score of them at least!"

"I never said a word," Limnar evenly answered. "In fact, I think you're right. Frankly, I don't know what has got into us, bickering like this."

Eldin shrugged. "It's just that I would have liked to get more out of old Hrill. We learned a lot, but there's a lot more we still don't know."

"And whose fault is that?" Hero tut-tutted. "It was you cut the rope, after all."

"Because I thought the damned gaunts would catch him!" Eldin exploded.

"Did you?" Hero snarled. "I saw the look on your face as the rope parted. You wanted Hrill to die—and so did I!" He frowned and paused, as if some new idea had come to him. "We all did . . ."

"Right!" Gytherik exclaimed. "We did—and my gaunts knew it. They can't smell, can't see, can't hear—not as we do. And so they work on instinct. And I repeat: they were right."

"So if we're all agreed," Limnar quietly asked, "what are we all growling about?"

A crewman of the watch appeared at the open cabin door. He nodded respectfully. "Moon's up, Cap'n. Just cleared the horizon. And bigger and fatter than ever!" He nodded again and returned to his duties.

"There's your answer, Limnar," said Hero. "Didn't Hrill tell us that the closer the mad moon gets, the madder we'll all become? It strikes me that from now on we'll all do well to hold ourselves rigidly in check."

They went out onto the bridge. The sky was indigo all around—with stars like jewels pinned on deep blue velvet—except for that region where the demon moon now floated free of the distant horizon. And gazing at the monstrous orb, which looked as if it might fall from the sky at any moment, Hero and his three colleagues knew beyond any further doubt that he was right. A tingling madness was in the air, radiating from the heart of the glaring yellow nightmare in the sky, and it set nerves ajangle and filled the blood with alien impulses and desires.

"Damn me!" Eldin irreverently muttered after a moment, his bearded, scarred face reflecting a sickly saffron glow. "Madness, is it? Well, only a madman would stay out in this in the first place. I've already had enough of it. If no one minds, I'll retire."

"Eldin's right," Hero agreed. "We should all get some sleep. And Limnar," he turned to the sky-Captain, "it might be a good idea if you got word to the other ships. Tell the Captains to keep their crews out of this mad moonshine. Too much exposure could become a real problem. One thing, though: I think we should all be given a shake if the moon starts acting up again. Oh, and one more thing: anyone who is wearing Leng gold must get rid of it right now!"

Limnar nodded, sent messengers down the rope ladders and across the stony desert to the other ships, issued instructions that he and his friends were to be awakened at first sight of any abnormal lunar activity; and without more ado the four sought their sleeping quarters.

It seemed that they were no sooner asleep than members of the night watch were shaking them into wakefulness. The moon was high now, filling a third of the sky, and the desert itself looked a moonscape of yellow gleam and stark black shadow. The tingle in the night air had become a physical thing, as of alien energies that played upon the skin and nerve-ends, causing a heightening of awareness which in turn inspired a terror of the fiendish forces now in play.

Meeting on the bridge, the friends were in time to see the magnetic moonbeam (as they now termed it) strike, but its target was too far away, somewhere in the east, for them to experience any of its associated phenomena. It struck, retired ... and then there came an even stranger, yet more ominous occurrence; if that were at all possible.

It was simply this: that before the beam shot down in a solid shaft of shimmering gold, the "face" of the moon had seemed to wear a frown; as well it might considering last night's abortive attack upon Ilek-Vad. But now, with the drawing back of the beam, it appeared that the "mouth" had turned up in a horrific grin, and that the "eyes" had narrowed to lustful slits. And in another moment, with the hurrying of clouds across the great golden disk, it seemed to the breathless watchers that the moon licked its lips!

As if in response, however involuntarily, Eldin used his tongue to dampen his own suddenly dry lips. "Another hamlet," he croaked, "perhaps an entire town—drawn up into the maw of the mad moon!"

And so yet again their sleep was destroyed, when for the remainder of the night they could merely toss and turn, sweating in the ship's stifling confines and feeling through the thick planking of her hull the mysterious madness blown on dreamland's winds. And slowly the night passed and the dim light of dawn began to glow in the east ...

And in that first dim half-light, as the crews of the seven ships stretched, yawned and scratched, the lookout in *Gnorri*'s crow's-nest gave a cry of alert that brought Limnar to the bridge and Hero and Eldin, in their nightclothes, to the ship's rail. There, fleeing east to west, the weirdest craft any

of them had ever seen scudded before a high, strong wind
whose eddies could be felt even down here; and Limnar gave
a gasp of surprise as he put his glass to his eye.

"Why, it's little more than a mainmast and sail!" he informed. "With a basket lashed below and the whole thing
suspended from a couple of flotation bags. Oh, yes, and a flap
of canvas on a knocked-together frame, acting as a rudder.
There are a couple of horned ones in the basket, working like
the devil to keep the thing stabilized. An ingenious affair—
but hardly maneuverable. And look at it go!"

The strange craft passed high overhead, rushed northwest-
ward, dwindled down rapidly to a speck and vanished in the
dawny distance. Gytherik, last to arrive, had seen only the
glow of the rising sun on the distant sail before the makeshift
craft disappeared, and he had heard only part of what Limnar
said. Rubbing sleep from his eyes, he asked:

"What was that? A gaunt fleeing the rising sun? Surely
not, for it was moving too fast."

"No gaunt," Limnar answered, "but a couple of clever
Lengites flying a bit of wreckage."

"What?" Gytherik cried. "I'll get my grim aloft at once!
Maybe they can catch them."

"Doubtful," said Hero, laying a restraining hand on the
youth's arm. "They were really moving. By the time your
gaunts give chase they'll be miles away. Also, we have to get
on. There can be no more diversions. Send a couple of your
rubbery chums out by all means, if you think it will do some
good. But they'll be on their own in the heat of the day, and
they'll have to find their own way back to us. Also, we might
just need 'em here, with the flotilla."

"But surely the horned ones are heading for Sarkomand,"
Gytherik protested. "They'll warn of our coming!"

"They don't know for sure that we are coming," said
Limnar. "Also, they'll be damned lucky to land that thing
without killing themselves. Also—"

"Also," grunted Eldin, "maybe this way we get a chance to
clear our collective conscience, eh? I mean, we cruelly killed

two of the squat little devils—in error, if you like—and so now we can even up the score by letting a couple go."

Gytherik relaxed and Hero released his arm. "Maybe," the youth said at last, "but I'm still not sure I like it."

"Like it or not," said Limnar, "it's done." And with that he set about readying his ship for the quest . . .

Sarkomand

PART 2

Voices in the Night

Limnar made running repairs to *Gnorri II*, whose damage was only superficial. She had been holed but her flotation engine was undamaged; one of her bags had exploded but had now been replaced; and as a safety measure, a temporary rail had been rigged in the stern. Now the seven ships sped north and somewhat west, as they had for ten days and nine nights, on that same high-blown current which had driven the crudely constructed Leng craft.

And it seemed the elements understood both the urgency of the questers and the nature of the threat against the dreamlands, and that they were sympathetic; for the wind had blown strong and steady and the nights had been unseasonably cold and cloudy. The mad moon had sent its beam Earthward once and once only (and then far to the south and gropingly, as if unsure of the target) and for the rest of the time had shown only as an ever-swelling yellow blotch or massive saffron blur behind the mercifully veiling clouds.

Always the way had led over ocean, but at midday on the tenth day they had sailed over a jagged granite rock that loomed up from the gray sea, when certain of Limnar's older sailors had shuddered and said that this was the shunned sentinel rock which guarded the shores of Inquanok. Inquanok was not their destination, however, and since Sarkomand was rumored to lie to the east of that cold gray land, Limnar now inclined to a course more nearly northward.

All through the tenth afternoon jagged mountains were visible in the north, later to become obscured by dense distant mists and dark low clouds, and as night came on the flotilla crossed a cold shoreline glimpsed through swirling fog and drifting cloudbanks. Here Limnar ordered the ships down to an anchorage above a bleak region of huge and tumbled black boulders like broken slabs of monolithic masonry, as if the entire land were remnant of some aeon-dead metropolis of strange gods. The whole area for miles around was dim, misty and darkening now with the fall of night; very little had been visible from the air.

Because he suspected that Sarkomand must now be close indeed, Limnar decided to wait out the night—and hopefully the mist—right here, moving on in the morning or as soon as the weather permitted. And knowing that if he was correct in his suspicions, then that action was equally imminent, he called for a meeting with his Captains. While the meeting was taking place, Gytherik went off for a long flight with his restless gaunts (ostensibly to spy out the ground, though in fact the gaunts loved nothing better than a good glide through the mist) and Hero and Eldin were left with nothing to do but bemoan their inactivity.

Now they leaned on the ship's fog-wreathed rail, their hoods up against the dampness of the air, and gloomed together into the chilly night. All around, the dim ghosts of sky-ships lolled gently at anchor, sails furled, their rigging creaking a little but muffled by the mist and seeming strangely distant.

"Somewhere up there," said Eldin after a while, inclining his leonine head toward lowering clouds, "the mad moon grows larger, closer, just waiting for a break in this weather."

"So are we," Hero reminded. "These clouds may be good news for the dreamlands—for by now the message must be well and truly out and about, and even the smallest hamlet must know of the danger—but they're damn bad news for Ula and Una. I *itch* to do something, to get into action, to—"

"—To rescue those poor lasses," Eldin growled. "I know, me too. And it's worst knowing that they may be somewhere close by, in the foul paws of those horned horrors from Leng."

"How close, I wonder?" Hero answered. "Westward lies Inquanok, and way beyond that Isharra. And here, somewhere, perhaps no more than a mile or two away—"

"Shh!" Eldin suddenly hissed, startling his younger friend and making him jump. He thrust his head forward, eyes wide and staring into the mist. "Did you hear that, or was it only my imagination? That cry in the night—that voice calling 'Eldin, Eldin?' "

"Eh?" said Hero. "I heard not a thing. It must have been the creaking of—" Abruptly, his eyes too went wide. "But I heard it that time!" he gasped. 'Hero, Hero,' it cried. A girl's voice—my Ula's voice! But how?"

"Again!" Eldin pointed a shaking hand. "Out there!"

"It *is* Ula!" Hero whispered.

"Both of 'em, then," said Eldin. "They"ve escaped from the horned ones. Perhaps they saw our ships in the sky, through a break in the clouds—saw us as we sank down into the mist."

"Aye!" Hero agreed, Eldin's imagination spurring his own. "And so they broke loose and headed this way. And they're out there in the dark and the mist, searching for us."

"Pursued by horned ones."

"And the lecherous, loathsome Dukes of Isharra!"

"And Zura."

"And Lathi."

"Damn me!" roared Eldin, shaking his fist at the night.

"*Shh!*" Hero grabbed the Wanderer's brawny arm, at the same time casting about through half-shuttered eyes at the crewmen where they went about their tasks on the deck. Wreathed by swirling mist, the sailors seemed unaware of the sudden tension in the waking-worlders, were deaf to the faint cries constantly ringing through the night.

"Listen," said Hero urgently, "we don't need this lot clattering about, attracting horned ones and such. There are two girls out there and there are two of us. I vote we do this job ourselves. They were our girls, after all."

"Agreed," said Eldin. "And there's not a one of these lads stealthy as you or I." He gripped the rail and peered again into the bank of mist where it swirled all about. "There," he said after a moment. "Did you hear it? From over there." And again he pointed.

Hero listened, frowned, then grimly nodded. "Right," he said, swinging himself over the rail. Ignoring a handy rope ladder, he grabbed an anchor rope and went sliding down into the mist. Eldin followed, and a moment later they landed like cats on the broken, slippery stone surface below. There they paused, listening intently for a moment, then set off silently and at speed in a generally northerly direction.

Keeping low, they automatically adopted the crouching lope of expert thieves and nighthawks—which indeed had been their trade before they became questers—and soon they had merged with the mist and the darkness to such an extent that no one would ever have known they were there. And the cries came echoing through the night—plaintive, seeming sometimes distant, sometimes quite close at hand—and yet somehow getting no closer, if anything retreating.

Following those distressed and distressing calls, the pair gradually grew suspicious. With the ships far behind them and swallowed up by distance, darkness and mist, they became aware of their own vulnerability in the night. They were good in the foggy gloom, certainly, but were they better than horned ones from Leng's perpetually nighted plateau? Better than Zura's zombies, creatures of darkness? Better than Lathi's termen, with their insect instincts?

"But I can hear Una calling!" Eldin protested in a low growl.

"I said nothing," Hero answered, his voice hushed.

"No, but you were thinking it, I could almost feel your lip twitching. It always does when you start to have doubts."

They found themselves in the depths of a steep-sided ravine whose walls pressed in on both sides. Now their pace slowed, they became cautious and stuck to the blackest shadows.

"That's just it," said Hero at last. "You can hear Una but I can't. In fact, I haven't heard Una once, only Ula."

The ravine widened out into a place of reeking vapors, silent except for the distant drip of nameless moisture. "And I haven't heard Ula," said Eldin. "Not once!"

The shadows closed in on the pair and the reek grew stronger. Now they knew that smell. It was the odor of decaying flesh, the stench of corruption!

"They're not calling now," Eldin breathed, his great hand reaching for his sword.

"I've a feeling," Hero answered, "that they never were!"

"Trap!" they both hissed together, and their swords sang in unison as they sprang from scabbards and sliced through a circle of hideous shadows. Shadows which were not shadows but—death!

Death fell on them in the night, in that terrible opening at the end of the ravine, in the mist and the reeking darkness. Suffocating death, rotting death. And hack and slash as they might—as they did, with all strength and in an utter frenzy of nightmare dread—still they could not turn the veritable tide of death which washed over them and bore them down.

Death in the shape of Zura's walking dead . . .

After leaving the deck of *Gnorri II*, Gytherik and his grim had headed north. Well wrapped against the night, against the rushing damp air and the natural chill of these northern regions, the gaunt-master had been happy to let his beasts fly where they would, secure in the knowledge that they would find their way unerringly back to the seven ships when they were done with exercising and enjoying themselves.

Actually, it was difficult to say for certain whether or not gaunts ever did truly enjoy themselves. They never showed emotion, or very nearly never (how could they without faces?) and unless directed their flying invariably seemed purposeless and gave them no visible pleasure. But Gytherik suspected that they enjoyed it anyway, and so did he.

They had briefly penetrated the cloud ceiling to fly in moonlight, but so yellow, hideous and dazzling had been that light—and so monstrously vast and close its throbbing source—that the gaunt-master had ordered the grim down again and back into the clean (by comparison) clouds and mists. Once, too, he had thought he spied a flight of shantaks, several of which had seemed to carry riders, but this latter effect might have been merely phenomena of the mist. Whichever, the hippocephalic creatures had been visible for no more than a second or so, nor had they caused Gytherik more than a moment's concern. Shantaks, despite their great size and strength, are utterly afraid of gaunts; even a flock of them would rather flee than face one lone gaunt in the night skies of Earth's dreamland.

On the other hand, it was known that Leng's horned ones had mastered and occasionally rode shantaks; which on second thought did give Gytherik a little more room for conjecture. And so for over an hour he had searched the misty skies and the needle peaks of clouded mountains—to no avail. He saw nothing more of either shantaks or horned ones, and so decided to return to the ships. In doing so he urged the grim to greater speed, for a nagging voice in the back of his mind was now becoming more and more insistent that all was not well; so that he hardly surprised himself by sighing out loud when at last the grim circled down to a landing on the mist-slick deck of *Gnorri II*.

Limnar Dass was there to meet him, and the look on the sky-Captain's face confirmed beyond a doubt Gytherik's own feelings of impending disaster. As the gaunt-master dismounted, so Limnar apprised him of the latest development. "Hero and Eldin," he said. "They're gone."

"Gone?" Gytherik ushered his grim below decks. "Where have they gone?"

"They went while I was in conference," Limnar answered. "Don't ask me where or why."

"But someone must have seen them go?"

"Indeed, several of my crewmen. I'm told that they appeared excited, then furtive—and that they slid down a rope into the night—since when they have not returned. They've been gone for some two hours, since shortly after you yourself went off with your gaunts. I was hoping that perhaps you had seen something of them?"

Gytherik shook his head. "Do you think they're in trouble?"

"Not necessarily. They're like cats in the night, those two, and fierce fighters to boot. But you know all that. It's just that I have this feeling . . ."

"Me too," Gytherik shivered. "Very well, let's wait until dawn. If they're not back by then I'll send out the gaunts to search for them."

Below decks, Sniffer shuffled uncomfortably and facelessly in the gloom of a cargo hold. Most of the other gaunts were already asleep (at least, they were in that huddled, wing-hooded state which serves for sleep in night-gaunts) but Sniffer was wide awake. He gave Biffer a nudge and they both inclined their monstrous heads upward, as if engaged in some sort of earless listening. In fact they were "listening" to Gytherik and Limnar's conversation: or more exactly, to the concern which radiated from that pair in very tangible waves, at least waves which were tangible to night-gaunts.

Having listened, they stared eyelessly at each other for a moment or two, and finally they each gave a single, simultaneous nod, as if in agreement to some mutual, unspoken suggestion. And half an hour later, when the ships were very much quieter and only the watch patrolled the decks, then they crept silently topside and launched themselves into the swirling mist . . .

The Dukes of Isharra

CHAPTER II

Trussed up in termen threads like flies in a spider's cocoons, with only their faces showing through glossy silken surfaces, Hero and Eldin were borne away like centuried mummies into the base of steep-rising cliffs, through reeking labyrinthine tunnels, interminably downward to vast caverns of elder horror. Among their captors were a few horned ones, a large number of zombies (which, being expendable, had performed the actual dirty work) and a handful of Lathi's termen.

Now they were bundled along horizontally through great caves, their way illumined by torches held in the paws of horned ones, amidst the massed and monstrous polyglot horde, toward some doom as yet unknown and probably best unguessed. And all around them the rush and patter of feet and paws in damply reeking bowels of earth.

"Mmf, mff!" mumbled Eldin, who couldn't get his jaws open wide enough to speak.

"Damn right!" Hero emphatically agreed. "Mmf!" And less restricted in respect of facial movements, he went on to berate his burly friend: "Of all the stupid, brainless, wild-goosiest wild-goose chases you ever got me into, this—"

"Mmf?" Eldin was astonished. "Mmf mff *mff*!" he in turn accused.

"It was you heard the cries first," said Hero.

"Mmf mff *mff* mff!" Eldin answered, his astonishment turning to outrage.

"Now just you hold on there, old lad," Hero snarled. "And don't go taking that tone of mmf with-" Abruptly he broke off as they were bundled out from torch-flickered gloom into an open space which stretched away for miles to the murmuring ocean. It was dark and misty and the pair could not see that distant shoreline, but they could hear the dull *hush* of waves and taste the salt in the dank night air.

Above—high, high above black cliffs that went up in massive and vertiginous steps—the phosphorescent clouds of the north hurried southwards in great belts; and such was their glow that the eyes of the pair soon grew accustomed to the weird light which they lent the place. And a strange and terrible place it appeared to be.

There were crumbling walls and shattered columns everywhere, and grayish shrubs that forced their way through weirdly-patterned pavements, breaking them upward and forming small piles of debris. The gaping ruins of great houses stood or lay fallen at every angle, and following the contours of their mounds the pair of trussed-up questers could see that this had once been a mighty and thronging city—but how many thousands of years ago? There were legends in the dreamlands which had it that a certain primordial city had perished a million years before ever the first true humans discovered and inhabited Earth's dreamland . . .

The thought must have found its way simultaneously into both Hero's and Eldin's minds; for as the truth of their whereabouts dawned on them Eldin gave an exclamatory mmf! and Hero whispered, "Sarkomand!"

"Sarkomand, aye," agreed an evilly grinning horned one, coming close and shoving his face near to those of the captive pair. "Sarkomand, which is where the glorious careers of dreamland's most famed questers must surely end—but not before you have seen the so-called Lords. And the so-called Ladies . . ."

"Ladies?" said Hero. "Ula and Una? They really are here then?"

"Eh? Oh, those two," the horned one answered. "Aye, they're here—but they are not the ladies I meant." And he urged the throng of monsters to more speed as they hurried through the dark and primal ruins.

Hero's eyes met Eldin's as the pair were rushed headlong through the centuried streets. "He means Zura," Hero grunted sourly.

"And—mmf!—Lathi," Eldin answered. He had finally succeeded in working his jaw loose and could now speak—with difficulty. "And speaking of—mmf!—Lathi, did you ever see a ship like that before?"

Hero, unable to turn his head, had to wait until he was jostled into the required position. There, looming in the mists some fifty or so yards away, a totally unique vessel was moored. The ship was a leprous white and its outline was indistinct, but even at that distance and in the misty gloom Hero was able to recognize the mushroomy color as one and the same with the city of Thalarion, the Eidolon Lathi's fire-doomed seat, which Eldin had razed to the ground by use of his firestones.

"So," Hero said. "The grub-Queen has ships now, does she?"

"One, at least," Eldin answered in disgust. "A vessel such as that could not belong to any other."

"And look!" Hero exclaimed. "That black ship there, with the octopus figurehead. We've seen her before, I fear."

"Zura!" Eldin spat out the word. "A pretty writhing of maggots here, Hero."

Now they were passing ship after ship, all gently rocking at anchor some twenty or thirty feet above the crumbling ruins of the ancient city. "Leng ships, these," said Hero. "Black as Zura's vessel but bigger, squatter. Looks like the fiendish females have only one ship each, and that the rest of the fleet belongs to the horned ones."

"That fits," Eldin muttered. "We smashed Zura's fleet at

Serannian, all except her flagship. As for Lathi: she didn't have any ships. That one we passed back there, it must be her prototype."

"And the Isharrans?" Hero wondered.

"Too small a community, ingrown, degenerate. A goldmine grown all out of proportion. Shantytown at one end, palatial residences at the other. A veritable slave community governed by the Dukes. Sky-ships would be too modern in concept for them. Yak-carts with wooden wheels, more like. I would guess that they've borrowed a Leng ship, and a Leng crew to boot. Knowing what's in store for them at the end—at least according to old Hrill—that would seem most logical, don't you agree?"

"Oh, I do, I do," answered Hero, impressed. "You've obviously given these Dukes of Isharra a deal of thought."

"I do my homework," the other stated, a little too smugly for Hero's liking.

"Oh, good!" he said, straining his eyes to peer up, down and sideways at the cocoon encasing his head. "Fore-warned is fore-armed, eh? Whatever would we have done if you hadn't done your homework?"

"Listen, scut—" warned Eldin, but before he could continue the ambush party came to a halt where the ruins of a house formed a square of broken walls. The walls were rough and thick, forming black shadows away from the building, while inside all was yellow and orange glare reflected from a central fire . . . and a circle of ruddy faces, turning as one to stare at the captives where they were bundled through a gap in the wall and into the firelight.

"A warm, healthy glow, that," Hero observed under his breath.

"A fire to serve human needs," Eldin returned, his ire quickly evaporating. "I think we're about to be introduced to those so-called 'Lords' our squat little friend was talking about. Namely, the so-called—"

"Dukes of Isharra," a steely, ringing voice cut him short. "At your service, gentlemen."

Two figures stood up and stepped clear of the seated circle, peering curiously at the questers where they were now propped upright in their cocoons. Held in that position by several of Zura's zombies, the pair could only stare back. The rest of their escort, having fulfilled their task, now melted away into the night.

The Dukes stepped closer, and it could now be seen that they were near-identical twins. Dressed in gold-threaded jackets and fur-lined silken breeches—with thigh-boots of red leather, belts bearing gold-filigreed swords, their hands and wrists heavy with gold—the only immediate difference between them appeared to be the livid scar which one of them wore above his right eye; whose gouge faded away vertically into his crew-cut hair, giving his eye a fixed and permanently devilish cast. Of the two, however, this one seemed most talkative; and if his voice had the ring of steel, certainly his words were no less cutting:

"You'll be Eldin the Wanderer," he said, prodding Eldin's cocooned chest with a stiff, blunt finger. "Oh, yes, you fit your description well enough. Ugly, brutish—full of a false bravado . . ."

"See here—" Eldin growled, the very rumble of his voice threatening to burst the cocoon. But the steely-voiced speaker merely flipped him in the mouth with a gold-worked glove. At that Eldin snarled incoherently, almost mindlessly, and gritting his teeth strained desperately against the tough strands which bound him.

"Be still!" snapped the Duke. "And be *quiet*! When I want you to speak I'll say so. No man talks back to Byharrid-Imon Isharra without his permission."

Now his brother came forward, tilting his head up a little to gaze into Hero's ice-blue eyes. Tall though the brothers were by the standards of dreamland, still Hero stood taller. "And you'll be David Hero," this one said, his voice like the smoke of hot oil. "Or Hero of Dreams, as you are known." There was a strangely hybrid look about his sallow, unpleasant, overlarge features—an almost feminine tilt to his cheekbones and eyebrows. "A singer of songs, eh?" he continued. "A poet . . ." He reached out to touch Hero's cheek with a pointed, manicured fingernail.

Hero drew back his head (as best he could) and spat straight into the Duke's eye. "And you'll be Gathnod-Natz'ill Isharra," he evenly answered as the other staggered away dabbing at his face. "As woolly a woofter as ever I saw—in dreams or out of 'em!"

"I do believe he's discovered one of your little vices, brother," Byharrid-Imon gave a dry, barking laugh.

"Damned right!" Hero quietly agreed. "And to think I worried about my Ula with him. Why, he'd not know what to do with her!"

"Oh, he surely would," laughed Byharrid-Imon. "His tastes are wide-ranging, that's all."

Now the circle of figures seated around the fire stood up as Gathnod-Natz'ill finally got Hero's spit out of his eye and drew his sword. "Damn you!" he cried in his girlish voice. "First you wound us sorely by stealing off with our future brides, and now you add insult to injury! We'll see how well you can spit without a tongue, David Hero."

The zombies holding the pair upright backed stumblingly away, leaving them to rock in their silk-paper cocoons—which it now fully appeared would be their coffins. Byharrid-Imon also drew his sword, aiming it at Eldin.

"Aye," he said, his voice low now but ringing still, "my brother's right. We've suffered enough from you two. Not only did we lose face when you stole our brides-to-be, but we lost money, too. Why, we've paid bounty-hunters a small fortune for your heads! And now you come along, delivering them to us yourselves, and all of your own free will." He chuckled, however bleakly. "Oh, don't worry, Hero, for I shan't let my brother kill you. Not just yet. If he desires your tongue, however—"

"Cowardly dogs!" Eldin roared. "If my arms were only free—"

"Your voice," said Byharrid-Imon warningly, "continues to

annoy me. It is altogether too deep and strong." He pointed his sword at Eldin's lower middle. "I think I should prefer it castrato. After all, if my brother intends taking a trophy . . . well, shouldn't I claim one also! Perhaps two?"

Now the figures about the fire came forward and closed upon the questers. Some of them were true men, Isharrans, with the same unhandsome looks as their leaders, and the rest were almost-humans. The men were silent, perhaps a little resentful of their masters (or else just naturally surly) but the Lengites were filled with a hideous excitement.

"Go on," one of them chortled to Gathnod-Natz'ill. "Take his tongue. Here, let me reach up and open his jaws for you." And Hero felt foul paws groping at his face.

Another tore at the terman webbing binding Eldin's lower body. "And you, Lord Byharrid-Imon. Here, let me fix this for you, so that you may take—"

"Take nothing—touch nothing!" came a commanding female voice from on high. And as the Isharran party fell back in astonishment, so a black shadow drifted slowly over the ruins. Up above, a leprous white ship had moved silently into view.

"I have first claim on those two," came the voice again, "for they have sinned more against me than any other. Lucky for me that my siblings brought word of their capture. Lucky, too, for you Dukes; for if you had harmed them you would pay. I have my own plans for them."

A window in the ship's side framed a face of incredible beauty. Rocking back on his heels to see that face more clearly, Eldin gasped: "Lathi!"

"Aye, Lathi," she answered, her voice utterly humourless. "The Eidolon Lathi, whose city, Thalarion, you burned to the ground!"

As she spoke, termen on the ship's deck let down sticky silken gobs of stuff on strong threads, swinging them until they contacted and adhered to the cocoons of the questers. Before the Isharrans could make a move, Hero and Eldin were hauled up from the ruins and out of their reach. In a matter of seconds they were being dragged aboard the white ship.

"Out of the frying pan," muttered Hero grimly as strong termen hands closed on him.

"And into the fire—" the Wanderer groaningly finished it for him.

Ship of Paper, Ship of Death

"Paper!" Eldin rumbled. "No wonder the ship looks so leprous and lumpy. She's made of the same sort of material they use to build their cities, a variation on this binding muck that's wrapping us."

"Pretty strong muck," Hero answered, "as witness our inability to break out of it."

"Aye, but it burns well enough," Eldin darkly reminded. "I may have lost my sword—that good one of mine, shattered and reconstituted by the power of the First Ones—but I still have my firestones."

"Fat chance you'll get to use them," Hero answered. "Not a second time. But right enough, the ship would burn like a torch. Take note: there are no lamps here. See, the light comes from those tiny luminous mushrooms growing out of the woodwork—er, the paperwork. And look—even the sails are like mighty shavings of softwood!"

Now they were bundled into Lathi's cabin and brought face to face with the Eidolon herself. Each quester was held upright by a pair of termen, whose wickedly curving knives were held poised to strike at first sign of a false move—though how the adventurers might contrive to make even a tiny false move was anybody's guess. And finally, her voice much quieter now but no less deadly, Lathi spoke:

"So, we meet again. You, David Hero, who sang songs to

me to lull me into sleep. And you, Eldin the Wanderer, whose firestones turned my lovely Thalarion to ashes. Ah, but this time we meet in a much colder clime. And there is a coldness between us that may only be dispelled when you two are no more."

Silently the pair stared at her, attempting to fathom the depths of her mind, to know her thoughts. She was as beautiful as Hero remembered her—the top half of her, anyway. But where her waist disappeared into silky ruffles of glossy pink and purple paper, there the horror began. For the hidden part of Lathi had more than ten times the mass of the visible; and like an iceberg's submerged portion, the unseen was far more lethal than the seen.

There were curtains to one side of her bench-like seat, which billowed slightly as Hero's eyes found them. Back there, where Lathi's termaids doubtless worked even now, massaging and smoothing with soft oils and supple hands, her monstrous lower body was that of a Queen termite—whose appetite was more monstrous yet. Hero could not help but shudder, and Lathi saw his grimace.

"Still you spurn me," she hissed, "who might have known the final, intimate ecstasy of my embrace. Well, that offer is no longer open to you. You are not worthy." Her eyes narrowed perceptibly. "How would you die, David Hero?"

"Any other way than—" he began, and instantly wished he could bite off his tongue. "With a sword in my hand," he hastily went on. "The way I have lived."

"Aye, likewise," said Eldin.

"Ah, Wanderer!" Lathi's voice was poisonous sweet as she turned her gaze upon Eldin. "But no . . . no, your fate was decided the day you doomed the hive city—by fire!"

"It was you played with fire first," Eldin reminded. "Threatening to burn down that poor defenseless Great Tree."

"The Tree, defenseless?" Her face twisted in fury. "Not since you two taught him how to fight! My termen dare not even approach him. His roots spring up underfoot to coil and crush; his tendrils flail like whips; dead branches are wont to fall like the hammers of gods!"

"Good for him!" growled Eldin.

"But not," she smiled beautifully, and yet hideously, "for you."

At that moment a terman entered through the cabin door and bowed low. "Lathi," he said in a curiously neutral voice, "they punish the horned ones."

She turned her face to peer out of the large, open circular porthole beside her and beckoned to the termen holding the questers that they should bring the two closer. They were bundled forward until they crowded beside her, but still their view outside the ship was restricted. Lathi impatiently shook her head.

"I wish to *see*," she snapped at one of the termen holding Hero. "And I wish our—guests—to see, so that they may know the severity of our punishments. Drone, get me up onto the deck at once."

Hero thought to himself: *"A neat trick if she can turn it,"* and was immediately astonished by an abrupt and completely unexpected turn of neat trickery. For as the terman hauled on a large lever in the wall, so the "roof" of the cabin slid back and the entire room became a platform which creakingly elevated to the now open upper deck.

Lathi's amazing paper ship had ascended somewhat and was now a hundred feet or so above Sarkomand's ruins. A Lengite vessel was rising fast behind, her sails unfurling, and the questers could make out the figures of the furious Dukes of Isharra on her deck.

"They intend to take you back," Lathi needlessly informed, "but they shall not have you." She turned again to her termen. "Release them from their bindings—but do not take your eyes from them. They are treacherous! Strip the young one, for nakedness makes humans weak. As for the other: lash him to the mast . . . for the moment."

Using their fingertips, which exuded a thin, melting fluid, the termen quickly cut the questers free of their cocoons.

Numb and cramped, the pair stumbled a little as the termen continued to obey Lathi's commands. Hero was quickly stripped of his clothes and Eldin was trussed up to the main-mast.

Now Lathi grabbed Hero's arm and drew him onto the seat beside her. He shuddered at the contact and she smiled, relishing his horror. "Ah, David Hero, but you shall never know what you missed. And do you tremble? I agree, it is cold in the north. There—" and she held him close and threw the folds of her voluminous gown about him. Crushed to her more than ample and very beautiful bosom, Hero cringed inwardly at the thought of what lay behind and below: the monstrous pulsating grub which was Lathi's lower body.

"Look!" she suddenly said, and turned his head toward a strange and cruel scene. "See, the Lengites punish their failed fellows. Oorn has ordered it. Her God-mate, Mnomquah, will suffer neither fools nor failures."

Hero looked, but his concentration was elsewhere. Moving as gently and minutely as he could, he flexed his muscles here and there, unwinding his cramped, cold body and willing feeling back into his arms and legs. He had not realized how crushingly restrictive the paper bindings had been, but as blood began to flow again so he felt the sting of pins and needles in all his limbs.

The eyes of the termen were no longer upon him; all eyes were gazing at the tableau laid out in the ruins of central Sarkomand down below, where the Lengites were camped in strength. And as Lathi had directed, finally Hero too looked. The mist had cleared a little and the glow of the luridly racing clouds was sufficient to lend the scene a sort of foxfire luminosity.

Thronging horned ones were jeering and laughing, dancing obscenely around a pole or totem to which they had tied two of their own kind. But now Hero saw that this was neither pole nor totem but a shattered mast, and seeing the basket at its base he recognized the contraption as weird makeshift vessel which alone had escaped the wrecking of Hrill's ship in the desert. The sail had been stripped away and a mass of flotation bags was now attached to the top of the mast, straining and threatening to bear the whole thing aloft. Several stout ropes anchored it to the ground.

"But what's going on?" Hero asked, intrigued despite himself. "Surely those are the Lengites who forewarned of our coming, so enabling you to trap us? And talking of traps: just how was that done? Or was it really Ula and Una calling to us in the night?"

"Too many questions, David Hero," she whispered in his ear. "Now be quiet and watch." But as he opened his mouth to speak again she conceded an answer to at least one of his questions. "Yes, you are correct. They are the survivors of your desert attack upon the Leng ship—the last vestiges of a miserable failure. They failed to destroy Ilek-Vad—thanks to you."

"But they *are* survivors," Hero pointed out, frowning. "Survivors returned from a dangerous, however treacherous, mission—and by ingenious use of their wits, at that! They are my enemies, certainly—but they're your allies. How can you punish what my kind would see as heroes?"

"That's where you human beings fascinate me," Lathi answered in a purr. "Your distorted sense of values, based on meaningless concepts like 'Honor,' 'Heroism,' and 'Loyalty'—especially 'Loyalty.' "

"Oh?" Hero argued. "And what of the loyalty of your termen?"

"The group instinct of the hive," she shrugged. "Not loyalty at all, really. Survival. You would give your life for the Wanderer there. One terman would not give his for another, only for his Queen. On the contrary, another terman's death would not concern him at all."

"But—" Hero would have argued (at the same time resting his eyes casually and fleetingly upon the loosely held, curving knife in the hand of the nearest terman).

"There are no buts," she cut him short. "Do you think that the horned ones returned of their own free will? They did not.

The wind brought them back here, Fate. They could not control their funny little vessel, that's all, and one of the Lengite patrol ships saw them, intercepted and brought them down. They were hoping to reach Leng, where doubtless they would hide themselves away and disappear. Oh, yes, David Hero, for they knew well enough the price of failure."

"The price of failure—" Hero mused, more to himself than to Lathi, as he weighed up his own chances. But perhaps she overheard him, or at least sensed his thoughts—and she saw his slitted eyes furtively casting about. Saw them pause, however briefly, once more upon the terman's knife.

"You are a devious man, Hero of Dreams," her purr deepened warningly. "When I might expect the hands of any other man to come a-fondling at my warm breasts—especially since they will be the last breasts to comfort you before you are folded to the cold and clammy bosom of Death herself—instead I discover your eyes upon a loosely-held weapon. You tremble not at my nearness or the desirability of my body, but at the contemplation of mad adventuring! Even now you seek your freedom, with enemies all around and escape utterly unthinkable. I begin to consider you a fool."

"Am I a male spider then?" asked Hero. "Who loves his mate until she delivers the death-bite?" His mind worked overtime to seek a plausible excuse for his recalcitrance, his ingratitude, before Lathi should decide to make a quick end of her cat and mouse game; and out of the corner of his eye at last he glimpsed his salvation—

—The Leng ship under the command of the Dukes of Isharra, where it rose up silent as a ghost on the port side, its deck a mere leap away. "You would eventually kill me," he gabbled, "whether I managed to grab your creature's knife or not—but *they* would kill me right now, which makes it a matter of survival." He freed an arm to point it at the Isharrans who came silently leaping between decks, their twin masters waving them in to the attack.

Lathi jerked her head round to stare where he pointed and

her hand flew to her mouth. "What?" she cried, her voice thick with sudden rage. "How *dare*—"

"I'll face the death you plan for me when—if—it comes," Hero yelled, hurling himself naked from beneath her paper gown. "But as you can see, the one they plan is rather more immediate!"

He leaped at the startled terman, wrested his curved knife from him and shouldered him over the ship's flimsy rail all in one fluid movement. As he turned toward the mainmast two more termen got in his way. He despatched them with coldly brutal efficiency and smelled the swampy fetor of their sappy blood as he sprang to Eldin's side.

Three strokes of the razor-honed knife sufficed to free the Wanderer, who immediately gave a deafening and ferocious bellow—the cry of a berserker plunging into battle!

He snatched up the knife of one of the termen Hero had felled; and the two adventurers stood back to back, Hero naked and deadly calm, Eldin raging and brassy as hell's fires. And the Isharrans came, swords dully glinting, eyes gleaming with an almost luminous rapaciousness. They came—and they met red death!

Death in the shapes of Hero and Eldin, for even with curving knives in place of their usual weapons, still the two were the craftiest fighters ever known. And though Lathi's termen also fought off the Isharrans, nevertheless the two cut down termen and Isharrans alike, indiscriminately slaughtering all who came within range of their borrowed blades.

Now the Dukes of Isharra themselves had boarded the paper ship—at which very instant Lathi's voice rose above the hoarse cries of battle and the *hiss* of slicing steel:

"Fools!" she cried. "Do we fight each other? They are our enemies!" And she pointed at Hero and Eldin where they stood, gory with blood and red-eyed from the fever of the fight.

At Lathi's cry the termen and Isharrans turned toward the pair, their eyes slitting as they stared at their true foes; and like some terrible tide they began to creep toward the beleaguered questers, hot death in their faces and cold in their hands.

"Farewell, Old Lad," said Hero, gritting his teeth in anticipation of the onslaught.

"We'll go to hell together," the other growled—and jerked back his head as a rope's knotted end struck him in the face. "What in all the dreamlands—?"

"Ask no questions," yelled Hero as a second rope dangled into view. "Climb!"

In the next second, knives clasped in grinning teeth, they were toiling speedily upwards toward the side of a ship whose keel wallowed a little where it showed through lowering clouds and swirling mist. The same thought was in both their minds as they heard the howls of frustrated rage from behind and below; that perhaps this was *Gnorri II*, with Limnar Dass come to rescue them.

But as at last they climbed toward the rail their hopes were dashed to pieces. The ship was black. Black as the shrivelled lips of a zombie—

Black as the putrid heart of Zura of Zura!

Aboard the Krakenship

As their heads came up level with the black planking of the deck, bony, briefly glimpsed feet kicked their knives roughly from their mouths. "A black ship!" Eldin croaked, spitting blood from a slashed lip. He rapidly climbed higher and hooked an elbow over the rail.

"Aye," groaned Hero following suit, "and I'll give you odds she has an octopus figurehead—and a crew whose graves have yawned empty since the day they were dug!" Even as he spoke, stumbling zombie forms came forward out of the ship's reeking blackness and rotting fingers clutched at the arms of the pair, hauling them over the rail and onto the tarry deck. Many an empty or worm-eaten eye-socket gazed dispassionately upon them; or at best rot-swollen orbs whose lidless glare was wet and fishy. And as always, Zura's zombies stank to high heaven.

"Here we go again," choked Hero as the smell suddenly engulfed him; and with his left hand he caught at the sword-wrist of the nearest zombie, while his right delivered a massive clout to the creature's crumbling face. The battered body flew apart noisomely . . . and Hero fought back nausea as the zombie body broke in half on the rail and the entire sword arm came loose in his grasp.

Eldin, not nearly so sensitive as his younger companion, grabbed a still kicking leg and tore it free from the corpse's lower half. Then, using the limb as a club, he set about to belabor the encircling horrors. Hero by now had managed to get grips both on himself and on the rusty weapon wrested from rotting fingers, and zombie bits flew as he worked sword-wizardry upon Zura's stumbling, crumbling minions—

—But only for a moment.

For as the zombie crew fell back before the fury of the questers, so Zura's voice sounded from the bridge, clear and sweet as some golden poison and issuing well-rehearsed instructions. Pulleys creaked as a rope was slashed through, and even as the adventurers turned their gaze upward, so a great heavy net fell out of the rigging and wrapped them in its mesh.

"Snared!" Hero gasped, slashing at the heavy ropes until his blade was trapped and wrenched from his hands.

"Snared, aye!" Zura repeated him, coming down from the bridge like some strange Angel of Death. "As I have longed to snare you since that day when you sank my skyfleet in the aerial Bay of Serannian. My ship was *The Cadaver* then, but I burned her because she reminded me too much of that black day."

"Black day?" Eldin grunted. "Funny, but I always thought black was your favorite color?"

"You—" she rounded on him, prodding him with her knife through the net, "will have little enough to joke about shortly. In the morning my ship will sail under new colors—its flag shall be the flayed hide of one Eldin the Wanderer!"

On hearing Zura's threat Eldin puffed himself up in mock rage; but he could not restrain the bobbing of his Adam's apple, and it is a difficult thing to maintain a berserker rage wrapped up in a great net. While the Wanderer vainly searched for a suitable rejoinder, Zura turned her gaze upon Hero.

Shrouded and weighed down by the heavy rope mesh, he asked: "And will you skin me also, Zura?"

"Oh, be sure of it," she whispered, moving closer. "Your skin shall stretch upon my cabin's wall, marked with all the

lands of Earth's dreams—a map of my future conquests. And
the skin of your head shall cover a small drum, with your
nose at one side so that the drumsticks may be sheathed in
your nostrils."

"Your imagination knows no bounds," Hero faintly answered, feeling goose-bumps rise up all over his (for the present intact, however naked) body, and knowing that they were
not entirely due to the chill Northern air.

Zura had seen his nakedness, however, and her eyes
widened in appreciation as she stared at his crouched and net-
weighted nudity. For his part he stared back. She was a lustful monster, this Zura of Zura, and perhaps her appetite might
yet work in his and Eldin's favor.

"I had forgotten what a man you are," she said, more softly
but no jot less dangerously.

"And I had forgotten your great beauty," he lied.

And yet in fact she was beautiful, or had been, though tell-
tale signs of corruption were now visible despite the artful
draping of her invariably adventurous attire. Hero deliberately
drank in the sight of her, as were she some sweetheart of his
younger, waking-world days; but all the while his mind was
working overtime to discover a way out of this new and em-
inently perilous dilemma.

While his mind raced he continued to look at her, and
knowing he stared, she posed for his eyes. Long and leggy,
she wore a scarlet sheath split from her feet to her waist.
Above that her body was naked, breasts large, brown-tipped
and firm. Wide golden bands held scarlet sleeves to her arms,
and her wrists were heavy with gold and silver bangles. Her
eyes were huge and black to match the ropes of shining hair
which fell about her shoulders.

With lips whore-red, and a thin film of oil to give her body
a milky sheen, Zura was all seductress and knew it. But Hero
knew it too—knew also that her gaze was the hypnotic gaze
of a serpent, that the scarlet-covered areas of her body wore
the purple bloom of creeping decay. And knowing all of this,

still he smiled at her—which was a hard thing for that Princess of Nightmares to understand.

"Ah, but you had your chance once, David Hero," she said.

"I merely lusted for life more strongly than I lusted for you," he told her. "You would have sucked me dry—like a vampire—simply to renew your own strength. But if there had been some other way . . ."

She considered his words. "Knowing me," she finally said, "knowing my story, still you—?"

"You are beautiful," he cut her short, "but so is life. If I could have you and not lose my strength, my life . . ."

For long moments she stared at him, directly into his eyes, until his head began to swim under that burning gaze. "Do you seek to share the Throne of the Dead, David Hero?"

"That would be vastly better than to serve as one of the undead," he answered. "Alive . . . I am a man in my full strength. Dead—" and he shrugged, "I would be just one more zombie."

"I must think on it," she slowly said, never taking her eyes from him.

"Then think quickly, Zura, for Lathi would take me from you—aye, and the Dukes of Isharra, too."

"The Dukes?" she laughed throatily. "One day they shall crawl before me; for living the way they do, surely they shall die monstrously and so be mine. As for Lathi: she rules over insectmen and females who are 'maids' in name only. I fear not that gross grub!" She called forward a pair of freshly dead (alive?) zombies to lift up the hem of the net, then beckoned Hero to come out.

As he stepped free of the heavy mesh, leaving Eldin still entrapped, a cry went up from far below. Stepping to the rail, Zura called Hero to join her. In the heart of Sarkomand a bonfire now blazed close to the place where the miserable captive horned ones waited for death. Even as his eyes took in the scene, Hero knew that the end was now in sight for that pair of survivors of the desert clash. One by one, the jeering, thronging torturers were cutting the ropes which moored the straining mast and basket to the ground.

Taking all of this in—and noting that the contraption lay almost directly below Zura's ship—a mad idea came into the quester's mind. He glanced at the net which still covered the struggling Wanderer, and at the hawser which had held it aloft in the rigging. At the end of the stout rope an iron grappling-hook lay upon the deck . . . As Hero's idea took on flesh, so there came a second concerted cry—this time of hellish glee—from below.

" 'Ware, Zura!" cried Hero. "See, the last rope is slashed through—and that rocketing thing speeds straight for your ship!" He threw her back from the rail, stooped and snatched up the grappling-hook, then leapt up onto the rail where he balanced desperately as the cluster of flotation-bags, shattered mast, basket and shrieking horned ones came rushing up toward him from misted Sarkomand. At the last moment, as Zura screamed a command and her zombies rushed him, he took aim, hurled the hook overboard and threw himself atop Eldin in his net entangle.

Sprawled there, half-on, half-off the cursing Wanderer, Hero squeezed his eyes shut and hung on for dear life. He felt zombie fingers clutching at him—heard Zura's harsh command that her minions should "Kill him! Kill him!"—and for a split second believed that his hastily conceived and yet more hastily executed plan had gone horribly awry. Then—

—A massive fist snatched him, Eldin, net and all crashing through the ship's splintering rail and up, up. Several zombies where they stood or stumbled amidst the net's mesh went spinning, some sundered, outwards in a rending of rotting limbs, and silently down in lazy arcs, like skeleton leaves fluttering from a winter tree. For Hero's shot had been a good one—the grapple had caught in the framework of the basket—and now the cluster of flotation bags hauled two extra passengers, one clinging like a leech, the other too stunned to do, say or even think anything at all . . . for a heartbeat or two, at any rate.

"Great heaving bloody hell!" Eldin roared then through mesh and rush of wind, his eyes bulging inches from Hero's own. "Don't tell me you've done what I think—fear—you've done?"

"As you wish," Hero shouted back through the mad howl of sundered air. "I won't tell you."

"Are you daft?" Eldin cried. "Have you finally succumbed to moon madness? Man, you've done for us! How are we supposed to get out of this one?—and why are you groping at my leg?"

"Bend your knee, great oaf!" yelled Hero as they soared upward into southward fleeing clouds. "Do you still wear that little knife which you used to carry strapped to your calf?"

"Aye, but it has no edge. It's for stabbing, not cutting. You'll not chop me out of this net with that."

"You're safest where you are—for the moment," Hero answered, his fingers creeping up Eldin's trouser leg until he found and slipped the small dagger from its shealth. Then, blade transferred to teeth, naked as a newborn babe and cold as the core of a glacier, he began to climb the rope from net to basket.

Eldin knew now what his companion was trying to do. If he could climb up to the flotation bags and rupture one or two—they both might still come out of this in one piece. Craning his neck to follow Hero's progress, the Wanderer saw that he had reached the basket and was now starting up the mast itself. Above him, lashed to that sole remaining timber of Hrill's destroyed craft, the cloven feet of the survivors of that same brief battle were barely visible through the rushing vapors of the cloudbank.

"Go to it, lad!" Eldin roared as loudly as he could. "Good luck, you skinny son of a monkey!" But he doubted if Hero heard.

Bitterly cold now but determined to do or (literally) die, Hero was clambering up the ropes which bound the horned ones to the mast. Incredibly, one of them snarled something inaudible into his ear and bit that same inoffensive organ.

With the knife clasped in his teeth, Hero could not tell the horned ones that he was attempting to save their lives, not to mention his own and Eldin's; better simply to ensure that the rest of his climb went unimpended. Thus he kneed his attacked in the groin and butted him in his wide-mouthed face, so that he at once lapsed limp and passive.

But even as the naked quester continued his climb, he guessed that he was fighting a losing battle. The mast was slick with moisture from the clouds; gravity pulled tirelessly and with much more than its usual force; his fingers were blue and every inch gained drained so much energy that there would soon be none left. Worse, the heaven—(or hell-) bent contraption finally burst out of the clouds and shot up into mad moonlight: a sick, blinding yellow glare emanating from that looming, bloated, cratered monstrosity which now seemed to fill the entire sky.

Hero felt his numb fingers slipping and knew this was the end. It had been a good game while it lasted (both in the dreamlands and, he supposed, though he could not really remember, in the waking world), but now it was over. For a moment he considered simply relaxing his hold and letting himself be swept away. But then he thought of Eldin. No saying what bother the old fool would get himself into on his own. No, better simply to cling here, like a limpet to a rock, and see what the future—if there was to be a future—held for them both. And if there was no future . . . well, eternity would welcome him frozen to a sky-ship's mast somewhere in the bitter reaches high above the dreamlands. At least this way he could never go as a zombie to the Charnel Gardens of Zura!

But damn it all, he had *almost* made it. The flotation bags were just up ahead, a couple of feet away. It might as well be a mile. He turned a frosted, rime-covered head slowly upwards, squinting his eyes against the painful glare of the mad moon—

—And saw a fantastic, impossible sight!

Black shapes, a pair of them, were outlined against a

bloated background of yellow craters and looming, golden mountains. Black shapes, horned, bat-winged, with forked tails—and carrying weapons?—circling the flotation bag cluster where it dragged its burden skyward, less speedily now but quite irresistibly.

"Gytherik's gaunts!" Hero whispered to himself as hope surged up in him once more. "But they must almost be at their limits in this altitude. Whatever they intend doing, they'd best do it quickly!"

And almost as if they heard him (which indeed they did, in their way) the weapon-wielding gaunts "did something." They angled their bodies into streamlined arrows, turned their swords—one curved sword, which Hero now recognized as his own, and one straight, which was Eldin's—toward the straining bladders of flotation essence, and came zeroing in on the bags in a crazy kamikaze dive like . . . like—

Like bats out of hell!

Hero's Plan

CHAPTER V

Morning light was still an hour or so away when Gytherik, unable to sleep, went up onto *Gnorri*'s deck to find Limnar Dass already up and about and pacing the planks in the chill, eerie half-glow of pre-dawn. Gytherik could tell from the sky-Captain's expression that nothing had changed: Hero and Eldin were not yet returned from their inexplicable and unguessed night-quest.

But it was not until he called his grim up onto the deck from their storage-hold quarters that the gaunt-master realized the real size of the problem. Not only had the ex-waking-worlders gone off into the night, but apparently Sniffer and Biffer had also heard and answered some unknown call. And in that last Gytherik was closer to the answer than he might ever had guessed.

"Those two gaunts," he told Limnar Dass, "are definitely a most unusual pair. They have developed characters—I mean *real* characters—at a frightening rate. Maybe I made an error when I gave them names. Perhaps it only served to accelerate the problem."

"You think they went off with Hero and Eldin?" asked Limnar.

"I believe they may have gone out on their own to search for Hero and Eldin," Gytherik answered. "Without my go-ahead."

"Look," said Limnar, "it will be daylight soon, or as close as it ever gets to daylight around here. I'll have the ships readied for flight, and when you think there's enough light you can go off with your grim and give this entire area a minute going over. Then, if you find anything, the flotilla will be ready to back up any action you may have started. How does that sound?"

"Mist's clearing, Cap'n Dass," came a cry from the bridge, complementing Gytherik's nod of agreement. "Air's pretty still. Sunup is forty minutes, full daylight in one hour forty-five."

"I may not wait for full light," said Gytherik to the sky-Captain. "I don't like the idea of just sitting here doing nothing. The feeling is growing in me that something is very wrong. If I get the grim airborne now, when daylight comes we'll be that much further ahead."

"Mist still clearing, Cap'n," came the watch's cry once more. "And—" the crewman's voice paused and went up a notch, "—and something coming this way. Something in the clouds!"

"Where?" yelled Limnar at once, his eyes scanning gray, sluggish heavens. And to Gytherik, in a lower tone: "Could it be your gaunts?"

"Could be," the youth answered, "—or a Leng ship!" And suddenly, excitedly he pointed up and north-westward into the sky. "There it is! But what in—?"

His question, unspoken, hung in the air in imitation of the weird aerial device which now hove into view through a gap in the clouds. The clouds, along with the mist, were thinning, but the mad moon was already down and disappeared beyond dreamland's rim. And blown on a falling north wind the thing in the sky loomed closer, until its outlines became unmistakable.

"Why, that's the mast and basket from Hrill's ship!" gasped Limnar Dass. "The contraption those horned ones used to flee from the wreck in the desert."

"Right," Gytherik agreed. "Except it no longer has a sail—and it's in tow behind Sniffer and Biffer!"

"There's someone in that net," Limnar went on, squinting his eyes as the aerial device drifted, was blown and towed closer to the ship.

"And someone else—three someones—on the mast itself," Gytherik added. Then, suddenly filled with urgency, he turned to his depleted grim and ordered them aloft. Moments later they joined the straining Sniffer and Biffer in the sky above *Gnorri II*, and in a short while the flying contraption was brought safely down and secured to the ship.

By then it could clearly be seen that two of the three figures on the mast were horned ones, lashed in position with ropes. Above them, Hero was quite literally frozen to the broken mast—while in the net Eldin blustered and roared as always until he was set free. Then the remaining flotation bags were punctured and the entire device allowed to collapse gently onto the deck, the horned ones were cut down and taken away for questioning, and Hero was gently prised from his position and carried into Limnar's cabin. There he was given brandy and covered with warm blankets.

With the horned ones out of the way, and after Sniffer and Biffer had been severely chastised—then petted and fondled to a ridiculous extent—by their youthful master, then Eldin, fortifying himself with a bottle of mellow golden wine, told all of what had happened. This was in the sky-Captain's cabin, where Hero, still recovering from his near-fatal freezing, merely sat and sipped at brandy while Eldin talked.

"And that was that," the Wanderer finished. "In like a flash—like twin flashes—came Sniffer and Biffer, puncturing half of the bags in as much time as it takes to tell, and down we came out of the sky. The wind was in our favor, of course, but those two bloody marvelous gaunts did most of the work!"

When he sat back with his wine, both Limnar Dass and Gytherik were rightly full of questions. "But who was it called you away in the first place?" the gaunt-master wanted to know.

"And how far away exactly is this centuried city?" asked Limnar. "And just how do we get to it?"

"And do you really think that these two girls of yours— Ula and Una—are there?" (Gytherik again.)

"Would we have a chance, do you think, in a surprise aerial attack?" (Limnar.)

And all the time Eldin's great bearded face turning first to one of his questioners, then the other, until his brows began to come down like angry thunderheads. Then it was that Hero managed to get his shivering and the chattering of his teeth under control, and with something of his old authority he commanded all:

"Now slow down, l-lads, and let's take it one qu-question at a t-time. Ula and U-Una, you ask: did they call us into a trap? I think n-not."

"Not them, no," growled Eldin, "but some dark demonic voice in our minds. They are there, though—of that we're pretty sure. As for the exact location of Sarkomand: we should find it again easily enough, simply by following the shoreline westward. We'd see the ruins from the air; and if we stayed close to the ground—"

"Then we m-*might* also have a chance in a surprise attack, y-yes," Hero finished it. "But I don't think we'd better let it come to that. I have a few ideas of my own—which I'll come to in a moment. But for now, since it seems we've answered most of your questions, I have one f-for you."

"Go ahead," said Limnar.

"F-first off, did Sniffer and Biffer bring back our swords? They did? Good! And secondly:" he lifted his blankets to peer under them at his nakedness and grinned ruefully, "does someone have a spare set of clothes I could use?"

Suitable clothes were sent for, and while Hero waited he

sipped more brandy and further recovered. His wits, it seemed, had been honed to a fine edge by his ordeal. As dawn broke on a drear but much less cloudy day, finally he gave his friends the benefit of his reasoning.

"We were above the clouds when Sniffer and Biffer rescued us. Out of sight of the Isharrans, Zura and Lathi alike. My guess is that they'll think we've gone right off into space. They'll think we're finally done for." He shrugged. "Well and good, let them continue to think so. And just in case they've spies out, let's have the mast from old Hrill's ship chopped up and destroyed once and for all. If it's spotted aboard *Gnorri II* it will be a dead giveaway. As for our prisoners—"

"I had all but forgotten them!" Eldin excitedly, rumblingly broke in. "They might know the whereabouts of Ula and Una!"

"Right," said Hero, "and if they do—"

"We'll launch a rescue mission," cried Eldin, "—a proper one this time. A full-scale attack, and—" He paused as Hero slowly shook his head.

"No," said the younger quester. "Stealthy does it this time, my friend: Slowly, slowly, catchee monkey!"

"Eh?" said Eldin, Limnar and Gytherik as a man. And Eldin added: "Has the cold addled your brains, lad? We're not after catching any oriental monkeys!"

Hero frowned. "That's a saying I remember from the waking world," he informed. "I think . . . Anyway, it doesn't matter, for even if we went at 'em full tilt we couldn't win. They outnumber us two or even three ships to one. Even if we *did* win our losses would be enormous—and probably unnecessary. No, that's not the way. Look, they think we two are finished. That's our trump card! See, I believe their snatching us was purely a delaying tactic."

He paused, then turned to Limnar. "What would your course of action be if we hadn't come back?"

"Why, we'd be airborne and searching for you—starting just about now!" answered the sky-Captain.

"So let's be at it," said Hero. "That's what they'd expect, right? All you have to do is *avoid* the coastal region to the west—Sarkomand—where the enemy is actually encamped. I figure it's not an easy place to spot from the air anyway. Toward evening, however—as night falls and before the moon rises—the flotilla can close in, seemingly haphazardly, until the last moment. Then—"

"Then we catch 'em with their pants, down, eh?" guessed Eldin, only to be frustrated once more.

"No," Hero shook his head, "for they'll have spotted our ships long before that. But while they're watching the ships, and as soon as the light begins to fail, you and me and Gytherik—and the gaunts of course—we'll be sneaking in on them at a very low level, perhaps out of the sea mists. While they're getting their fleet airborne to fight off Limnar's possible attack, we'll hit 'em from the rear and snatch Ula and Una."

"But what's to stop them attacking our ships during the day?" asked the sky-Captain, not unreasonably. He frowned. "If they have superiority of numbers—"

"That's a chance we'll take," Hero answered. "But personally, I don't think they will attack. This is the way I see it:

"This whole thing has got to climax soon. Perhaps tonight, maybe tomorrow, certainly within three days. When we were up there above the clouds I saw the moon, and I just know that this can't go on much longer. That being so, the dreamlands are in for one hell of a battering—from which they're not supposed to recover. Now then, the root of the problem lies in Sarkomand—"

"Oorn," put in Eldin. "Mnomquah's mate."

"Aye," said Hero, "Oorn."

"So the horned ones and their allies are here simply to protect Oorn," said Gytherik, pulling at his chin. "Is that the way you see it?"

"Something like that, yes," Hero agreed.

"And you think they'll be loath to risk any sort of fight

where there's a chance Oorn's life may be jeopardized?" This from Limnar Dass.

"Right again," Hero nodded, then pursed his lips. "Well, not her life, exactly. No, for I'm told it's difficult to kill these Great Old Ones. Come to think of it, I've also heard that they have telepathic powers. They can call with their minds!" He glanced at Eldin. "Maybe that explains last night's little trap, eh?

"But at any rate, the way I see it is that the enemy won't want anything to go wrong with Mnomquah's leap to Earth, which is why they'll sit still and chew their fingernails while our seven ships are nosing about. And while they're all concentrating on a possible attack from the air or the land, we must try to get Ula and Una out the back door. Our ships will be the decoy, if you see what I mean. They're faster after all and can easily outrun the Leng ships."

"Outrun them?" Limnar Dass still seemed a little uncertain; his tone was a trifle indignant. "We are to run before them?"

"Now don't go getting upset," said Hero placatingly, holding up a hand. "Actually, I believe my trip into the heavens has done me a lot of good. Cleared my head, as it were, of the mad moon's influence. I can see things a lot more clearly now."

"Oh?" rumbled Eldin. "Well, I wish to hell I could! You'd better explain yourself fully."

"Look," Hero sighed. "If there're going to be large bits of moon's crust flying about, and tidal waves and all, and Mnomquah—in whatever shape or form he takes—streaking from broken moon to dreamlands, and this place is to be the epicenter, more or less—"

"I begin to see," whispered Gytherik. "Why, it's obvious! The last place on Earth that Zura and Lathi and all the others would want to be is here, right?"

Smiling, however wryly, Hero nodded. "The way I see it, they'll be off into space—maybe even a safe spot on the dark side of the moon itself—until it's all over. That's why the horned ones have gathered together a regular fleet: so that they can make a mass escape. When it *is* all over, then Lathi, Zura and the Dukes get theirs—whatever has been arranged for them—and Mnomquah and Oorn, and their workshippers the moonbeasts, and the horned ones too, inherit the dream-lands. Except—"

"Yes?" the others queried as a man.

"Except we're not going to let them." Hero's smile was grim. "As soon as they make tracks for the moon—signalling the beginning of the end—we sail in, find Oorn's pit and do whatever we can toward preventing her aeon-deferred reun-ion with old Mnomquah."

"Brilliant!" said Eldin with feeling.

"Glad you like it," Hero remained grim.

"But *how* shall we deal with Oorn?" Gytherik was less sure.

"We might seal her pit," Hero shrugged. "Something like that."

"How seal her pit?" Limnar now demanded.

"Hell's teeth, I don't know!" Hero growled. "With an av-alanche, maybe. A landslide."

"With fire!" cried Eldin. "A blazing ship to scorch her . . . well, whatever she's got."

"Good!" cried Hero, shaking a fist. "That's it! Now you've got the idea. Now get on with it. *Think*, you dodos—get your damned brains working! Me . . . I'm knackered. As soon as I get some clothes on that fit me half decently, I'm for bed. I've had a rough old night, one way or another.

"As for you lot: Cap'n Dass, you'd best get the flotilla mobile. Eldin: you can talk to the horned ones. Find out where the girls are. But don't hurt 'em, mind! Well, not a lot, anyway. And then you'd best get some sleep too."

"What about me?" asked Gytherik, full of excitement.

"You look after those gaunts of yours," ordered Hero. "Make sure they get a good day's rest. And Gytherik—"

"Yes?"

"Give Sniffer and Biffer a kiss from me, will you? Not only did they track us, recover our swords, follow us to

Sarkomand and save our lives, but they did it with a great deal of . . . of . . ."

"They did it right, eh?" grinned Gytherik.

"*Damned* right!" Hero emphatically agreed. Then, seeing the gaunt-master's sudden grimace, he added: "Well, if not a kiss, a hug at least!"

Strange Sanctuary

Ula and Una, as fine and desirable a pair of ladies as ever were lusted after (and won, however contrived the double "conquest" had been) by dreamland's most fabled-to-be questers, were in dire straits. Well-proportioned girls—to say the least—from an early age, their father Ham Gidduf of Andahad had used not so jokingly to threaten them with chastity belts if they so much as looked at boys. (Not that this had stopped boys looking at them!) How dearly they wished they might be secured in just such weighty nether-garments right now ...

Dark-haired, green-eyed and delicately elfin-featured, despite their very worldly prominence in other areas, they were supple and willowy ... and very much on edge. Neither one of the girls had slept but in brief snatches for two days now, since the first reports had reached their captors of the approach of a flotilla of ships out of the south. For Ula and Una had known that they were merely bait on the hook, and that the hoped-for catch would be David Hero and Eldin the Wanderer.

If the Lengites and their allies could only remove these two obstacles to their Master's plans, then all should go very well indeed. Since it had been known well in advance that eventually the pair must be recruited on the side of the dreamlands, plans had early been laid first to lure, then to dispatch them. And if anything at all were guaranteed to bring the questers a-running, surely it was the knowledge that former friends of theirs—and most certainly former lovers—were in trouble. Hence Ula and Una's this time very genuine abduction.

And yet strangely, they had not been harmed. Perhaps there was logic in this, too: if the questers should get it into their heads that the girls had been mistreated, then perhaps they might carry such a notion to its ultimate conclusion and suspect that they had been murdered—horribly. Which in turn would doubtless provoke or precipitate a berserker attack in which the men of the flotilla would fight like madmen, regardless of the cost. This might well endanger not only Oorn but the aeon-awaited arrival in the dreamlands of her Lord, the moon-god Mnomquah himself.

Last night, however, the luck of the twin beauties had seemed dramatically to change, and then it had become apparent that a certain promise made by the Dukes of Isharra to the degenerate human members of their ship's crew was about to be kept. Namely: that as soon as Hero and Eldin were in chains, then the twin daughters of Ham Gidduf would be handed over to the crew for their amusement. And the horned ones, who formed an even larger percentage of the ship's contingent, had likewise been offered whatever was left when the Isharrans were finished!

Which was why, as soon as they heard jubilant whispers that indeed Hero and Eldin had been trapped, Ula and Una—who thus far had enjoyed a small measure of freedom—had contrived to lock, bolt and bar themselves into the comparative opulence of the Dukes' own cabin aboard the bad ship *Shantak*. Which was also why, when the questers had been delivered to the Dukes, the meeting had taken place in Sarkomand's ruins and not aboard *Shantak* herself. No, for there the crew's more rapacious members had been dicing for the doubtful privilege of being first, second, third and so on to attempt forced entries on the twins in their retreat.

One enterprising youth, the highest scorer and therefore the first to try his hand, had got himself down in the ribs of the ship beneath the cabin refuge, where he had loosened a floor-board; and had then made the mistake of exploring the gap with a free hand. For the girls had found an assortment of weapons in the cabin, the outcome being that the luckless bravo had lost two of his fingers and one thumb, and had earned for himself a broken thigh in the resultant plunge from precarious perch in the rafters to hold's thick-planked bottom.

When a second man had smashed in a small-paned leaded window, and after he had been fatally skewered through the left eye for his pains, then the horned ones had been invited to join in the game. Why, after all, should the humans hog all of the fun? Fair-minded fellows these Isharrans . . .

The Lengites had fared no better, however, though one of them made an attempt of sorts; had managed at least to carry out the preliminaries. He had climbed up onto the cabin's roof, stretched out flat and found himself a tiny peephole where a knot had fallen from the timbers. He had forgotten, alas, a basic principle (what may be seen into may also be looked out of) and paid the price of his folly. A single great *thump* had been heard; his prone, roof-hugging body had been seen to give a jerk; and when his corpse was taken down a second knothole had been discovered in the region of his heart, through which had been driven with considerable force a stout, sharp, six-inch ship's nail.

The girls had then plugged all remaining knotholes, rein-forced the tiny windows and further barricaded the massy door; and so far no further intrusions had been attempted upon their privacy. Eventually they would weaken through starvation, or if things got desperate the cabin's door could be broken in with axes, though that would hardly be to the liking of the Dukes of Isharra. But in any case, all of this frustration and waiting about could only serve as fuel for lustful imag-inations; and oh! the plans which were made for Ula and Una—and all within their hearing—while their tormentors prowled outside, black-hearted and red-eyed.

And the girls had been there, barricaded in their cabin,

when the Dukes gave chase to Lathi's ship *Chrysalis* and Zura's *Shroud*: and with pounding hearts they had listened to the sounds of fighting: the clash of weapons, screams of crippled and dying men, and a certain bull-voice roaring which Una was almost certain had belonged to the Wanderer. And following all of this, much groaning and many low-muttered curses; and all through the night the girls had been left to themselves, to snatch what sleep they could during this brief respite, while the Dukes of Isharra counted the cost of the fighting and the wounded tended their injuries. And in their waking hours the girls had done a great deal of sobbing, for it seemed certain to them that Hero and Eldin had been overwhelmed and murdered.

"That time in Baharna," whispered Ula tearfully to her sister in the night, when they both sat awake and trembling in the creak-timbered cabin. "We used those lads so cruelly."

"With never a thought for their welfare should they be caught," Una added. "Indeed, our plan required that they be caught—or at least discovered. And them branded rapists and abductors through our accusations! And getting nothing out of it at all."

"Except us, our bodies."

"Huh!" answered Una, bitterly, as might be imagined. "Even that was plotted, so that father wouldn't marry us off to these vile Dukes of Isharra. But Eldin . . ." (and she sighed), he was . . . such a capable lover."

"Hero too," sobbed Ula quietly. "At least, I've always assumed he was—having no standards of reference, I mean."

"Those two would be good by any standards, I'm sure," Una sighed again. "And just think: we could have sailed away with them over the Southern Sea!"

"Instead of waiting here to be raped and soiled and murdered," Ula added. "We didn't know what we were doing until it was much too late—for all of us."

"We could have sailed away with them," Una repeated in a low whisper, dabbing a teardrop from the end of her pretty nose. "Well, they'll go no more a–sailing now, poor lads. We played them for fools and were ourselves fooled—and look what it's all come to."

And so their tearful conversation had gone on until Una had fallen asleep. Later she had sat alert in the darkness while Ula drowsed and nodded fitfully; and so on until morning, when the *Shantak* had grown very still in the calm of the new day. Then the girls had heard a hubbub of seemingly concerned voices, and later they had opened up a peephole upon a scene of puzzling activity.

The Lengite fleet was apparently preparing for battle while yet at anchor, and every crewman seemed busy and full of feverish excitement. Even the lurkers about the cabin refuge aboard *Shantak* were called away to various tasks, and again the girls grabbed at this welcome respite from filthy jokes and horrifyingly depraved whispers, promises and threats. This activity of preparation went on through the whole of the morning without let-up and was not completed until shortly before noon, when a series of frightening events took place as harbinger to the great maelstrom yet to come.

For it was then, as the Captains and crews of the black (and one white, or at least gray) ships relaxed a little and the sniffers returned to prowl and threaten vilely through the stout planking of the cabin's walls, that the mad moon's proximity to the dreamlands began to make itself felt more physically, more fearsomely. Hearing cries of awe and wonder without, the girls once more employed their spyhole to see what was going on. At first they saw nothing; all looked gray and dreary as ever, and the only real change seemed to be in the weather, which was now utterly calm, with grim and motionless clouds above and eerily dissipating mists below (except in the cliff-guarded byways of primal Sarkomand itself, which seemed permanently misted); but then, seeing where *Shantak*'s crewmen were pointing, the eyes of the twins gazed toward the seaward horizon.

Strange shiny tubular structures stood far out at sea, towering like the legs of giants over the apparently still deeps and rushing to and fro, occasionally colliding and collapsing in torrents of spray. Waterspouts, in amazing profusion, parading like blind suicidal guardsmen across the face of the ocean! Some of these monsters towered even higher as they approach the primal city's quays, and one even pushed its way to the mighty, ancient sea-wall itself before subsiding and melting down into the sea. For hours the display continued until, suddenly, the nodding colossi made off, rushing south in a seeming panic and disappearing over the gray horizon.

And as if to explain their panic-flight, in the space of a few more minutes a great wind began gusting that blasted the startled clouds southward in the wake of the waterspouts and screamed banshee-like through the fleet of moored ships. Several of the vessels were torn free of their moorings and driven out over the sea before their Captains could regain control—by which time the winds were dying away as quickly as they came.

Then, in the gray northern daylight, before thoughts could be expressed or even gathered: a meteor shower! Great blazing boulders that howled across the tortured sky and hissed down through holes in the clouds to fall explosively into a now surging sea. And where they fell columns of steam rose up and the waters boiled, however briefly, to mark their deep green graves. Several of these aerial fireballs struck Sarkomand, shattering ruins yet more ruinously and spraying fire everywhere; and one, in its fiery passage to earth, scorched the topsail, rigging and mast from a Leng ship. Then, once more, all was still. Except for the sea . . .

Beyond the massive sea-wall the ocean seemed now to rush, first west in a racing tide, then east in choppy disorder, where mighty whirlpools formed swirling tunnels into tumultuous depths. And this was the highest tide the primal city had every known; or at least the highest since the raising of the hoary sea-wall, in predawn days by hands other than Man's. Great waves pounded against the wall, flinging spray a hundred feet and more into the air. And the rush and roar of ocean could be heard and felt more clearly, even aboard the ships of the Lengites, even though the wind blew steadily southwards once more.

And so the day grew to its close, and evening blew in with the winds from the north, and Ula and Una resigned themselves to another fearful night in the cabin aboard the creaking, rolling *Shantak*. Here was a very strange thing, however, and one which struck the girls as monstrously sinister. By now the Isharrans and horned ones of the *Shantak*'s crew must know that they had peepholes from which they could gaze out upon whatever was happening; but something must now be happening (or about to happen) which the Dukes of Isharra did not wish them to see; for blankets were brought and nailed up all around the cabin, and as the evening grew toward night so the remaining light was entirely shut out.

Then, for a further half-hour or so, all that the terrified girls knew was the quiet creep of many feet and the occasional furtive whisper. They heard, too, the unmistakable but subdued accents of the Dukes themselves, and so knew them to be aboard; and of course they suspected that this was some new and elaborate plot to snatch them from their now very fragile-seeming sanctuary.

A plot it was, most certainly, but the girls could hardly have guessed that it centered not about them (although they stood in fact at its center) but about a certain pair of questers, late of the waking world, who were on their way here right now through darkening northern skies—

—And who the Dukes of Isharra, their motley crew, and the entire Lengite alliance *knew* were coming!

The Best Laid Plans . . .

CHAPTER VII

All about the deck of *Shantak* her crew crouched and waited, weighed down with weapons and nervous in the knowledge that they awaited the advent of three of dreamland's most fabulous citizens—not to mention an entire grim of its leathery, most legended beasts. They hid in open holds ready to spring out at a moment's notice, behind and atop the cabin on the deck, beneath canvas covers and in the folds of furled sails—so that with the sole exception of a lookout on the bridge, the ship looked and seemed completely deserted.

And yet the entire crew was there: humans (however degenerate), Lengites, and pseudo-aristocrat "masters"; and all of them grim-eyed in the surety of the imminent arrival of their enemies—and then that there would be a deal of blood before that trio was subdued. Some there were aboard *Shantak* who, having previously felt the fury of Hero and Eldin, would gladly be elsewhere; but Oorn herself, through the medium of her High Priest, had ordered the taking of the three. Moreover, they were not to be harmed, not seriously—not immediately.

No, for these ex-waking-worlders had become so pestilential—so dangerous and damaging to the schemes of the Great Old Ones, even to the Great Old Ones themselves—that they must now be handled personally. And Oorn had been given that honor, that small but significant task of removing

them forever from Earth's dreamland and so from the immemorial battle between Good and Evil.

As to how they had come to be worthy of her personal attention: they were too rapidly grown into legends. Legends
were dangerous; living legends even more so. There were
others like these two (these three, if Gytherik were included).
There was Lord Kuranes of Serannian and King Carter of
Ilek-Vad. Aye, and that damned de Marigny—his meddling
son, too, and the equally troublesome Titus Crow—but none
of the latter were here now. Present or otherwise, all had been
responsible, in one way or another, for the suppression of the
darker side of dreams.

Had not Hero and Eldin destroyed Thinistor Udd, a powerful ally of the Forces of Evil? And the centuried, mad First
One who could have been such an asset to the darkside powers? Even Yibb-Tstll's dreamland avatar—in the shape of a
huge stone idol carved in His likeness—had fallen to their
mischief and gone down in fragments; and who could say
what other blasphemies might yet be ascribed to their devious
hands if they were allowed to continue?

The Dukes of Isharra (those bungling dupes) had tried to
deal with them and failed miserably; so too the Eidolon Lathi
and Zura of Zura. And as for the horned ones of Leng—those
alien minions of the moonbeasts who served Mnomquah and
Oorn—why, they had proved less than useless! That was why
Oorn Herself must now take vengeance upon them and see to
it that they offend no longer. Indeed, that they *exist* no
longer!

All of this Oorn had explained to her High Priest where he
dwelled at the rim of her pit prison, and he had dutifully
passed it on to dupes and worshippers alike. The questers
were to be taken alive, aye—and then sacrificed to Oorn Herself; fed to her in her pit, a delicious repast to give her
strength for her impending mating . . .

And now they came—out of curling, night-thickened mists
of ocean—came from the south on great membrane wings. A
triangle of stealth in the sky, with Gytherik above, riding the

huge gaunt which was his personal mount, and Hero and Eldin below, where each dangled from the paws of lesser beasts. Hero was suspended beneath Sniffer and Biffer, that pair of most splendid night-gaunts, while Eldin (because of his greater bulk) had been given into the care of two somewhat sturdier if duller creatures.

Unerringly they came—over the now submerged quays, flitting bat-borne across the mighty sea-wall where the mad ocean raced mere feet from the worn and weathered rim—beneath wings trimmed for speed, and now for rapid descent as Hero pointed out *Shantak* where she was moored, somewhat apart from the bulk of the Lengite fleet. Down they swept, a black blur of motion in the near-darkness, a glint of steel, of slitted eye, the merest *hiss* of air across arcing membrane vanes.

"The females you seek are aboard *Shantak*," the horned ones had informed without the slightest hesitation. "They have locked themselves tight in the cabin of the Dukes of Isharra, which they now defend for their very lives!" For which information they had been granted *their* lives. The grim had flown them to a mountain pass at the foot of that great range which went up to Leng's forbidden plateau, from where they had gladly scrambled into obscurity. With luck they might return to their homeland of eternal twilight and desolation, and without luck . . . that was their problem. They had been only too glad to be released alive and intact, and free to use what little time remained in putting as much distance as possible between themselves and damned, doomed Sarkomand.

. . . Now the watchman on *Shantak*'s bridge—an Isharran—spied the three where they soared down silently out of darkness. A large and fearless brute of a man, he gave the alert, cried out once and once only as Eldin sprang down beside him, knocked aside his weapon, hoisted him up bodily and threw him down across the rail and into space. Then the rest of the gaunts were down and Hero and Gytherik crouched together on the deck, ears alert, listening to an almost painful silence.

"He cried out," came Eldin's hoarse whisper from the bridge. "If others heard—"

"Where the hell *is* everyone?" asked Gytherik, his voice hushed in the darkness.

"They must be asleep," answered Hero. "Land-lubbers, these Dukes. You'd not expect to find them aboard. Still . . ." and he paused, then shook his head. "It doesn't smell right to me," he said, "but no time to worry about it now. So let's be at it, eh? The girls are in the main cabin, so—" He strode up onto the bridge beside Eldin, and together they turned to face the humped, blanket-draped bulk of the Masters' cabin.

As Gytherik joined the pair, Eldin yanked aside a blanket and found the sturdy door. "Ula," he hoarsely called, keeping his voice low and gently rattling the iron doorknob. "Una, it's us—Hero and Eldin."

Inside the cabin the girls had heard the single cry of the watchman in that moment before Eldin launched him into eternity. Now they heard the Wanderer's gruff query and sprang to the door—where caution froze their hands even as they trembled on bolts and bars.

"Quickly, girls!" came Hero's unmistakable voice, vibrant in its urgency. "We haven't much time. We're here to take you out of this."

Yet still they hesitated, and as Eldin rattled at the doorknob a second time Ula's fearful, breathless voice demanded: "Show your faces—at the small window in the door."

Hearing her muffled cry, the questers pressed close to the tiny barred window and Eldin struck hot sparks to a taper taken from his pocket. In an instant the faces of the two showed a flickering yellow through grimy glass, and as Eldin snuffed out the little flame so the girls gasped their recognition and began tugging at bolts and removing heavy bars. Another moment or two and the door flew open, and female forms hurled themselves into powerful arms while Gytherik blushed with pleasure and youthful shyness in the darkness to one side.

"Hero!" the girls cried softly in unison. "And Eldin! Alive when we had feared you dead!"

Ula, peering about fearfully in the darkness, saw the gaunts where they clustered impatiently on the lower deck. She gasped and her hand flew to her mouth—

"*Shh!*" Hero warned. "They're only night-gaunts—and they're on our side."

Now Una spotted Gytherik's shadowy form and she pressed closer to Eldin's massive chest. The Wanderer patted her soft shoulder and said, "This is Gytherik, and he too is a friend. He's the master of the gaunts there."

"But where are all the Isharrans and those horrid Lengites?" questioned Ula. "There seemed to be so many of them . . ."

Hero's skin seemed suddenly to prickle and he felt the shadows closing in on him. "So many of them?" he repeated the girl's words. "Here? . . . When?"

"An hour ago at most," she answered. "We heard them come aboard and thought the ship must sink with their weight, they seemed so many." She clutched the quester tighter. "And Hero . . ."

"Yes?"

"We did not hear them leave!"

Hero and Eldin had time for one gnawing, agonized glance into each other's eyes. Then—

"We did *not* leave!" came the scornful, ringing voice of Byharrid-Imon Isharra. "And this time we have three of you—aye, and the girls too."

Many things happened then—happened together, with mind-dazzling, stupefying speed as the Isharran trap was sprung. Black-robed figures fell from the roof of the cabin like giant spiders, slamming shut the door and placing their backs against it even as quester steel slithered from oiled scabbards. Gytherik called out to his gaunts, his youth's voice shivering in the night air. Holds were thrown open and squat, knife-wielding shapes poured forth. A gaunt leaped high— and fell soundlessly to the deck, its neck severed half through. The rest of the grim lifted on violently throbbing wings; torches hissed into life, blinding with their glare; and out from their numerous hiding places sprang the rest of *Shantak*'s crew, swords aloft to ward off swooping gaunts, all making for the bridge where already a frenzied crush surged to and fro in a mad melee.

The questers fought like madmen, hacking and slashing at all who stood before them; Gytherik too, fighting like a veteran alongside his mightier, meatier friends. Screams filled the night and blood splashed wetly in the torchlight, washing the bridge. Then the trio was inundated—borne under, Ula and Una too—by sheer weight of bodies, and vile paws and calloused hands grabbed up all five of them and rushed them to the ship's rail.

Blazing torches were hurled aloft to ward off fluttering, disorganized gaunts; hard fists delivered final blows to panting, scratching, biting, desperately kicking forms; and five figures were tossed from ship into cold night air. Gytherik was last to go, and as he shot headfirst overboard so he called out to his gaunts. Two of them, unafraid of the noise and the affray (Sniffer and Biffer, as might be guessed), having seen the descent of the girls and their would-be rescuers, were already diving through the night. Reacting to the gauntmaster's cry with impossible speed, they snatched his tumbling body from thin air and bore him swiftly away.

"Damn, damn, *damn!*" cried Gathnod-Natz'ill Isharra from *Shantak*'s deck. His high-pitched, near-feminine voice was full of fury. "Those blasted gaunts have rescued their master!"

"But only him," answered his brother in typically ringing tone, "and without his friends he's harmless. As for this so-called Hero of Dreams and his good friend Eldin the Wanderer, this time they are ours. Or rather—they are Oorn's!"

The brothers gazed into the torch-flickered shadows of *Shantak*'s bridge. Corpses littered the planking and blood dripped blackly from bridge to lower deck. The ship stank of blood. A groan sounded where bodies sprawled thickest and an arm lifted jerkily—only to fall back as life winked out. Pale for a moment, the Dukes turned back to the rail and their eyes stared with those of their depleted crew down at the scene some forty feet below.

There, caught in nets as they fell and now tight-wrapped in ropes, like human bobbins, the questers cursed and their women sobbed. Byharrid-Imon grinned cruelly and called down: "Curse and cry all you want, you four. Believe me, when you meet Oorn face to face you'll be glad you practiced!"

Hero stopped struggling and glared his hatred into the mad faces which grinned down on him from *Shantak*'s rail. "So we're to have an audience with your monster Goddess, are we? Well, we've met such before. She can be no worse than the stinking scum she commands."

"Can't she, indeed?" Byharrid-Imon roared with half-crazed laughter. "And who said anything about an audience, eh? No, no, my friends, not an audience exactly. You see, to propitiate Mnomquah's final plunge from moon to dreamlands—you four are to be sacrificed to his hungry mate!"

"Aye," added his brother in shrill glee, "and sacrificed this very night—right now!"

. . . Of Men and Gaunts

Bruised, bloodied and only half-conscious, Gytherik made no complaint but merely hung limp in the prehensile paws of his charges as, joined by the other pair of nightmarish creatures, they sped him back to the coast, across sea-wall and submerged quays, and up into the night sky toward Limnar Dass where he waited aboard *Gnorri II*. Had things gone as planned, this would have been a joyous trip, a victory flight. The five gaunts would now be flying in line abreast, with Gytherik riding his great gaunt on the flank and the questers and girls suspended beneath the rest of the line. The gaunts would be overloaded, to be sure, but not for long. Out over the sea they would be met—as even now they were met—by the rest of the grim, all three of them, who would then have taken their share of the burden.

That was how it should have been. Now, with the sole exception of the gaunt-master himself—all dazed and battered and shaken up—there was no burden; and the grim had lost a brave and worthy member.

With *Gnorri II* in sight Gytherik regained his wits and began to react to the cold night air gusting into his face. Sensing his recovery, the great gaunt which was his chosen mount slid beneath him where he dangled and took his weight. He held tight to the saddle, swaying a little as the grim descended to *Gnorri*'s welcoming deck.

By this time the rim of the moon was showing like the crack of some false golden dawn all along the night horizon, but mercifully the heavens were still full of vapor, thin banks of cloud which obscured the mad yellow glare. In the sea, however, waterspouts were marching as before, and meteorites blazed across the night sky in fiery profusion. On the western horizon orange fires lit the land and made ruddy haloes on the underside of ashen clouds, and thick columns of smoke and tephra were aglow in the glare of freshly spawned volcanoes. The very air seemed charged with weird energies; and the thin clouds twisted and writhed as if tortured, even though the wind had fallen utterly away.

"Well," said Limnar Dass when he had heard Gytherik's brokenly gabbled story, "at least with the wind fallen there'll be no chase, no unequal fight. But how did they know you were coming?"

Seated in the sky-Captain's cabin with his bruised head in his hands, Gytherik could only offer a miserable shrug. "I don't know," he answered. "I only know that the whole thing was a mess, and that I'm lucky to have come out of it in one piece. If I hadn't been kicked half senseless—" He shrugged again. "Certainly I would have tried to rescue them—and that would have been the end of me, too."

"You think . . . that they're dead, then?" Limnar had difficulty forcing the words out.

"No, not dead, not yet. As I fell I saw nets set to catch us—saw the others bounce and tumble—and the hordes who waited to leap upon them! No, not dead. They wanted to take us alive."

Until now Limnar Dass had been calm, cool as a sky-Captain's training had made him. Training which had it that in a tight spot—when confronted by apparently insurmountable circumstances and difficulties—still there was always something one could do, as long as one refused to panic. Fine and proper advice coming from the lips of some hoary old Admiral who never in all his long career was so confronted . . . but now? Limnar sprang to his feet and dragged Gytherik upright and out of his chair. Face contorted in a fashion most unsuited to a man born of dreams, Limnar stared into the other's startled eyes, then shoved him roughly out through the cabin's doorway onto *Gnorri*'s bridge.

"Listen, lad," the sky-Captain ground the words out of his mouth. "It's not just Hero and Eldin—though without a doubt they're the finest, bravest pair of rogues a man ever knew—not just their lives we're talking about. Not even the lives of a pair of poor innocent lasses. No, this time it's everything! Everything, d'you hear?" And again he grabbed the youth's shoulders, his hands trembling with the urge to shake him.

At that Gytherik came out of his waking nightmare. The lines which made his young face haggard in the light of the ship's lamps took on a sterner mold. In ten seconds he seemed to mature by at least ten years—and abruptly he shook himself free from Limnar's grasp. With haunted eyes he looked at the moon, still rising, potent as some demon drug in the sky.

"You're right," he told Limnar Dass then. "These two have become everything to me, but it's no longer just them. And Limnar . . . tonight is the night! It must be. So what can we do? Is there anything we *can* do?"

Suddenly the sky-Captain's bearded face, whose lines never seemed quite so soft as those of other dreamlanders, broke into a craggy grin. He slapped Gytherik on the shoulder and jostled him back into the cabin, quickly poured two fat glasses of brandy and tossed his back. Gytherik followed suit and pulled a face.

"You know," said Limnar, "you had me worried there for a moment."

"You had *me* worried!" answered Gytherik with feeling. "But I know what you mean. At least I think I do."

"Do you? Listen, we're dreamlanders, right? We're what Eldin calls *Homo ephemerans*. Which means that however we play it, our actions are governed by the dreams of men in the waking world. Our entire world has been built of their dreams since the first man dreamed his very first dream! And even when they make the transition from waking world to dream-lands, still they seem to run the entire show—just as we've seen in Hero and Eldin. Am I right?"

Without waiting for an answer, Limnar thumped the table and jumped to his feet. "Maybe it's just that something of those two has rubbed off on me," he continued, "I don't know for sure, but I'm no longer satisfied merely to drift wherever dreams take me. Damn it all—I reckon it's about time we started to play our own cards!"

As if caught up in Limnar's fervor, lit by inspiration, Gytherik's face brightened for a moment. Then he relaxed and asked: "But what cards do we have to play? What can we do? Everything seems to be against us. If they were here—why, they seem able to *make* things happen, and—"

"But they're not here," Limnar cried, "and *we* must make things happen!" He thumped the table again. "Now sit," he said, "and let's work things out." They sat and Limnar poured more brandy.

Gytherik sipped, thought, and frowned. He said: "Though the clouds boil, there's no wind. Our sails hang slack, so we won't be fighting any sky battle."

"No," Limnar answered, "but the enemy is stuck too. Until the wind rises we're becalmed—all of us—it's as simple as that."

Gytherik nodded. "But we have the gaunts!"

"Too few," said Limnar. "We can't launch an attack with a mere handful of gaunts. And that's not to belittle them, you understand."

Gytherik began to grow despondent and it showed in his face. "You see? If those two double-damned questers were here—why, they'd turn events in their own favor, make adversity work for and not against them!"

"Good thinking," Limnar nodded. "So let's work on that. We don't have a lot going for us, so how can we use what stands against us? What, exactly, does stand against us?"

"The mad moon, for one thing," Gytherik shuddered. "She rises even now, and if this really is the night—"

"The last night, for the dreamlands," Limnar finished it for him. "Unless we can come up with an answer."

"The mad moon," Gytherik repeated, his frown deepening, fingers tapping on Limnar's table. "The last night. It's going to happen tonight." His fingers tapped faster and his jaw began to fall even as his frowns lifted.

"What is it, lad?" Limnar asked, leaning forward to gaze into Gytherik's face. "You look as if you've seen a ghost. I can almost count your goosebumps!" But it seemed that the youth no longer saw him, only the idea growing in his mind.

"Turn adversity to our favor!" Faster still his fingers tapped. "Waterspouts and whirlwinds, volcanoes and earthquakes and roaring, raging tides!"

"Yes, lad—go on."

"Tides!" Gytherik whispered almost inaudibly, his eyes wide and staring. "*Tides*, by all that's—"

"What is it?" Limnar now pressed. "Come on, out with it."

"The sea!" the gaunt-master suddenly shouted, springing to his feet. "The blessed sea!" Now it was his turn to lay hands on Limnar Dass. "The highest tides you've ever seen, lapping at the rim of the old sea-wall. What a knock in the eye *that* would be! Hero wanted to do it with earth, and Eldin with fire—but they were both wrong. There's another element which they overlooked—another way . . ."

"To do what?" Limnar now roared.

"To trap old Oorn in her damned pit!" cried Gytherik. "That's what!"

Limnar gaped, shook his head. "I don't follow you."

"Of course not, for you weren't there. You haven't seen the old sea-wall and the waters raging, ready to break through . . . Limnar, how much powder does *Gnorri* carry?"

"Powder?"

"Yes, powder—for the cannon, man!"

Taken aback by the heat of the gaunt-master's excitement, Limnar could only gasp, "Enough to blow the ship to hell—if all barrels went up at once."

"Oh, they will, they will," chanted Gytherik, and he began

to dance in his fever. Then he rushed out onto the bridge, where a bemused and breathless Limnar Dass caught up with him.

"Up onto the deck," cried Gytherik like a madman. "The powder, let's have it! Let's have it! Let's see what we've got. And Limnar—where's the nearest ship of the flotilla?"

"Right there," the sky-Captain answered, beginning to fear for the youth's sanity. He pointed off to starboard, where the lights of a ship winked beneath weirdly rotating skies. "Becalmed, of course."

"No matter!" cried Gytherik. "All to the good. If we're becalmed, they're becalmed. You said so yourself. They can't strike back." Before Limnar could question this, he added: "A note, quick! A note to the Captain of yon vessel. We want her powder—all of it. My gaunts shall bear the note, return with the powder. Return loaded down with the black, beautiful stuff! A few trips and we'll have it all."

Now, as the sum of Gytherik's babblings began to add up, Limnar became fired with the youth's enthusiasm. "Are you saying that you intend to blow a hole in Sarkomand's seawall?" he breathlessly asked.

"Right!" Gytherik hugged him. "*Damned* right, as Hero would say! We'll drown the damned place, seal old Oorn in her damned pit, smash the encampments of the damned horned ones, termen, zombies and Isharrans flat!" Then, eyes still burning behind dark bruises but softer now of voice, he added: "But we must be quick. The mad moon rises Look—"

Dreamland's rim seemed to burn beneath a mighty golden dome, to burn with a yellow glare the night mists could no longer hold at bay. Confused clouds cleared a path for mad moonbeams which put down their sick tendrils on the land like a glowing, cancerous horror of cosmic magnitude. Great waterspouts beyond number rushed here and there across heaving deeps—as if the very sea were trying to invert itself—and a dull, continuous rumbling filled the air, subdued now but growing ever louder. Volcanic fires burned in a score of distant places, and meteorites blazed and hissed in the heavens in such numbers that the sky became bright with their fire. Nothing like this had ever been known before in all the history of the lands of Earth's dreams.

For long moments the two stared at a world gone mad. Then—

"Ahoy the crew!" cried Limnar Dass. "There's work for you. I want all the powder brought up onto the deck right now ... and steady as you go. No accidents, if you please. Bundle the barrels together in scraps of net, gaunt-manageable in size, and get it done as quickly as you can. Come on, lads, bustle about. And listen, keep your chins up. We're not licked yet!"

To Gytherik he said, "I'll have that note for you in a dozen flaps of a night-gaunt's wing. And talking of gaunts, while I'm writing the note you'd best have an earnest little chat with the entire grim. Gytherik," he squeezed the youth's shoulders, "I think your answer is the right one, possibly the only one. I think it will work."

"Think it will work?" the gaunt-master answered, his eyes aflame with reflected meteorites. "My friend, you'd better pray it will work. It *has* to!"

Oorn!

A thousand torches blazed all through the streets of centuried Sarkomand from its oceanmost limits to Oorn's temple, lining the route for the triumphant procession which now wound its way through the alien ruins, bearing aloft the bound, bruised and battered forms of Hero, Eldin, Ula and Una. And there could be no mistaking the fact that now—setting aside all matters of earlier, personal squabbles—the entire enemy alliance was truly allied and in one accord in its current task: namely the physical destruction and spiritual damnation of the four prisoners in a mad and monstrous sacrifice to Oorn.

Zombies marched (or shuffled) with the throng; horned ones leaped, cavorted and played grating, inhuman tunes on nameless instruments; termen, however woodenly, paraded with the rest; and the Isharrans, led by their twin masters, slouched along in their generally degenerate fashion. And never an argument nor indeed any single sign of discord along the way. Noting this absence of enmity, Hero and Eldin began to wonder if they might not breed a little in the minds of their captors. The Dukes of Isharra were sticking close to them (their bearers were burly members of *Shantak*'s depleted crew) and so the questers decided to work first upon the minds of the sinister brothers. The decision was unspoken, mutual; even in adversity—perhaps *especially* in adversity—Hero and Eldin worked as a team.

"Hey, Byharrid-Imon," called Hero, sucking sore lips and teeth where a fist had bruised his gums. "You realize of course that you and your fellow Isharrans are the only true humans in this entire bunch—except for us, I mean? See, I'm puzzled. I can't figure out why you've teamed up with these damned monsters."

"You should listen to him, Isharran," Eldin gruffly put in. "We don't know what you've been promised, but we certainly know what's in store for you! We had it from old Hrill, the horned-one Captain of a ship we sank out in the desert west of Ilek-Vad."

Byharrid-Imon turned to smile grimly up at the two where brawny arms held them aloft. Without breaking his stride he said, "Talk all you like, questers. That's your right. But don't you think you've left it a bit late to try wriggling your way out of this one, eh?"

"It's late for all of us, Byharrid-Imon," Hero eagerly answered. "Can't you see that with the dreamlands destroyed there'll be no room for you in the moon-God's plans? What possible service could you perform for Mnomquah?"

Now it was Gathnod-Natz'ill's turn to speak. In his shrill, half-female voice he said: "We have been promised a complete monopoly in the trading and control of all precious metals and stones throughout the length and breadth of the dreamlands. Moreover, we are to be Satraps of Oriab and the Southern Isles, Kings of all the lands and cities bordering on the Southern Sea—with the exception of Zura and Thalarion, of course, for which we've no special desire—and High Lords of sky-floating Serannian."

"Oh?" Eldin lifted painfully puffy eyebrows. "But surely Lathi will have something to say about that? I mean, she's been promised a nest of hive-cities stretching right across the dreamlands!"

"And what of Zura, Princess of Zombies?" asked Hero. "She has plans to go a-conquering wherever her fancy takes her. And remember: all who die monstrous deaths become Zura's to command." He gave a wholly genuine and involuntary shudder. "By all that's rotten, her armies will be swelled this night—and that's for sure!"

"We know nothing of all that," Byharrid-Imon returned, but his voice rang a little less stridently now and his tone appeared less certain. "We do know, however, that we've always had fair play in our dealings with the horned ones and their masters."

"Of course you have," Eldin readily agreed. "They were setting you up, using you. They needed you to distribute their damned moon-gold, so that Mnomquah would know where to fire his double-damned beam on cities full of innocents. Beware, Isharrans, for you've been out in the mad moon's glare too long! You say you'll be Kings? Kings of what? Who will your subjects be when the slaughter is over? Who will you trade with then? With Zura and her million undead?"

"Bravo!" whispered Hero admiringly as they were bundled along. "Good stuff, that. Are you sure you weren't some sort of orator in the waking world?"

"I doubt it," muttered the other, "for then I might expect to be making an impression. But these buggers—why, they're mad as March hares!"

"Don't you realize what's going to happen here?" Hero raised his voice again. "There'll be fire and destruction and innocent blood spilled in a torrent! Would you set your seal upon that?"

"We shall not be here to see it," informed Gathnod-Natz'ill. "By the time the moon-God arrives here we shall be on our way to collect our tribute from his minions on the moon."

"To become slaves of the moonbeasts, you mean!" cried Eldin. "Or worse . . ."

"We shall fill our ship to capacity with moon-gems before returning," replied Byharrid-Imon—but there was a sudden tremor in his powerful voice, which sounded just a little like the strained gonging of a cracked bell.

"Before returning to what?" cried Hero. "Look about you, man! Look at the sky, the seas, the very land itself. And this is only the beginning. Can't you see you've been duped? When Mnomquah comes the dreamlands will run red with lava and blood. Smoke will hide the sun for centuries and the skies will rain volcanic ash. The seas will be of mud and the green fields barren deserts. And as for towns and cities—they shall be obsolete as this very Sarkomand!"

"You'll not make fools of us!" Gathnod-Natz'ill cried, more shrilly than ever. "Not as you've done with Lathi and Zura. We are destined for greatness. We always have been!"

"I'll bet you sang the same song in the waking world," returned Eldin. "Even when they were dropping you in the river with your feet set in fresh cement. You're not only born losers and fools, you're madmen! Especially you, you damned—*crone*!"

At that, and with a shrill, piercing cry of rage, Gathnod-Natz'ill hurled himself at the bearers who held the questers and girls aloft. For Eldin had been quite right and he had hit upon a very sore spot. In Byharrid-Imon there probably remained something of sanity, but his brother was utterly mad. It might well be an inherited madness—though more likely it resulted from long-term proximity with "Leng-gold" and, more recently, the influence of the mad moon—but certainly the effeminate brother was completely deranged.

And such was his fury that he might well have killed all four helpless captives there and then, except that this was not to be. For even as he punched and snatched at them to bring them tumbling down from the now tired arms of their bearers, so the procession arrived at its destination, the immemorial Temple of Oorn; and from then on events were taken right out of Gathnod-Natz'ill's painted and manicured hands.

For now, as the questers and girls fell upon crumbling flags—even as the crazed Duke laid a hand across the hilt of his sword and snarled his madness at them where they rolled in dust—so a sigh went up from the assembled polyglot masses, and all heads turned toward Oorn's temple where its low, circular wall showed a jagged, broken rim in the center of the centuried city. Outside that wall a black silken tent had been erected, with yellow tassels and runic, lunar symbols: the sumptuously cushioned and noxiously scented pavilion of Oorn's High Priest. And there between the arched gate in the wall and the silken wall of the tent—the High Priest himself.

A large lumpish figure, he stood (or rather slumped) and regarded the small knot of humans, captors and captives alike, at the head of the massed, torch-bearing parade. His robe was of yellow silk figured with red signs and moon-symbols, and a yellow silken hood covered his head; with circular eye-holes almost at the sides rather than in front, where human eyes should be. Behind those holes unseen orbs stared, under whose steadfast gaze the crowd fell back, until none stood between humans and High Priest; yet still he remained silent.

Beside him, smaller and standing in his shadow, a similarly robed, bare-headed horned one waited attentively until the High Priest placed the mouth-piece of a black flutelike instrument beneath his hood to blow a series of seemingly unconnected notes. When finished, the horned one—patently an acolyte—turned to the vast congregation, especially to the Dukes of Isharra, and spoke these words:

"I speak for Him:

"You seem to forget yourself, Gathnod-Natz'ill Isharra. The questers and their females were to be unharmed, and yet it seems to me that you were about to harm them. Indeed, it seems you intended to kill them! Would you defy Oorn?"

Hearing these words, the crowding horned ones—who far outnumbered all other types in the assembly—crept almost unnoticeably closer to the small knot of humans. All madness had fled out of Gathnod-Natz'ill by now, however, and his aspect was a ghastly white in the light of numerous torches. He stood unspeaking, seemingly hypnotized by the High Priest's staring, unseen eyes, until his brother urgently grabbed his arm. Then he gave a start, swallowed rapidly once or twice, and made a visible effort to pull himself together.

"Lord High Priest," he began, his girlish voice quavering. "The questers angered me with their blasphemies against

Oorn and their lies concerning the validity of your own promises, made to us on behalf of the moon-God Mnomquah Himself. I would merely have chastised them, nothing more."

The High Priest raised his flute again to blow several softer notes; which his horned-one acolyte translated thus: "It is well, for Mnomquah's word is the law, and the law is inviolable." Now the crowding horned ones relaxed a little and a soft, concerted sigh was heard. All, it seemed, had been holding their breath, as if in anticipation of some terrific event.

Yet again the lumpish, silk-clad figure blew upon his carven instrument, more urgently this time, and again his acolyte translated, directing his words at the entire congregation. "The time draws nigh and we must soon away. Mnomquah's coming will be a wonderful, terrible thing. Even now the Lord of the Moon gazes down upon our works—see!" And triggered by his acolyte's words, the High Priest's jellyish—arm?—lifted to point down the wide, cliff-lined rift of Sarkomand's ancient valley to a horizon already lost in the yellow glare of the rising moon's leprously scarred and pitted dome.

Once more the weird fluting, and again the translation—a question this time, and a command. "Is the gold positioned? Then let it be revealed, that Mnomquah may know his true destination when he rushes to Oorn's fond embrace!"

More torches were lighted, a vast circle of them on the outermost extremes of what was now seen to be a tremendous cleared area; and at numerous points about this huge outer circle tarpaulins and other coverings were thrown back to reveal veritable mounds of gold—moon-gold, as the captives well knew.

Of the questers themselves while all this was taking place: they had not been utterly idle. Trussed up as they were, they could still speak to each other ... for the moment at least. Eldin, in the curious way he had of detaching himself from current events—even when they promised to become fatal—had asked of his younger companion, "Hero, late as the hour appears to be for us, there's something that bothers me a bit."

"A bit?" grunted the other, spitting out dust and gravel. "Myself, I'm bothered quite a lot—but say on, if it will give you peace of mind."

"It's just this: how did they know we were coming? I mean, there's a fair old bit of preparation gone into this lot. And that ambush was a superb job of planning and timing."

"Old lad," Hero had answered after a moment, "brace yourself—and try not to think too badly of me, but—" at which point Eldin had closed his eyes, groaned and cut in:

"You're not going to tell me you knew? Please don't tell me that, lad, for if you do I'll know for sure that you're as mad as these bloody Isharrans!"

"Oh, I didn't know for a certainty," Hero answered, "or I surely would not have come, but I have to admit that I suspected. You see, knowing that Oorn had used that mind-call of hers to trap us in the first place, I reasoned—"

"—That she might also be able to read our minds, eh?"

Hero tried to nod but only succeeded in bumping his head on a broken pavement. "Except . . . well, I hoped that after our trip into the sky they'd all believe us dead—Oorn included. If so, she wouldn't be on the lookout for us."

"And you were wrong!" Eldin groaned again.

Again the younger quester bumped his head. "It appears so," he said. "She knew we lived, kept her cosmic ear on us, told her High Priest when to expect us. Why, she's probably listening to us even now; splitting her sides—I hope!— laughing at us."

In the next instant as if to confirm Hero's suspicion, the questers heard again that voice in their minds which had first lured them from *Gnorri II* and into the mists, through the bowels of the mountain buttress to dread, primal Sarkomand. But this time they knew the true source of that mental voice, and it made no further pretense of disguising itself. "*Hero . . .*" it eerily mocked, clammy and alien in their heads. "*Eldin . . .*" And yet even now there remained echoes of that earlier, sweeter calling, left there deliberately to linger in their minds and remind them what fools they had been.

By this time the horned ones on the perimeter had done with their uncovering of glowing piles of moon-gold, so that their torches now struck yellow fire from a vast circle of the stuff. Even where they lay, the questers could see its shimmer beyond the thronging forms of their captors; and now Hero whispered: "So that's how old Mnomquah will find his way here, eh? A golden bullseye, with Oorn's pit at its center!"

Before Eldin could answer they were roughly hoisted aloft once more—the sobbing, fearful girls, too—and borne into Oorn's temple through the worn and pitted archway. At one side of that entrance as they passed stood Zura, with a retinue of zombies; at the other lay Lathi upon a large platform, surrounded by termen and -maids, her lower body silk-draped and fitfully pulsating. Vile females that they were and utterly different, still their faces shared the same expression: fury and dark hatred, for Hero had spurned and made fools of both of them.

"No hope from that quarter, lad," said Eldin.

"No hope from any quarter, questers!" chuckled the horned-one acolyte as he stuffed greasy gags in their mouths. "There! That's to ensure that you lie there nice and quiet throughout the ceremony—until the rising moon calls Oorn up from her pit to claim you. After that we must leave—but at least the Goddess shall have feasted before her Great Mating!"

Now they were placed at the four cardinal points of the pit, face down with their heads just over the rim, so that they might gaze into the very throat of Oorn's lair; and now too there commenced the sounds of an ancient, evil ritual as demon flutes piped and bone-dry crotala clacked and rattled. And the questers and their ladies knew that indeed this must be the beginning of the end, and that there was nothing at all they could do about it.

Minutes lengthened into an hour, two, as the moon rose higher and the hideous music grew more frenzied and alien yet; and as that sick yellow light flooded the land so the four bound humans found the dark shaft of the pit dimly illumined, and Eldin in particular began to find a special loathsomeness in the shiny smoothness of its perfectly circular wall. It was not unlike the pearly mouth of a conch, this pit, except of course that it was not coiled but fell straight into the bowels of the very earth. Or did it?

No, for down there, at the limits of vision, a vast nacreous slab plugged the shaft like a cork in the neck of a bottle. And this huge disc of stone persisted in attracting the Wanderer's attention; persisted too in reminding him of . . . of what? Staring again at that great plug in the bottom of the pit, suddenly Eldin fancied he saw it moving, inching *up* the shaft, slowly but surely shortening the distance from bottom to top. And with this creeping, insidious movement there came such a rush of foul gases that, had he not been gagged, the Wanderer was sure he should be violently ill. Hero and the girls also smelled this awful fetor and felt the nausea it brought, but as yet they had not guessed its source.

Eldin, however, no longer had any doubt. He now *knew* what he was seeing. Knew that the vast slab which continued to inch its way upward was no slab at all but something far more monstrous. Monstrous beyond words . . .

It was a gigantic operculum, the protective plate or lid which secures a snail inside its shell—*or, in this case, that most ghastly of all gastropods, Oorn in her lair!*

Moonfleet

Other things were happening in the night, things perhaps divinely provided by beneficent gods of dreams to keep the Wanderer's mind from dwelling too deeply upon the imagined nature of the inhabitant of the pit. The sky was ablaze with hissing meteorites and the ground trembled now and then with seismic convulsions. A rumbling growl was plainly discernible, as of far distant mountains on the move; and as the moon rose higher so the rumbling increased, becoming an almost continual tremor in the foul night air.

Turning their heads—which was about as much freedom as they had—the questers and their women were able to see the moon's rim where it climbed steadily above the jagged wall of the temple. Bloated beyond belief, the thing seemed no longer a satellite but a sister planet suspended magically in the sky just beyond dreamland's edge. Its needle-toothed mountains, oily oceans and sinister valleys looked no more distant than, say, the coastline of the Southern Sea as viewed from Serannian on a clear day, and its great evil "face" seemed to leer with an expression at once human and yet unutterably alien. Seen so close, the questers could well understand the madness which the moon had brought immemorially to sensitive minds in the waking world—and which now it was visiting upon the lands of Earth's dreams.

Then, abruptly, the monstrous music of the horned ones

rose to a screeching crescendo and faded out in a final clash of brazen cymbals. Mnomquah's propitiation was complete; His way was made plain; His mate prepared to partake of her bridal feast!

Eldin's bound body jerked violently as a cloven foot kicked him in the side. "Goodbye, questers," came the guttural, nasal tones of the silk-clad horned one. "Oorn's High Priest bids you a fond farewell, and so do I."

Now the High Priest himself came to the pit's rim, slumping forward and wriggling beneath his robes as he peered through his wide-spaced eyeholes and down into the throat of that nameless shaft. He saw how close the pearly door had climbed toward pit's rim; and if he could smell at all he doubtless smelled the hideous effluvium of the Thing beyond that door. His robe shivered fitfully and Eldin was aware of a pink writhing beneath its momentarily parted folds as carven flute was set to unseen lips. The notes this time were high, urgent, filled with a certain glee—yes, and a certain fear, too.

"The time is nigh," the acolyte translated. "We go!" And he gave Eldin a final kick with sharp, cloven hoof. Then they were gone, leaving the four bound humans to wait out their final nightmare.

Eldin, knowing (or at least having very strong suspicions) just what the nightmare would be, now worked feverishly to release the bandage which held his gag in place; and seeing their friend so urgently at work, Hero and the girls did likewise. Finally, hooking the rag over a sharp knob of rock where it projected at the pit's rim, and tearing his face a little in the process, the Wanderer was first to free his mouth.

For a few seconds he paused to draw air deep into his lungs—but only until he began to taste upon his tongue the musk of the horror which crept ever closer—and then he choked back his nausea to call out across the pit, "Hero, have you guessed yet what this she-monster is?"

Spitting out his own gag, Hero called back, "Man, I don't dare guess! But if she looks half as bad as she smells . . ."

"Oh, she'll look worse than that," Eldin promised. "You see the great slab which creeps ever closer up the shaft toward us? That's part of her, attached to her like the lid on an oyster's cup. She's beneath it—immediately beneath it—and once that lid begins to open—"

"Are you deaf, man?" Hero snarled. "I said I don't want to know—and I'm damned sure the girls don't! What Oorn is isn't important. How to get the hell away from her is. If only these ropes weren't so damned, *uh*!—tight . . ."

"Can you roll?" Eldin asked.

"Eh?"

"Can you rock your body until it rolls?" Eldin repeated. "At least that might get us away from the rim."

"Damn me," answered the other after a moment's thought, "I'm not sure I want to try it. We're so close to the edge that if we roll the wrong way—"

"Well, we're going to have to try it sooner or later," said Eldin. "Another few minutes and she'll be here." So saying he began to rock his trussed body to and fro until he rolled once, twice, three times away from the pit. Seeing his success, Hero and the girls did likewise.

Both Ula and Una had their mouths free by now, and as the latter rolled once in the wrong direction she gave a shrill little cry. The others held their collective breath until she corrected the motion and began to roll away from Oorn's monstrous shaft, after which they breathed out a single, concerted sigh. Then, for long minutes, all that was heard was a great grunting and panting—and the occasional curse—as all four strained to put distance between themselves and the reeking horror which crept upon them.

And it was as Hero rolled onto his back for the fourth or fifth time that he noticed the strange thing taking place in the sky. Where before the clouds had seemed to churn and tumble mindlessly, now they moved with a peculiar, an almost sinister purpose. They were forming a coil, like some impossible languid tornado, whose tenuous funnel spiralled visibly toward the ever-rising moon. And down from the looming

face of that mad golden monster, as if to greet the funnel of
clouds, sick moonbeams crept to form a yellow path or river
in the sky.

Then, climbing the spiral of clouds, the quester saw the enemy's squat black ships; saw them drawn steadily around the
whorl and away across the heavens toward the moon . . . and
never a breath of air to fill a single sail!

Soon the entire enemy fleet was airborne and adrift on the
great aerial whirlpool, climbing ever higher, ever moonward.
And all across that demon-painted sky the meteorites blazed
and hissed, and the effect of this spectacular sight upon the
four humans (for by now all were watching) was near-
hypnotic. Until, as if to break the spell, there came a vast
grating and shuddering, and in the center of the temple
Oorn's mighty, softly shining operculum appeared like the
pearly eye of some creature of the deep.

"Here she c—" Eldin commenced a growled warning, only
to choke on the last word as the great lid cracked open to ex-
pel the foulest stench any dreamer ever dreamed. Zura and all
her zombies together in the fathomless sewers of Baharna
could not have equalled such a stench; but mercifully it lasted
no more than a second or two before the worst of it hissed
visibly upward and dissipated into the chill night air. And after the release of these pent-up gases, this condensed essence
of Oorn—

Then came Oorn Herself!

. . . But slowly, cautiously (perhaps savoring the moment?), else the questers and their women were certainly
driven mad in the merest moment. And if ever they had seen
all of Oorn—

First there were the eyes.

Beneath the part-raised, yard-thick hatch—eyes! A dozen,
circular, burning and unblinking, big as plates, staring out in
all directions from a dark, as yet only half-seen, half-
suspected bulk. Then—tentacles! Tentacles like nests of fat
pink worms . . . Or were they merely cilia?

Cilia, yes—tiny feet to carry the larger, heavier, true tenta-

cles wherever Oorn directed them—like the myriad feet of
starfish. And out from the pit, out from beneath the luminous
eyes, out from the darkness under the vast and pearly slab
those true tentacles now uncoiled, pink and translucent but
pulsing with a green fluid that made mobile veins on their
slick, viscous surfaces. Thicker than a man's body, one, two,
three—ten of them in all. Like the suckered arms of some
sentient squid, but huge beyond belief!

They coiled, those arms, winding about the great slab
where it now tilted more steeply, and as they wound so they
spread outward from the pit toward the questers and the girls
where they now lay backed up against the temple's wall.

"Gods!" Hero gasped. "But this is no way to go." And the
girls, brave lasses though they had proved to be, now began
to sob and shiver in the shadow of the wall as the tips of the
tentacles, swaying like the heads of blind snakes, moved ever
closer.

A loathsome slobbering sound commenced, and a hissing
and gasping as blood-red siphons appeared from the shaft to
sway and writhe and suck convulsively at the still, dank air.
And the tips of the hovering tentacles opened like mouths as
they began to descend upon the terrified forms of Oorn's living sacrifice.

"Lad," called Eldin gruffly but with no trace of the old
bluster, "I don't think I can stand much more of this. Forgive
the prattle, David," (rare day when the Wanderer used Hero's
first name!) "but if I don't talk I'm sure I'll start to scream."

"Talk away, old son," Hero croaked in return. "As for
me—I'm already screaming! Inside!" And as if encouraged
by his words, an open tentacle-tip descended upon his thigh.

Hero did scream then—but more in agony than in horror,
and more an outraged cry than a scream proper. Green juices
flowed from the open mouth of the pseudo-pod and dissolved
away a patch of his tough leather trousers in a second—
dissolved, too, the skin of the thigh beneath. And now that
mouth became a sucker, slurping back the *solution* which the
green juice had become. Seeing and feeling this, Hero cried

out again—this time in true horror—for now he knew how Oorn fed!

For the merest fraction of a second then, time seemed to stand still—a moment's pause in the rhythm of the dream-time universe—before the green juices flowed more copi-ously in the veins of the tentacles and their snake-head tips descended with more purpose . . .

Somewhere, at some indeterminate distance in the night, a mighty explosion sounded as a dull rumble, and a second later the earth gave itself a small shake—and Oorn froze! The monster . . . listened! Yes, she listened, her every molecule tuned . . . to what? Then, a rapid retraction, a frenzied scur-rying of a million tiny limbs and a slithering of tentacles withdrawn—and the vast bulk of Oorn, still mainly and mer-cifully unseen, drew back down into her centuried pit. In an-other moment the siphons were withdrawn, the eyes lowered themselves into darkness, the lid sighed shut with one last great exhalation of poisonous gases, and the monster was gone. There came again that grating and shivering as the mas-sive operculum began to descend the shaft.

"What the hell—?" Eldin croaked, and the others began to breathe again as his voice broke the stillness.

"Something frightened her—*it*—off!" Hero tried to say, but only succeeded at the third attempt and after many a gulp.

"The explosion," came Ula's shivery voice.

"The shaking of the earth," said Una.

"Did she harm any of you?" Hero asked, strength fast re-turning. "No? She—tasted me!" He shuddered. "Just a taste, but I'll never forget it. Damn her loathsome eyes!"

"You know, lad," rumbled Eldin, his voice ringing in a barely controlled hysteria, "sometimes I've envied you this fatal fascination you seem to have for certain females. But there are other times when I'm not so—"

"*Shh!*" cried Ula and Una together. "Listen!"

From somewhere to the south there came a foaming, rush-ing sound that rapidly built to a roar whose tremor could be felt as a vibration in the earth itself. "What now?" growled

Eldin—and gave a massive start as night-black shapes fell from the sky and gray paws grabbed him where he lay.

The others were similarly snatched up—not without shrieks of renewed terror from the girls, despite Gytherik's young voice crying out that it was only him and his gaunts—and all four were borne aloft in the last moment before the released fury of the sea smashed through Oorn's temple and raced in a deep tidal surge through the now deserted streets of Sarkomand.

Above that curling, hissing wall of water, which inundated all in its path, the questers felt spray on their faces and a gaunt-wing wind that dried cold sweat on their bodies and left them shivering uncontrollably. Perhaps Ula and Una had fainted (better for them if they had, thought Hero) for they were now silent; but Eldin had already begun to roar his delight in a manner well remembered of old. And as for Hero himself—though later he would not admit it—he was baying like some great crazed hound, laughing until the tears flowed down his face and dripped into space . . .

In a very little while Gytherik eased his grim down onto *Gnorri*'s deck and the swooning girls were carried away to be cossetted and comforted. Hero and Eldin were their own men again and more than sober. They had good reason to be, for during the gaunt-flight many things had changed. The sea lay flat once more and relatively calm, except for a certain bubbling and frothing and choppiness of the waters where they lay deep in the one-time Vale of Sarkomand. The meteorite shower had petered out and the expectant thrumming of the ether had been replaced by a clammy stillness, as if the very elements were shocked. And most important of all, it seemed that Mnomquah's devastating leap to earth had been averted or at least postponed.

Other things, however, had not changed; and one thing was very new and very frightening. Though there was still a complete absence of wind, *Gnorri II* and the other six ships of the flotilla were now in motion. They had been drawn by some nameless magnetism into the great whorl of clouds and were beginning to spiral up into the sky and along the moonbeam path toward the moon.

—That mad, mocking moon whose "face" was now a threatening mask of depraved hatred and anger beyond the mundane minds of men to comprehend!

Moon Madness

PART 3

Tunnel in the Moon

"Can we still use the gaunts," asked Limnar Dass of Gytherik, "to carry messages to the other ships?" (For some reason the dreamlands had never adopted semaphore.) "I mean, will they be capable of inter-vessel flight way out here between moon and dreamlands?"

"I really don't know," the gaunt-master answered, frowning. "This is a new situation for me—for my gaunts too, I'm sure." Down on the main deck the grim pressed close together in a sullen huddle and shuffled uncomfortably in the streaming, maddening moonlight. *Gnorri*'s sails provided a good deal of shade from that glare, but still its awfulness could be felt as an almost tangible thing.

"Of course I could always ask the gaunts," Gytherik continued, turning toward the grim and leaning across the bridge's rail. Before he could inquire, however, Biffer (it could only be him!) thrust out his neck, fanned his membranous wings and soared aloft—just as if he had heard the sky-Captain's question and his young master's answer, and thought that this display should settle the matter to everyone's satisfaction. He disappeared overboard to port, passed beneath the ship and came up to hover for a moment before perching on the starboard rail.

"Well," said Limnar, nodding his acknowledgment at Biffer, "that seems to be the answer to that one!"

Of course, in the normal way of things his question would have been redundant, for gaunts are superb fliers who have no aerial peers in all the dreamlands; but the flotilla was no longer *in* the dreamlands, and no one seemed able to say for sure which laws might or might not apply out here. Several so-called "natural" laws, or laws which the questers had always considered natural, had already been shattered beyond repair. For one, there was the matter of the temperature.

It was cold, most certainly—extremely cold—but not nearly what they had expected. They needed the heavy garments in which one and all were now draped, to be sure, but all were in agreement that it was only slightly colder than a bad northern winter. Hero in fact was astonished by what he leniently termed "an amazingly mild, not at all uncomfortable atmosphere."

Of course he had experienced the dreadful cold of dreamland's upper atmospheric reaches (and naked at that), which not only made him something of an expert but also accounted for his present astonishment. If it could be so bitterly cold just a few miles above the dreamlands, how come it was not utterly freezing way up here? Eldin suspected that they were moving through a sort of Gulf Stream of warm air which existed permanently in the previously supposed "void" between the atmosphere of dreamland and that of the moon.

These and many other matters had occupied the questers in the relatively short span of time since the commencement of their involuntary journey, but once the halfway point had been passed their talk had turned again to more pressing questions: chiefly Mnomquah's purpose (for it was plainly his doing) in drawing the flotilla up to the moon, and what would be waiting for them when they got there.

And yet even that simple statement "up to the moon" was invalid here; for they no longer spiralled up but down—down toward the surface of an utterly inhospitable world. Not at all the airless inhospitality of the waking world's moon, no—rather that of the vile and inhuman race of moonbeasts, whose *habits* and *appetites* did not, according to legend, bear mentioning.

As for the trip itself: it had been as strange a voyage as any of the questers had ever undertaken, and they had made several fantastical journeys in their time. Not the least of its strangeness lay in the speed with which it had been accomplished; for while on leaving the dreamlands the spiral flight had seemed slow and strangely languid, since then they had attained a monstrous velocity. Something of this had been seen in the speed with which the dreamlands had dwindled in their wake, and in the rapid bloating of the moon from a sky-filling bulk to an intricately etched world of golden plains, yawning, secretive craters, dark, oily oceans and black shadows. And yet there had been no sense of acceleration, no slightest billowing of slack-hanging sails, no agitation of air as one might expect to be occasioned by their passing. Unless their journey was totally magical in nature (which Limnar Dass frankly believed must be the case), then Eldin's Gulf Stream of air must be travelling apace with them.

Quite apart from discussion and conjecture, the trip had not been without occurrence. On the contrary, Mnomquah's outrage at being denied—however temporarily—access to the dreamlands and oneness with Oorn had made itself very plain in the way he three times aimed (indiscriminately?) his solid-seeming tractor-beam across the now narrowed distance to strike at certain defenseless cities. This had been during the earlier part of the trip when the dreamlands were less obscured with clouds and their contours still visible and more or less identifiable.

And when *Gnorri*'s Master got round to studying his maps and charts he had found a very strange thing . . . three of them, in fact. The moon-God's rage must be violent indeed that he should so drastically and consistently mistake his targets! Or had he mistaken them? The horned-one fleet up ahead, which of course included *Shantak*, *Chrysalis* and *Shroud*, must also have witnessed the triple striking of the beam, and the questers could not help but wonder what Zura,

Lathi and the Dukes now thought of their splendid alliance with the moonbeasts and their horned-one minions. For Mnomquah's targets had been none other than the Charnel Gardens, twice-builded Thalarion, and the degenerate and decaying township of Isharra! How now for promises and fair play?

"Is it because they fouled up?" Limnar Dass, at the time, wondered aloud. "Or simply because they're of no further use to him?"

"A little of both," Hero had suspected. "Of course, they were easy targets. What with all the movement of moongold this lot have been engaged in, there were bound to be stockpiles of the stuff in their various headquarters."

Eldin for his part had gone a little deeper into the subject. "With the moon so close to the dreamlands now," he reasoned, "you'd hardly think old Mnomquah would need his golden zeroing-in device anymore . . ." And he had frowned thoughtfully. "How come he doesn't use his beam more often?"

"I believe," Hero had answered, "that he's been trying to, well, *fuel* himself. Do you know what I mean? You remember what Hrill told us? That the peoples of the dreamlands would be fodder for Mnomquah and the moonbeasts? I really think he meant 'fodder' quite literally, and that Mnomquah has been, you know—"

"Yes, lad," Eldin had stopped him short. "We all know what you mean. But if he's so damned hungry, why doesn't he just go right ahead and gorge?"

"He *is* hungry, I'm sure of it," answered Hero. "See, his beams consume energy, magical or otherwise makes no difference, and he needs to make it up as fast as he uses it. Which shouldn't be a problem, really. Except—" and he paused to snap his fingers.

"Well?" they had all wanted to know.

"You remember what Randolph Carter told us in his letter? About Theem'hdra in the primal waking world, the land at the dawn of time? They had two moon-gods in those days,

Mnomquah and Gleeth. Now Gleeth, if you recall, was an elemental god, not really there at all—and he was blind! What I'm saying is: perhaps the old legends got it all mixed up. Perhaps Gleeth, who never was, got credited with certain characteristics—one at least—of Mnomquah, who was and still is! Do I make myself plain?"

"As mud!" Eldin had grumbled.

"You're saying that Mnomquah is—" began Limnar Dass.

"Blind?" Gytherik Imniss finished it.

Hero nodded. "I'm beginning to think so. That's why he daren't expend energy on tractor-beams which stand only one chance in, say, ten thousand of hitting anything worth eating. He took the cities of his allies because they had been made easy targets. Also because Zura, Lathi and the Isharrans are of no further use to him. *Also*, I suspect, because we'd put him in a bit of a tantrum—but mainly because he was hungry."

"And now that he's fed he'll be fully fueled for his plunge to Oorn's pit, eh?" questioned Limnar. The others looked startled, suddenly reminded of a nightmare they had all hoped was over and done with. "After all," Limnar continued, half apologetically, "the moon does govern the tides, you know. What comes must go—including the waters which at present cover Sarkomand."

"Personally," said Hero after a moment's silence, "I don't think Mnomquah will have derived much benefit from Thalarion and Isharra. And as for Zura's Charnel Gardens— why, he's probably throwing that lot up right now! No, I rather fancy that we ourselves are intended to provide the energy for his big jump. If we let him get away with it, that is."

"Well, we're certainly not going down without a fight!" Eldin had rumbled then.

"—In which we'll be outnumbered three or four to one," Gytherik had pointed out. "Also, the enemy fleet will be battle-ready, just waiting for us to come spiralling down out of the sky. Why, we'll be sitting ducks!"

Which had taken them to the point where Limnar Dass in-

quired about the airworthiness of the gaunts in these inter-
planetary regions. And as soon as Biffer confirmed that indeed gaunts were capable of flight in the Gulf Stream ether,
then the sky-Captain explained the reason for his anxious in-
terest.

"Gytherik is right," he said, "we'll be sitting ducks. And,"
he reminded, "we have no powder. Nor has *Starspur.* We
used it to crack Sarkomand's old sea-wall. Without powder
we can't fight, so—" he turned to Gytherik, "your gaunts are
going to have their paws full for the next couple of hours.
They'll have to resupply *Gnorri* and *Starspur* from the other
ships. Fortunately this crazy whorl has kept us all fairly close
together, so the gaunts shouldn't really need to exhaust themselves."

By the time the grim fully understood their task and had
been given letters marked for the flotilla's Captains, a gradual
deceleration was already making itself felt. This showed itself
not as any return of weight (which had never departed and so
could not return) or change of motion (which had also
seemed to remain constant, despite the enormous speed they
must have attained), but in the gradual recognition of a sense
of *spiritual* weight and direction; as if the souls of all concerned had passed through an area of freefall, and that now,
as they approached journey's end, some mechanism of the
psyche was alerting them to that fact.

Strangely enough, the gaunts seemed similarly alerted and
showed an urgency all their own. Sniffer and Biffer, however,
before commencing their powder-ferrying tasks with the rest
of the grim, shuffled down into *Gnorri*'s hold and returned
with Hero's curved Kledan sword and Eldin's straighter
blade, handing (pawing?) them to the questers in a sort of
solemn but almost tangibly sarcastic silence. Just how they
managed to express their disdain without the facility of facial
expression or scathing words would be difficult to say, and
yet both Hero and Eldin did feel a peculiar embarrassment.

"I had forgotten about your swords," Gytherik now explained. "The gaunts picked them up from the spot where we

were tossed overboard from the deck of *Shantak*. They went off on their own to recover them while Limnar and I were placing the powder charges below the old sea-wall."

"Like a dog when you throw a stick for him, eh?" Eldin hopefully grinned.

"No," replied Gytherik in a very dry tone, "I think not. More like a patient valet whose senile master keeps forgetting his trousers!"

By this time *Gnorri*'s crew had done what they could to ready her for battle, likewise the crews of the other ships, and all that remained was to watch and wait for the gaunts to finish with their transporting of powder barrels. This, too, was rapidly accomplished; and now the seven-strong flotilla slowly spiralled down out of a black, gold-streaked sky toward the surface of the moon.

Ruins which from afar had merged with the mountains now became visible, dead temples to defunct and forgotten deities; and on the shores of oily oceans stood cities of thickly-clustered, leaning gray towers, windowless and inherent with a nameless menace other than that of their obvious and ugly alienage. The spiralling moonbeam path straightened out and was soon seen to be drawing the ships down toward a mighty crater of at least a mile in diameter and completely conjectural depth, whose throat occasionally belched rings of orange smoke or vapor and about which the Lengite armada sailed in a huge circle, keeping a healthy distance from the menacing rim.

"That great hole," observed Eldin, "seems more a gigantic tunnel in the moon than a crater in the proper sense."

"Mnomquah's lair," opined Hero with a grimace. "A vast burrow indeed. And somewhere in the middle, the blind beast himself—all horrid, hateful and hungry!"

Strange Alliance

Some three miles over the mouth of the great moon-shaft, the flotilla recommenced its weird rotation; and despite maximum use of flotation engines, the seven ships began to be drawn inexorably down out of the lunar sky. As they corkscrewed ever lower the cannons were loaded with powder and balls, the crews took up weapons and readied themselves to adopt defensive position, and all was put in order for the battle which seemed about to break.

Limnar Dass, however, ever the sky-Captain, was sorely puzzled. Granted, the enemy had an overwhelming majority—they had freedom of movement, too, for it could be seen that their sails were filled and that they navigated quite normally outside the spiral whorl—but should these advantages make them *so* contemptuous of the flotilla's firepower? For the ships of the Lengite fleet did not seem to be taking up battle positions at all but were merely milling about like a crowd of excited spectators!

Only one small group of enemy vessels seemed to display any real purpose at all, and these hemmed in an even smaller nucleus of ships—three in number—which tacked to and fro as if seeking an exit through the cordon. Seeing all this from on high, from a vantage point no sky-Captain could possibly resist, Limnar put his glass to his eye and scanned the scene more minutely. What he saw then caused him to beckon both Hero and Eldin to his side.

"Those three ships down there are *Shantak*, *Shroud* and *Chrysalis*," he informed, "and it looks like their master—or mistresses, as the case may be—have finally come to their senses. They appear to be trying to make a break for it!"

"Huh!" the Wanderer callously grunted. "Well, good luck to them."

"We, too, have had our eyes on that lot," said Hero, indicating the milling fleet far below. "Frankly, we don't give a hoot for the problems of Zura, Lathi and the Isharrans—but there's something decidedly wrong with the rest of this set-up."

"So you've noticed it too, eh?" Limnar raised his eyebrows. "Well, say on. Let's see if we've arrived at the same conclusion."

"The way we see it," Eldin took it upon himself to explain, "is that these Lengites are either damned poor sailors and strategists, or else they're plain stupid. Just look at 'em down there. They've not bothered to make ready for battle at all. Their formation—if you can call it a formation—is a total mess!"

"Seems to us," Hero now put it in a nutshell, "that they're merely jostling for a ringside seat!"

"My own conclusion exactly," Limnar grimly nodded. "They're not here to fight, simply as spectators. They're so sure we're doomed that they're just going to sit there and watch us go plummeting into that hole—like so many leaves swilled down a gutter."

Suddenly Hero, whose eyes were still taking in the scene below, gave a start and leaned farther over the rail. He pointed excitedly downward. "Look there! Yon cordon's left a gap and our black-hearted friends from the dreamlands are making a run for it!"

Limnar again put his glass to his eye, said: "Fools! They're being shepherded into the spiral, fed directly into Mnomquah's maw!"

"Aye, and they've twigged it," cried Eldin. "See how they turn and fight!"

Shantak and *Shroud*—and Lathi's paper ship *Chrysalis*, too—all had turned back from the moonbeam whorl to fire massive broadsides at the harrying horned ones. One Lengite ship was severely stricken, losing all of her canvas and much of her superstructure in the first withering fusillade; and a second vessel literally blew to bits in the sky as a lucky shot found her magazine. And despite the fact that the three fugitive ships had been mortal enemies, still *Gnorri*'s crew gave a cheer at the sight of the closest Lengite vessels turning tail. Any glee was short-lived, however, for more enemy ships were soon on the scene. Slowly but surely the three at bay were forced into the outer edge of the shimmering spiral.

By now the flotilla's altitude was much decreased, and it could be seen that the seven ships must soon sink down to the level of the three refugees as they were drawn deeper into the whorl. The Lengites on the other hand were now drawing well back, beyond the range of the flotilla's cannon, content to let the spiral moonbeam complete its work. And as the whorl tightened so its speed increased, drawing all ten ships closer together like bits of flotsam in a whirlpool, until all rotated within hailing distance of one another.

Finding Zura's *Shroud* suddenly alongside and seeing the zombie princess herself defiant on the bridge, Hero called out: "How now, Zura? Are you beginning to regret your alliance with the moonbeasts? You've seen their cities, how alien they are, and you've surely learned the bitter lesson of any contract made with them. Why, they almost make your zombies seem wholesome by comparison!"

"Ever the witty one, aren't you, David Hero?" she called back. "But I have to admit, it seems you're right. Shall we call a truce and fight side by side?"

"Aye, if it suits you," he answered, "though I can only see us going down to hell together!"

At the stern of the ship Eldin made similar overtures toward Lathi, whose lovely face showed pale and outraged from her cabin's window. "What's it to be, Lathi?" he roared across to her. "Are you with us now that you've seen Thalarion destroyed a second time?"

"You burned my hive city to survive," she shouted back. "Mnomquah acted out of greed, deceit and treachery! I am with you, quester—for now."

Farther afield, *Shantak*'s rigging was decorated with dangling corpses. Most of them were horned ones, but two ... they wore the apparel of the Dukes of Isharra, their silk-clad necks in nooses where they hung. "No need to ask whose side the Isharrans are on," said Limnar Dass to Gytherik. "The crew has mutinied—and it seems their masters remained madmen to the bitter end. Well, there are damned few of them, and they're poor sailors at that, but any port in a storm ..."

And tighter the whorl drew the ten ships as their plunge became steeper and the mouth of Mnomquah's lair loomed up from below. Now they were within the shaft's jagged rim and level with the bulk of the Lengite fleet, and now they began to descend into darkness ... Which was when Hero gave a great yell and cried:

"Well, lads, what are we waiting for? We know who is reeling us in like a prize catch, don't we? We know who waits at the bottom of this damned pit! Come on, Gytherik, lad, wake up! Don't you see? If gunpowder can crack a great sea-wall, shouldn't it also be able to give old Mnomquah a knock?—Enough of a headache, perhaps, that he'll shut off this damned beam of his?"

As if to emphasize Hero's words (which really required no emphasis at all, since the funnel of the pit picked up his voice and magnified it ringingly, so that all aboard all ten ships heard it simultaneously) a great orange smoke-ring came rushing up from below to escape into the light even as the flotilla spun down into subterranean night. And still the echoes of Hero's cry rang from the walls of that mighty stone throat.

Then—

A sudden stir of purposeful movement in the gloom! A flaring of ships' lamps! The slamming of hatches thrown back and the rumble of rolling barrels! And above all Limnar Dass in command, controlling all, hurling out instructions, his voice utterly nerveless, steady as the moon-rock through which the flotilla now descended.

"Hear me all Captains," he cried. "Use only half your powder made up into two equal lots. And to be on the safe side, two fuses to each lot. Long fuses, I think, to burn for at least a minute. First lots not to be dropped until I give the signal, second lots to be released automatically as soon as the first detonations are heard. And lads, they'll be loud bangs to be sure, so stuff your ears good and tight! Let's give this moon-God more than he bargained for, eh?"

He paused and breathed deeply of tunnel air, thought for a moment and listened to the sounds of urgent preparation in the gloom. For even down here the light was not wholly extinct. The atmosphere of the great shaft seemed sprinkled with luminous gold dust—yellow motes that streamed upwards and reflected the light of the lamps—Mnomquah's beam exerting its monstrous, irresistible magnetism.

"And listen," Limnar's voice rang out again. "All you engineers stand by your engines. Let 'em go full rip! Fill your flotation bags to bursting point. And if all works out the way we plan—well, you cannoneers will get a crack at the enemy yet! Now work, lads, work—and let's hear you yell when your bombs are ready, right?"

Minutes passed and the temperature mounted, and not merely as a result of the energy burned in frantic toiling. For as the ships of the flotilla descended toward the moon's core, a monstrous heat and the very fetors of hell rose up to meet them, telling their crews that time was now limited.

Sweating in the weak light of the deck lamps (for they dare not strike fire to unshielded torches), Hero and Eldin worked alongside *Gnorri*'s regular crew, their bodies naked from the waist up and gleaming as if oiled. Now the kegs of powder were shaped into makeshift canvas bundles with fuses protruding, and sections of the ship's rail were removed to ensure safe and easy ejection. Then—

"*Starspur*—ready!" came a cry from somewhere to port.

And, "*Skyhaze*—ready!" from starboard.

And, "*Shroud*—ready!" (A female voice, this time, and one Hero had never thought to hear with such relish!)

"*Skipcloud*, ready!" As the echoes of one cry died away another took its place, until at last all that remained was an eerie silence. A silence broken only by the sounds of creaking rigging and the whoosh of an occasional smoke-ring as it rushed up, encircled, and rushed on—

—A silence out of which Limnar's words now fell like hammer blows on the ears of all who heard him: "First powder-bombs . . . *ready!*" he gave the signal. "Light fuses . . . *now!*" And finally, "*Bombs awaaayyy!*"

In the dim light, angular black masses were seen to fall from the sides of the ships—appallingly slowly, it seemed—tumbling into the abyss and trailing sparks behind them. Then, seconds passed like hours while scores of hearts jumped and fluttered. Aboard *Gnorri*, Eldin closed his eyes, caught Hero's arm in a steely grip and began to whisper:

"Forty-six, forty-seven, forty-eight, forty-nine, *fifty!*"

With Hero taking up the beat: "Fifty-one, fifty-two, fifty-three, fifty-four—"

And Gytherik's youthful voice, beginning to show a few cracks now: "Fifty-five, fifty-six, fifty-seven—"

Limnar, "Fifty-eight—"

Eldin again, "Fifty-nine—"

Hero, "Sixty!"

And a pause, until . . . "*Sixty*, damn it!" Hero hoarsely repeated himself, making his words a command.

And as if in response to that command—

From somewhere far below a dull boom sounded, blossoming into a fully-fledged roar as the first bomb exploded. And upon that instant, triggered by the blast, a ragged but concerted shout of approval rang out from the crews of the ten ships (excluding Zura's crew who could not shout, and

Lathi's who did not understand) and the second stick of bombs went whistling down to unknown depths.

More explosions sounded, and one stupendous blast as several bombs detonated together in a chain reaction—and then the ships were reeling in a sulphurous, tearing wind from below, where a great expanding fireball lit up the bowels of the shaft as it rose menacingly toward them.

Deafened, blasted and half-blinded, the crews of the ten ships hung on for dear life in the maelstrom of mad, scorching winds and reeking odors which then engulfed them. But below decks the engineers stood to their engines, and on the bridges the Captains were there with whiplash commands, words of encouragement and praise; so that not a man knew panic where none was necessary. And again that ragged cheer, but louder now, as the moonbeam whorl blinked out—as the ships gave one last, simultaneous lurch—as the crews felt an unaccustomed surplus of weight beneath their staggering feet.

The flotilla was ascending!

Ascending, yes! Borne up by powerfully pulsating flotation engines, lifted on gunpowder thermals, tossed aloft by fire and thunder and all the stenches of hell—ascending to a battle whose echoes would live in dreamland's legends for all time to come!

Battle at the Moon-pit

To the horned-one Captains of the many vessels which swarmed at a low altitude about the moon-pit's rim, it must have seemed that Mnomquah had taken his prey and that he now enjoyed the feast greatly. Certainly he was making enough noise about it, as the subterranean booms and belchings erupting from below clearly showed. Indeed, there had never been such sounds from the moon-God's lair before, not even on those occasions when he had drawn entire towns full of souls down into the black depths.

Of course, there were those several individuals among the prey this time whose activities had caused the darkside powers a great deal of dismay—and Mnomquah himself great rage and frustration—so perhaps it was only natural that he should now vent his full fury upon them. How the oily waters of the Black Lake of Ubboth, the moon-God's sanctuary and former prison at moon's heart, must boil and froth now! And with these delightful thoughts in mind the almost-human Captains crowded their ships closer to the crater's rim, perhaps hoping for some sign or other proof positive from their blind and monstrous Master of Masters that their suppositions were well-founded.

A sign? If that was what they desired then they would soon be satisfied beyond their wildest expectations, but not with any sign of Mnomquah's planning.

On the contrary. For following close on the heels of a gushing emission of black smoke and sooty vapor, which acted as a smoke screen for the rapidly ascending flotilla, the bemused Lengite fleet suddenly found itself confronted with the damnedest and most unbelievable thing. Namely the ten "doomed" ships, most of them scorched and blackened—especially *Chrysalis*, who even smoldered a little—but air-worthy as ever and, now that Mnomquah's moonbeam whorl was no longer in evidence, marvelously maneuverable.

And now, knowing that their powder was limited, the gun-ners of the ten ships seemed possessed of an uncanny accuracy as they began to pound away at close quarters, ravaging those enemy vessels whose Captains had allowed them to stray too close to the rim. Dumbfounded, the Lengites stood in the sky over that hideous gray and yellow moonscape and shook with the savagery of the flotilla's roaring cannons.

Those Lengites well away from the center of activity re-covered first, but were unable to return fire in fear of hitting their already reeling and embattled comrades in the forward ranks. And as Limnar's little fleet sailed the circle, so her gunners crashed home shot after telling shot mercilessly into the now hopelessly confused and stampeding mass of enemy vessels. For this was what the flotilla's Captains and crews had been waiting for: something tangible at last, real targets upon which to wreak vengeance for all the atrocities perpe-trated against their fellow citizens in the land of Earth's dreams.

Skipcloud's cannons boomed fire and smoke . . . and in an-other moment a panicked Lengite ship lost her bridge and aft superstructure before blowing herself to bits as a shot found her magazine. *Starspur* blew away a black vessel's keel and substructure amidships, her flotation engines, too, so that in the space of a few seconds she began to teeter, then slide, then plummet from the sky amidst clouds of roiling green gas. And from all about the sky above Mnomquah's crater, bits of debris rained slowly down; shattered planking and tan-gles of rope and canvas falling alongside the squat bodies of silenced horned ones, and many who were not yet silent. So that to any observer—and there were observers—it must seem that despite the utterly overwhelming odds, if the Lengites did not soon pull themselves together, Limnar's flotilla must surely win the day.

But indeed some of those sinister black vessels were now rallying, though as yet their wild and spasmodic fire was proving as great a danger to friend as foe, and the large fleet was beginning to move into a battle formation of sorts. This sudden dawning of common sense and comparative calm-headedness among the enemy, however late, had coincided with an outbreak of shrill and urgent piping from on high— audible even over the roar of battle—and with the appearance in the sky of a figure at once alien and commanding. It was Oorn's High Priest, risen up from one of the Leng ships astride a great horse-headed Shantak-bird to a point of central elevation from which he now plainly directed the horned-one counterattack.

Other Shantaks—mammoth, scaly creatures of notorious and half-fabulous repute—were already winging down from the Leng fleet toward a low domed hill crowned with a monolithic stone or pillar. The hill stood at the rim of the moon-pit, and Eldin, watching the descent of the Shantaks, lowered his eyebrows and wondered at the doubtless baleful portent of what was taking place. He tugged at Hero's jacket to attract his attention, and in the next moment the eyes of both questers went wide as a great door opened in the side of the hill to discharge a dozen or more beings whose appearance could only have been born of Man's worst nightmares. They were moonbeasts, and such were their jellyish movements that the questers now knew for a certainty just exactly who—or what—Oorn's High Priest was. Except that he wore his robe of yellow silk while his cousins, who were pulling themselves up onto the backs of the Shantaks, had never known the need for any sort of subterfuge and were quite naked. Horribly so . . .

Neither Hero nor Eldin would ever be able to describe the creatures accurately, and this despite the fact that they would soon have much to do with them; for such were the *anomalies* of the amorphous monstrosities that one no sooner got used to one such when another, usually worse, would take its place. They were gray, toadlike in a certain way, jellyish, blunt-snouted, in some cases blind (but in no way incapacitated) and in all cases utterly nightmarish to behold. They carried strangely carven flutes—for just like Oorn's High Priest they could not speak in any normal tongue—though about their mouths and in other areas of their beings wriggled bunches of pinkish tentacles like loathsome anemones, with which they appeared able at least to converse with one another.

"More priests of the moon-God," said Eldin in disgust. "And do you see that tall boulder at the summit of the hill? Is that a statue, an idol, or—"

"An idol, yes," answered Hero. "Or at least it was, at some dim time in the moon's youth . . ." He stared harder, his view obscured by smoke and the settling of debris from shattered ships. The outlines of the idol were hard to make out despite its huge size. Carved from some single block of primeval moonstone, there were vaguely reptilian lines to it. It stood upright like a man, but its forelegs were held in front like the paws of some great and scaly dinosaur from Earth's prime.

"A lizard-thing," Hero finally decided. "Old Mnomquah's a lizard—but a damn big one, you can bet your life on that!"

Until now Ula and Una had obeyed Limnar's orders and stayed out of harm's way in his cabin; but now, fully rested and mostly restored to their former loveliness, they could no longer restrain themselves from joining the questers at their position on *Gnorri*'s bridge. And in all truth that smoke- and soot-grimed pair were glad to see them, for with the din of battle all around and the sky full of milling ships, smoke and green gas, Hero and Eldin were the only ones with nothing much to do. Gytherik had gone off at the double to bring his gaunts up onto the deck, and Limnar Dass commanded his ship with extraordinary skill as she spat fire and death at the enemy; but the questers were at a complete loss.

Eldin, itching to get into the fight, growled, "I could just

use a little close-quarter combat!" At which Una at once produced a rapier from her swordbelt and said:

"If it comes to a fight, we stand right alongside you two!"

"Too true!" agreed Ula. "We're not quite shrinking violets,
you know," and she too produced a slender, gleaming blade.
"Ham Gidduf, our father, believed a girl should be able to use
a sword as well as any man—if only to protect herself from
men!"

"Aye," Hero nodded, "well, you're brave lasses, both of
you—but right now it's not men you've to worry about. Also,
it's not likely to come to hand-to-hand fighting. We're heavily outnumbered and the horned ones are rallying. Especially
now that the moonbeasts are directing their tactics. Look—!"
And he pointed to where one of the flotilla's ships shuddered
mightily as shots poured into her flanks. Suddenly the
stricken vessel expanded as if taking in a great breath of air—

—Expanded in fire and smoke and noise as her magazine
blew her out of the sky in one great roaring detonation. "That
was *Skipcloud*," Eldin's voice was sick, "and *Cumulus* is also
in trouble."

Their eyes followed the Wanderer's pointing finger to
where a second ship of Limnar's command went limping
down toward the pit, her sails in tatters and her hull gaping.
Even as they watched, a Lengite vessel vented flotation essence and followed her down, blasting off a mighty fusillade
that completely shattered her substructure and sent her plummeting moonward. She missed the pit's rim with nothing to
spare—only to blow up in a bright gout of fire where she
struck the ground.

Now the great scaly Shantak-birds were back in the sky
above the battling ships, their toadlike riders tootling loath-
somely on their talking instruments. "That's what I was waiting for," cried Gytherik, as he swung up onto the bridge
alongside his friends. "Those Shantaks haven't seen my grim
yet—and there never was a Shantak-bird could stand the sight
of a night-gaunt!"

With a single gesture he called the grim aloft—was himself

picked up by Sniffer and Biffer and lowered into his saddle below the neck of the great gaunt—and in a moment the entire grim was climbing toward the four corners of the sky on powerfully pulsing membrane wings. The questers watched them grow small with distance, saw them veer toward their chosen targets—then roared their encouragement aloud as panic pierced the Shantaks to their very hearts!

In scant seconds the piping of the moonbeast riders grew frantic with terror as their mounts spied the gaunts, reared back, half-heartedly attempted to rally, and were routed in a panic-flight across the moon's sick sky. Such was their horror of night-gaunts (the reason for which no legend ever told) that they ignored utterly any commands their riders might have given them and fled; indeed, several of them actually threw moonbeasts from their backs to make for greater speed!

And no sooner were the Shantaks routed than the Lengite fleet once more fell prey to panic and mindless disorder. They had come to rely so heavily upon the instructions of their moonbeast masters that without them—

"They're useless!" Eldin spat out his distaste. "Damn me, if we had ten more ships we could win this fight outright! Just look at Lathi's *Chrysalis*!"

At that very moment the *Chrysalis* was sailing between a pair of enemy vessels at such close quarters that with a good run a man might leap between decks. The Lengites were pounding away but their shots were simply punching through the paper ship just below deck level and passing out the other side—to crash resoundingly into stout Lengite timbers. They were destroying each other! As Lathi's leprous ghost of a ship emerged from between them, holed but otherwise unharmed, one blew up in a sheet of fire and the other commenced a slow spiral into the moon-pit.

Now a third Lengite closed with *Chrysalis*, but before enemy guns could be brought into play, Lathi's termen produced a "secret" weapon of their own. The watching questers gaped as muscled termen whirled fluffy white balls above their heads and released them at the astonished enemy. Where they landed, these strangely plastic missiles burst and hurled out strands of sticky webbing in all directions, so that in a matter of moments the entire ship—rigging, decks, cannon-ports, even the almost-human crew—were caught up in the stuff like flies in a spider's web. Then Lathi's own cannons— lightweight weapons, to be sure, but deadly for all that—were brought into play to finish the job.

And so the battle raged.

Then—disaster!

Two enemy vessels, converging on *Gnorri* in an unplanned but nevertheless deadly pincer, saw their chance and began to pound away. Limnar's gunners fired back; his engineer vented essence and *Gnorri* began a rapid descent; but the keel of one of the Lengites smashed through the rail amidships, bit deep into the deck—and jammed fast! Locked, both ships immediately began to sink down toward the rim of the moon-pit; and as horned ones came pouring down through the rigging onto *Gnorri*'s decks, so Hero, Eldin, Ula and Una joined the fray.

It was a short fight for the four, but bitter and vicious. The almost-humans had superiority of numbers and were half-crazed with a strange mixture of fear and bloodlust, so that even as they died they drove the four back against *Gnorri*'s shattered rail. There, at the edge of the sprung deck beneath the squat prow of the Lengite vessel, Hero saw the danger too late. The rim of the pit seemed to spin with the motion of the locked ships; the pockmarked surface loomed close; and as *Gnorri*'s keel bit shudderingly into moondust so the enemy ship slipped free, broke her back on the jagged rim and slid aft-first into the pit.

Masses of rope and rigging fell from the doomed ship's side as she went, knocking the questers and their women overboard through *Gnorri*'s shattered rail and hurling them into chaos!

Marooned on the Moon

For a moment Hero thought they must surely follow the broken, careening Lengite ship to hell, but then he felt himself bouncing on spongy soil before coming to rest at the pit's rim. Eldin and the girls sprawled beside him, a little winded but apparently unharmed, caught up in bits of broken timber, scraps of canvas and slithering lengths of rope.

"Free yourselves, quickly!" Hero gasped as the doomed ship dragged sails and rigging, ropes and debris and all after her into the abyss. And in another moment the questers and their women were quite alone, strangers on the strange and sinister surface of the moon.

No one had seen their plight; the fighting aboard *Gnorri II* was still in progress as she rose up again into the sky; and shout as loud as they might the questers would attract little attention in the alien, cratered, utterly unknown and inhospitable environment in which they now found themselves. Disbelievingly, Hero watched *Gnorri II* sail higher into the sky; and seeing a sudden rain of almost-human bodies from her sides, he cupped hands to mouth and tried one last time to make himself heard over the din of battle.

"Limnar!" he roared. "Ahoy, *Gnorri!*" But no one heard.

"I don't believe it!" Eldin growled then in disgust. "Have we come all this way just to get ourselves marooned on the moon?"

"We need to get to a point of higher elevation," Hero told him. "From which we can see and be seen. Here, amidst all of these small craters, grimy and dressed in these drab-colored clothes of ours—and with no way of attracting attention—we're goners for sure." He turned to Ula and Una where they still sprawled on the spongy moon-soil. "Girls, are you all right? Come on, we have to be going."

"Going where?" Eldin asked, helping the girls to their feet.

"There," Hero answered, pointing at a tangent across the crater to the low domed hill with its idol-crowned summit.

"What?" the Wanderer cried. "But we've seen the great door in that hill and know it for a temple to Mnomquah! Who can say how many more moon-horrors are lurking there right now? And—"

"And it's the only hill for miles around," Hero calmly pointed out. "And this is no time to start an argument. Hell's bells, you were crying out for a bit of action not so very long ago! Well, perhaps you're about to get some."

"I think Hero's right," Ula agreed. "At least we'll be visible atop that hill. If we're going to be picked up at all, that's the most likely spot."

"Well?" asked Hero. "Is it unanimous?"

Eldin and Una looked at one another. The Wanderer's voice was gruff as he answered, "You bloody well know it's unanimous! You don't think we'd let you go adventuring on the moon without us, do you?"

Hero sprang to the top of a small crater's rim and balanced there, putting a hand up to his eyes and scanning out the way between their present location and the hill of the temple. "There's a sort of small forest or dene," he informed, "half-way between, which should give us a little cover. After all, we don't want to be seen until we're ready."

"Couldn't agree more," said Eldin. "I want to be picked up, yes—but not by a damned Lengite!"

"Right," said Hero, rejoining his friends and dusting himself down. "Let's go. If we stick pretty close to the rim of the

pit we'll have less distance to cover. It should take us no
more than fifteen or twenty minutes at most."

They stepped out, skirting the larger craters and keeping
the yawning mouth of Mnomquah's pit in sight at all times,
and soon approached the moon-forest. Entering into gloom
beneath the domes of vast and leprous fungi, they wrinkled
their noses at a cloying musk of rotten vegetation and over-
ripe puffballs.

"Toadstools!" Eldin grunted disgustedly. "Wouldn't you
know it? No sane or healthy forest on the moon." He gave a
shove at a thick and fibrous stem, then stood back as the huge
mushroom toppled and crumbled into chunks of sticky decay.
Hero and the girls at once held their noses as a vile stink rose
up all around.

"Do you mind?" Hero finally, patiently inquired. "I mean,
it's a wonder these old hooters of ours haven"t given up the
ghost long ago, the stinks they've had to endure; and there
you go creating more of them!"

They pressed on without hindrance and shortly left the fungi
forest to hurry across an open, fairly level and unpocked area
where the ground was made up of a sort of loose, lumpy pumice. Now they were able to scan the sky once more and see
how the battle was progressing; and all were delighted and
heartened to note that there still remained seven ships of the
flotilla in the mad moon's sky. The seven were scattered far
and wide now and sailed at various altitudes, but they were
giving the Lengites such a time of it that the enemy still had
not fully recovered from his initial surprise. More than a dozen
of his shattered ships lay burning and wrecked across the yellow moonscape, and others drifted with neither sails nor sign
of life, crippled and helpless.

"They're doing fine!" cried the Wanderer—but in the next
moment his cry turned to a gasp of dismay as a badly battered *Shantak*, that ship of the once-Dukes of Isharra, fell foul
of a Lengite fusillade to blow asunder in gouting fire and
ruin.

"Well," said Hero grimly, "they made a fair fight of it—

considering they were such lousy sailors! It surprises me they lasted so long."

Eldin nodded his silent agreement, gave a little salute, and all four paused for a very brief moment. Then they turned their faces once more toward the domed hill where it now stood less than a quarter-mile away. The way was easier now and they made good speed, but even as they reached the foot of the hill, the door in its side began to open, causing them to dive for cover in the shallow well of a nearby crater. From there they watched the emergence of half-a-dozen moonbeasts, dressed this time as Oorn's High Priest had been and wearing tall, pschent-like headgear. They carried long wands and there was that in their bearing, however ugly and alien they might be, which seemed to set them aside from others of their kind.

"Wizards!" Eldin hoarsely whispered.

"Eh?" said Hero. "How do you know?"

"All gods have wizards to attend them," Eldin explained. "See those wands? They're the wizard's symbol of office. His weapon, too. Mnomquah will have chosen these lads from his worshippers, taught them how to work a little magic—or given them powers for the same purpose—and set them over his commoner priests and priestlings to keep a tight rein on things. Wasn't old Thinistor Udd just such a wizard, who tended Yibb-Tstll's idol in the mountain heights? Oh, yes," and he nodded toward the moonbeast wizards, "they'll have lots of powerful magic, these lads."

As he spoke, the weirdly clad moonbeasts had moved forward away from the great door until they stood clear of its shadow on a level part of the hillside. They moved with the peculiar, wobbly, jellyish motions common to all their kind, and yet with a special sort of groping ponderousness that set them apart. Seeing this, Hero whispered:

"Blind! The moon-God has blinded them in his own image."

"To heighten their other senses," Eldin informed. "To increase the potency of their moon-magic."

Now the six sorcerers faced blindly outward over the pit, raising their gray, gold-speckled wands before them and stabbing skyward with them, in the manner of serpents thrusting with their heads. Six sinuous gray beams sprang from the tips of the wands, converged like thick braids of smoke high over the heads of the wizards—then raced as one beam into the sky toward the battling ships.

To the questers in their crater observation post it seemed that the gray beam curved over like the head of a snake, pausing in the sky over the battle-locked fleets as if to choose a prey, before lancing down and striking at one of the remaining six ships of Limnar's flotilla. And after that . . . then there could be no further doubt about the efficacy, the terrible potency, of the wizards' pit-spawned moon magic.

Nimbus was the name of the stricken ship, and her fate was utterly unlike that of any other ship as ever sailed. For on the instant of the gray beam's striking she was lost from sight in a thick bank of smoke that rolled up from nowhere, then just as quickly revealed as the gray smoke drifted away. Ah!—but in that moment when *Nimbus* was hidden, she had suffered a terrible transformation.

The ship had turned gray as the wizards' beams, leprous as the ephemeral smoke-cloud, leaden as thunderheads in a winter sky—*and heavy as the rock from which she now seemed carved!*

"Stone!" Eldin's voice was hoarse with horror. "She falls out of the sky like a stone!"

And it was true. The leaden sails of *Nimbus* no longer billowed but stood stiff as if starched; her stony hull and decks showed all of a ship's detail without its life and movement and texture; the gray ropes of her rigging were rigid as stalactites, and the crew that lurched from her decks into space looked lifeless as lead soldiers. *Nimbus* was a ship of the clouds no longer but a hurled stone plummeting to earth! And she struck like a stone, shattering into a thousand pieces . . .

Almost before the four witnesses of this monstrous magic could catch their breath, Mnomquah's wizards raised their wands a second time. But before they could thrust them snakelike at the sky—

"No more of *that!*" cried Hero aloud, springing from the crater and rushing in to engage the wizards at close quarters. "No more wand-play, monsters. Let's see how your spells face up to cold steel!"

Nor was Hero alone in his headlong attack, for hot on his heels came a roaring Eldin and a pair of lithe vixens with eyes full of hell's own fire and fury. And as the blind moonbeasts turned to face this new threat, so they found themselves confronted with four bright and dazzling scythes of death that gave them no time at all to work fresh wonders.

"This for *Nimbus!*" cried Hero, driving curved Kledan steel through pschent, writhing pink face-tentacles and pulpy head alike.

"And this for *Skipcloud!*" roared Eldin, severing the wand-arm of his prey and gutting him with the next quicksilver stroke.

"Let's not forget *Cumulus!*" trilled Ula, her rapier ripping the throat of a third wizard.

"Even *Shantak* deserves her share of vengeance!" sang Una, decapitating a fourth, "—though her memory shan't find me shedding a great many tears."

By now the two remaining monsters were shambling back toward the great door in the hillside, their magic forgotten in the face of quester fury—but Hero was not willing to let them escape so lightly. "After them," he growled. "Don't let them get away. Who knows how many more of these priest-wizards there are in the hill, or what they'll be up to next? We've more than ourselves to think of now."

Close behind the moonbeasts, he paused for a moment at the great pivoting slab which was the door to the temple. Then he beckoned the others on and crossed the threshold. Eldin and the girls hurried after him, into the blue-litten dimness of an extensive cavern system which reached back like some unholy warren of evil into the heart of the hill. And indeed at this point they might just have turned back—but with a sigh and a rumble the mighty door pivoted shut behind them, bringing down dust from an unseen, centuried ceiling.

"Well, that's that," whispered the Wanderer in a tone of disgusted finality. He spat into corpse-fire gloom. "We can't go back, so we have to go on."

"Stay close behind me," said Hero with an economy of words. "We're not finished yet. We've done our bit—but perhaps we can still do a bit more."

"Right!" Ula quietly but emphatically agreed. "In the very guts of Mnomquah's temple, surely we can make a nuisance of ourselves before we're done?"

"We can at least try," whispered Una with equal fervor. "And if these are his guts, what say we give him a pain in 'em? . . . Which way did the moonbeasts go?"

"Down there, I think," answered Hero, pointing into gloom. "Come on, let's go. But carefully . . ."

Left on his own for a moment, Eldin gave himself a little shake, as if to make sure he was awake. "Damn me," he muttered then. "As if Hero weren't bad enough on his own, it seems I've now got three of 'em to worry about!" But as the shadows began to close in on him, he hastened in pursuit . . .

Moonmoth

As the four moved forward through the temple's labyrinth, their eyes grew accustomed to the gloom. Getting used to the utter silence, however, was a far more difficult thing. After the boom of cannons, the splintering of timbers and the shrieks of doomed men and monsters, the unbelievable *quiet* of this subterranean maze was almost deafening in its intensity. It was a silence such as might live in the tombs at the end of time.

"Have no fear, girls," Eldin whispered, his very whisper echoing in the hollow stillness. "We've been down to the pits of the underworld, Hero and I—to the Vale of Pnoth itself—and came back alive and sane. Well, alive anyway . . ."

"*Shh*!" Hero hissed. "Quiet, man! In this place a whisper has the volume of a warcry." He lowered his own voice to a mere breath. "If you must talk at all, then do it like this. Merely breathe the words. All right?"

Eldin tried it and found that it worked. "You know," he breathed, "I'm not blaming you, lad, but I think we erred coming in here. I mean, we don't seem to be serving a great deal of purpose here, if you see what I'm getting at."

"Oh, but we are!" Ula protested, her voice the smallest shiver in the pale blue light. "For one thing, we've distracted the attention of the moonbeast wizards away from the flotilla."

"That's right," put in Una. "Trapped in here, they can't use their magic on Limnar's ships."

"Oh, we have *them* trapped, do we?" said Eldin, at the same time avoiding the luminous glow of a great stalactite where it hung from the dim and uneven ceiling. "See, to my mind it's more a case of—"

"*Shh!*" Hero hissed again. "I'm sure I sense some movement then. Also, I believe I heard something."

They had reached a great junction of burrows, emerging into a large, low-ceilinged cave whose walls were literally honeycombed with tunnels which led off to unknown destinations. The floor was very slippery here, worn smooth by the feet of Mnomquah's priests and wizards and worshippers since an age when the moon was in its infancy. Most of the tunnels were artificial, but there were natural fissures, too, and the low ceiling was split right across in a deep, dark gash.

"There!" said Hero as they paused. "Did you hear it that time?"

"Aye," breathed Eldin after a moment's rapt attention. "The moonbeasts at their adoration. Demon flutes massed in low key, like a distant booming of crazed frogs."

Hero shook his head. "No, there's more to it than simple worship," he said.

"A sort of urgency," added Ula.

"An urging," Una corrected her.

"A *calling!*" Hero named it. "They're calling Mnomquah up from hell, calling him out of his pit!"

"And that's not all," said Eldin, "for now I hear something else."

"A hissing, perhaps?" Hero inquired.

The Wanderer nodded his great head. "Aye, like flotation essence venting from a ruptured bag."

"And growing louder," Una confirmed, dread of the unknown trembling in her voice.

"Coming this way!" gasped Ula.

"Quickly," Hero hissed. "Follow me." He crouched down,

sprang aloft and hauled himself up into the great crack in the ceiling. The fault was more horizontal than vertical, sloping away from the junction of tunnels at a shallow angle. Hero lay down and reached out his arm to help the others climb, and in a little while they lay close together and peered breathlessly down at the area just vacated.

Nor had they been any too quick off the mark, for scant seconds later the hissing suddenly increased threefold and the darkness in the cave visibly lessened. The questers and their women drew back into shadows then as a strange dim glow entered the cave, a shaft of gray half-light liberally sprinkled with golden motes. Writhing and twisting, that awful beam— like smoke braided into a plait—paused in the space beneath; and indeed the four knew that this was none other than a shaft of monstrous magic, sent from the tips of moonbeast wands to seek them out!

For a moment or two the head of the snakelike beam, a foot thick and flattened like the head of a cobra, swayed and hovered in the center of the cave before sinking down to floor level, almost as if to sniff in the manner of some hideous hound. Then it lifted and recommenced its swaying motion, and finally it wove away down that tunnel by which the four had entered. Unbroken, the swirling, gaseous body of the beam followed its head, interminably writhing through the junction chamber.

Not one of the four made the slightest sound, nor even breathed aloud—for all had seen what the gray beam did to *Nimbus*, and to her crew.

Then, tugging at the sleeves of his friends, Hero crept backwards away from the mouth of the crevice, turned on all fours and began to feel his way into the near-darkness of the unknown fissure. Soundlessly the others followed, eager to put distance between themselves and the sentient-seeming beam of gray light. Once more their eyes were required to grow accustomed to the gloom—a deeper gloom here, where there was an absence of all but a trace of the blue luminosity—and as they went so the fault expanded until they were able to stand erect. After that they made good speed until the crevice turned abruptly upward to become a tight and stygian flue or chimney.

"Now we climb," Hero brushed the silence with a breath of speech. "We questers are used to this—you might even say we're experts—but what about you girls?"

Dark heads gave shining, negative shakes and green eyes widened in elfin faces. "Sword play, yes—" said Ula.

"Fool's play, no!" Una finished it. "Ham Gidduf used to say our legs were far too pretty to break taking tumbles."

"The silly old short-sighted sod was probably right," commented Eldin without malice. "Ah, well—we'll just have to teach you."

"Aye," Hero grimly agreed, "but we could have asked for better conditions."

The questers climbed into the volcanic rock chimney, finding it easy going and passing the girls between them from stretch to stretch. By this time full twenty minutes had ticked away since they entered the door in the hillside, and they could not help but wonder how Limnar's tiny fleet was doing now. They wondered, too, about the very faintest of tremors which were beginning to make themselves felt in the rock all around them—as if a giant stirred in the depths below—and they shuddered as they remembered the cryptic bass pipings of Mnomquah's moonbeast priests. Then, to speed them on their way, there came again that hissing of escaping gas, and they knew that the gray beam was hot on their trail once more.

As that fearful sound grew louder below and behind them, suddenly the chimney became a blow-hole that opened abruptly into a huge but patently unfrequented cave. Here the blue light was stronger, where great stalactites festooned the ceiling and pumice dust lay in a thick carpet all around. It was a natural cave and must be totally unknown to the moonbeasts.

Eldin was first to emerge and he quickly hauled the others

up to stand beside him, ankle-deep in the drifted dust of ages. "Where now?" he queried Hero in a breathless whisper.

The other shrugged helplessly, staring this way and that. "Damned if I know—but we have to make up our minds quickly, before—"

"*Who comes?*" a crystal voice full of fear sang out in their minds, causing all four to start violently and hug each other tightly at the shock of the thing. "*Who disturbs me in the Sleep of the Change? Is it moonbeasts, come to cut out my great heart while I helplessly hang here? Oh, who shall protest my unhatched sisters now?*" And as they gradually relaxed, the tinkling telepathic voice filled the four with its fear and sadness.

Meanwhile, the loathsome, near-distant hissing sound had subsided a little, telling them that the gray beam had picked up a false trail; but the tremors in the earth were grown much stronger, more frequent and threatening; and all taken into account, it seemed to the questers and their women that they were being driven toward some unknown precipice from which there would be no escape. This new thing—this telepathic voice in their heads—was just something else to set nerves a-jangle, to increase the hysteria building inside them.

"Who?—what?—dammit!—*where* are you?" Hero asked at last, barely remembering to keep his own voice to the merest whisper. "And listen, whoever you are: if the moonbeasts are your enemies, then you have nothing to fear from us."

For an answer he felt a crystal tinkling in his mind—a searching, a seeking-out of truth—and knew that his three friends were similarly affected. Whatever the presence was which dwelled in this cave, it quickly satisfied itself that there was nothing of harm in the questers . . . certainly none directed toward its at present unknown self. And again it spoke to them:

"*I am Eeth, a moonmoth maiden—or I will be when my metamorphosis is complete.*"

"Hero!" Eldin hoarsely whispered and clutched the other's elbow. "One of these stalactites is alive!" He pointed a shaking finger at a stony, stubby column of rock where it de-pended from the ceiling. "The thing's moving," declared the Wanderer. "Will you look!"

Hero looked, the girls too, and they all commenced to back away as the great stalactite's surface *pulsed* . . . and rested . . . *pulsed* . . . and rested . . . *pulsed*, and—

"Like a heart!" Hero whispered.

"Oh, yes, it is my heart you see beating," the crystal voice told them. *"The casing is not a stalactite, however, but a co-coon. Nature has designed it this way to deceive the moonbeasts, who find moonmoth flesh irresistible."*

Still backing away, Ula gave a little cry as the backs of her legs struck something and she tripped and sat. When the dust settled she got to her feet in a circle of five great white ovals, each one large as a decent-sized boulder. The things looked for all the world like huge—

"My sisters!" cried the telepathic voice. *"Oh, be careful! They are not yet hatched—and there are so very few of us!"*

Hero helped Ula step out from the circle of great eggs and turned back to the living stalactite. "You mean you're a chrysalis?" he said, astonishment coloring every whispered word.

"That is correct," answered the voice, *"but in a little while I shall be Eeth, a moonmoth maid—if the moonbeasts don't find me first!"*

"Eeth," Eldin now stepped boldly forward, a hopeful rum-ble in his echoing voice. "If you got in here there must be a way out. Now do be a good chrysalis and—"

"Shh!" Hero fairly danced in his torment, leaping on Eldin and clamping a hand over his mouth. "Great oaf! Be qui—"

But too late . . .

From somewhere deep in the heart of the hill a droning of triumphant flutes reached out to them, and at the same time the moonrock beneath their feet gave a sharp and very dis-tinct lurch. Important and ominous as these signs were, Eldin's ill-timed outburst had not been responsible for them. It was, however, responsible for the other thing:

Namely, a more deliberate and knowing renewal of the horrid hissing! For even as the ground bucked again and dust shivered from above, so a grim gray light gleamed from below; and up from the hole in the cave's floor rose a vast nodding head of writhing, gold-speckled smoke.

"The magic of the moonbeasts!" cried the crystal voice in the minds of the questers. *"Farewell, my new-found friends—for we are all doomed now!"*

Mnomquah!

At that precise moment when the smoke-formed wandsnake of the moonbeast sorcerers thrust its hissing head up through the chimney and into the moonmoth's cavern, an equally terrifying emergence was taking place on the lunar surface. Namely, that of Mnomquah's head from the mouth of his vast burrow. More of that in a moment . . .

In the meantime, all had not gone well for Limnar Dass and his now greatly reduced flotilla. He had recently lost another ship; powder was so low as to be almost exhausted aboard his remaining vessels; and *Gnorri II* herself, having suffered structural damage in the collision with the Leng ship and her subsequent plunge to moon's surface, was not answering the helm with half her usual willingness. The enemy fleet, on the other hand, had rallied from its initial pounding and was now well deployed to apply maximum firepower in the task of reducing the flotilla to aerial rubble.

This, despite the continuing loss of their own vessels to the flotilla's superior gunnery, was exactly what the Lengites were doing; even now an enemy cannonade removed the bridge from one of Limnar's surviving nucleus of ships. And still the flotilla fought back, though for a certainty the end was nigh.

Zura's *Shroud* continued to do remarkably well—so well indeed that Limnar was given to wonder how the zombie gunners fared in the massive recoil of their cannons. The living dead, by their very nature, are highly vulnerable to hard knocks and shakes; so that by now *Shroud*'s deck must be a veritable nightmare of detached, kicking limbs and various other more or less mobile bits and pieces.

As for Lathi's *Chrysalis*: just how that paper ship held together at all was a mystery Limnar Dass would never fathom. She was a very light vessel, of course, and perhaps that had much to do with it; but long after better ships had plunged to their doom, *Chrysalis* continued to give back blow for blow, even though she was little more than a torn rag in the sky. Yes, and if Hero and Eldin were here now, Limnar was sure that they would applaud the tenacity of these inhuman once-enemies no less than he himself.

Hero and Eldin ... Their loss over all else was the one blow which had troubled the sky-Captain beyond endurance. For he felt certain that they had gone down into the throat of the moon-pit along with the Leng ship. The questers and their brave ladies, fighting to the last, gone down to the bowels of the moon to spit in Mnomquah's blind eyes.

Well, they had left a rare legacy behind them; for it was as if something of the questers had found its way into the hearts of each and every surviving human, as if they fought even now right alongside their old enemies, Zura and Lathi, urging them to greater excesses of effort. And right there and then in the midst of the battle, even as the sky-Captain was given momentarily to admire the grit—the sheer fighting spirit—of dreamland's handful of battered ships, so there came that one cry he had most dreaded to hear: the despairing voices of his gunners, reporting that the powder was finished, that *Gnorri II* had fired her last shot.

One by one the rest of the ships fell silent as the Lengite hordes closed in, and Limnar knew that this was the end ... But still he refused to accept defeat, not while there was an ounce of fight left in him. If the dreamlands were doomed, then this son of the dreamlands would take as many as possible of the enemy with him!

"Weapon yourselves up, lads," he roared at his ragged crew. "We're going right through the middle of 'em. Let's ram the dogs down hell's throat!"

Gnorri II, as if hearing her Master's battle cry, rallied herself one last time to answer the helm with something of her old vigor; and the ramlike prows of three brave ships turned alongside *Gnorri*'s and advanced in line abreast, under all available canvas, straight toward the wall of Lengite vessels where they offered their fat black flanks.

Knowing that this must be the beginning of the end, Gytherik Imniss quit his present task (which was to direct his gaunts in their efforts to cut enemy rigging and sails to ribbons) and called the grim to him in the sky. Unashamed tears washed the youth's face as he counted just three of the creatures, four with his great gaunt mount, and knew that the rest had been slain. His sorrow would increase tenfold when he learned the loss of Hero and Eldin, but for now he urged the grim back to *Gnorri*'s deck and reported to the sky-Captain where he commanded a debris-littered bridge.

"Gytherik," said Limnar as the lad sprang up beside him, "save yourself. Take your gaunts and run for it. See if you can find the aerial Gulf Stream and let your grim glide you back to the dreamlands. Go home to your mother and father in Nir and comfort them as the land of Earth's dreams totters and dies. We've lost, lad. This is the end."

And as Gytherik stood there aghast—with enemy shot whistling through the rigging and squat black hulls looming larger by the second—Limnar told him of Hero and Eldin, of Ula and Una, and how he feared all four dead and gone forever from the dreams of men. How Gytherik cried then, and how he cursed the moon and its inhabitants, and the horned ones of Leng, and the very fates which had seen fit to end it like this, at this time and in this place . . . Then—

"I'll go if you'll come with me," he told the sky-Captain. "Only then. Most of me has died here, and you are another part of me. If I can't salvage something of my life, then I'll have none of it. Won't you come with me, Limnar Dass?"

The other shook his head, steered *Gnorri* on, aimed her wicked ram of a prow amidships of a squat black hull no more than forty yards ahead. "I go with my ship," he said.

Gytherik grabbed his arms. "And you are the one who would find his own destiny," he sobbed, "who was never satisfied merely to drift with the dreams of men. Do you forget so easily?"

"This *is* my destiny!" Limnar cried out in his agony. "But it doesn't have to be yours. Now go while you still may."

"Gaunts!" cried Gytherik, turning to gaze with burning eyes upon the grim. "Arm yourselves. Fight like . . . like men! Kill! *Kill!*" And as *Gnorri II* smashed shudderingly into her target he slid sword from belt and hung on grimly to the rail alongside Limnar Dass, youth no more but a warrior full-blown. A warrior doomed!

In the last few seconds before Limnar's brave ship rammed the Lengite, his engineers had boosted their engines and caused *Gnorri II* to gain altitude. Thus her keel tore away great chunks of the enemy's decks, superstructure, and all her canvas before *Gnorri* herself scraped on into free sky and left a gutted black wreck in her wake. One of the flotilla's other three ships had used similar tactics, and successfully, but a second, Zura's *Shroud*, had not been so fortunate. She had stove in the side of a Lengite and locked there; and now horned ones swarmed everywhere on the decks of the two ships, hewing away in hand-to-hand combat with Zura's zombies.

Seeing the way the fight was going, that Zura—whose crew had been severely depleted even before the commencement of the aerial battle—must lose in the end, Limnar quickly brought *Gnorri* alongside and called on the Lady of the Charnel Gardens to come aboard. Being no fool, Zura took a flying leap between decks—at which precise moment the gap chose to widen as the locked ships tilted and began to slip from the sky. Vainly the Mistress of Death reached out her hands toward *Gnorri*'s rail, and certainly had she fallen— but Gytherik's gaunts were there to pluck her from thin air and land her safely on the bridge beside their master and the sky-Captain.

As for Lathi's *Chrysalis*: that tattered rag of a vessel had not attempted anything so utterly insane as ramming tactics; no, for to her that must certainly have proven fatal. Instead, cutting between a pair of enemy ships, the Queen of Thalarion had had her termen enshroud those luckless vessels in their strangling strands and webs; and still *Chrysalis* remained aloft, though more out of miraculous chance than anything approaching skill on the part of her Captain and crew.

And now only three ships stood in the lunar sky amidst an enemy fleet which outnumbered them eight or nine to one; and the Lengites loaded powder and shot for one final, massed cannonade. Knowing what was coming as the enemy turned his gunwales broadside on to the tiny flotilla, Limnar Dass took Gytherik's hand in firm grip and shook it, much in the manner of the waking world. Then the two faced Zura and nodded her a curt farewell. Gytherik whistled back his exhausted gaunts—only two of them at the last, Sniffer and Biffer—and went down onto the littered deck to be with them.

Leathery monsters that they were, they tugged at him and thrust their featureless heads aloft, urging him to come with them; but he shook his head in one last denial. "You go," he told them, "back to your dreamlands, if you can. For me it ends here."

They would not go, however, but merely covered their heads and shuffled beside him in the manner of gaunts; and so they waited for the end.

—And had they but known it, this was the very moment when the wand-snake erupted into the cave of the moonmoth . . . and more terrifying by far, it was the instant when Mnomquah chose to thrust up his vast and scaly head from the mouth of the moon-pit!

The events heralding this awesome occurrence—the moonquakes and the sudden increase in frequency of the mighty orange smoke-rings from the pit—had of course gone unnoticed by the battlers in the sky, but not by Mnomquah's priests. Even now a horde of robed moonbeasts swarmed from the door in the hill and gathered at the side of the great crater, piping upon their hellish flutes to hasten the moon-God's emergence—and stumbling back in blind terror when in fact he *did* emerge!

Up came that massive scaly head into view, pushing ten thousand tons of rubble and rock before it, and such a roar and a blast echoed from the great hinged jaws that whatever else was happening stopped immediately, and all eyes turned to the moon-pit and Mnomquah where he rose from the depths of moon's heart. Mnomquah!—and how that awesome name suited this awesome monster.

His lizard's head and flabby wattled neck filled full half of that mile-wide pit, and his clawed, webbed forepaws were each two hundred yards long where he pushed them out to rest them on the rim. One of those paws, falling carelessly half across the base of the domed temple hill, effectively obliterated the pivoting door, caved in the hillside and crushed half of the moonbeast priests flat—but the rest fluted on in an apparent frenzy of adoration. For a moment or two the moon-God appeared to listen to these demon flautists, inclining his vast head while strangely sensitive organs bulged and pulsed beneath the membrane layer which covered otherwise empty eyesockets—but only for a moment or two.

Then his great jaws opened and with an outpouring of orange vapor his forked yellow tongue flickered forth. The moonbeasts—all but two of them—stuck to that tongue like flies in honey, were drawn back in an instant of time into his gaping maw. And now at last it was plain that Mnomquah was not pleased. Indeed, that he was utterly furious!

Very well, he had punished his moonbeast priests—but for what? They had not been to blame for delaying his great leap to the dreamlands. And by now the tides must surely have rolled back from Sarkomand, exposing Oorn's temple and Oorn herself where she doubtless waited in gastropod glory

and expectancy. Why did Lord Mnomquah wait? Why did he
not use his great magic right now, this very second, to hurl
himself and a billion tons of moon-rock across the vault of
space and down upon the cowering dreamlands? His
moonbeast priests had called him up from Ubboth's oily
wells, so what more could he expect of them? Perhaps he desired personally to destroy the aerial intruders for all the trouble they had put in the way of his great plan . . .

Two trembling moonbeast priests played on, and it seemed
Mnomquah heeded them for now he turned his blind eyes
skyward. Again the mighty hinge of his jaw opened to vent
orange vapors, and his flat yellow road of a tongue coiled itself back, back like a spring, poised in his gullet for a nightmare thrust. Then, as a stroke of lightning, that tongue
uncoiled—a mile of it that lashed the sky—and where six or
seven Lengite ships had sailed, only scraps of smoking
wreckage drifted on the moonwind!

How the two remaining priests piped then, guiding their
God more carefully, lining up his great head as it turned at
last to point at Limnar's tight little trio of crippled ships,
Gnorri, *Starspur* and *Chrysalis*. But did the moon-God really
need his priests? And if not, why had he first chosen to punish the horned ones and not these pitiful interlopers? Or perhaps he had merely desired to display to them his awesome
might—before letting them feel it for themselves.

Can a lizard smile? It seemed so to all who watched from
the rails of the three ships. The moon-God's scaly lips turned
back and his jaws cracked open yet again. Those hidden and
nameless organs pulsed and bulged behind the membrane of
his sightless eyes, and slowly but surely the great tongue
coiled itself into a tight, elastic mass.

. . . Then, on the very brink of nightmare, the moon-God
froze; and in the next moment he had jerked his vast head
round to gaze blindly but yet with superhuman instinct at the
mountainous, needle-tipped horizon. Sightless, yes—in the
mundane way of blind, lesser creatures—but still Mnomquah
sensed what was coming, what rose into view even now from

behind those looming peaks. Sensed, "saw", and his jaws instantly opened wider yet in a rictus of hatred and ... yes, fear!

All heads had turned with the moon-God's head, and where alien eyes now widened in terror, human eyes stared in utter disbelief and a kindling of incredible hope.

For this could not possibly be—and yet it was!

Magic of the Moonbeasts

On the instant of the rearing of the wand-snake into Eeth's cave, Ula and Una had instinctively drawn back, Eldin had drawn a sharp intake of breath, and Hero had drawn his sword. Just what the younger quester hoped to achieve with that blade against this most inimical magic of the moonbeasts is conjectural; but nevertheless he weighed curved Kledan steel in his hand and faced the nodding, fearsome head of the horror in true hero fashion.

Eldin, on the other hand, had noticed something which escaped the other's attention; namely, a jagged crack in a massy stalactite which hung from the ceiling directly above the shaft's mouth. Thus when that great ape of a man finally drew *his* sword, it was with a definite purpose in mind; and for the very first time he recognized a potential which never before had made itself apparent. For in an earlier adventure this very blade he now held had been first destroyed, then reconstituted by the science of the First Ones (a mighty race from extra-dimensional gulfs, whose aeon-slumbering survivors had sent Hero and Eldin questing for the Wands of Power), and thus the sword was imbued with a very special strength of its own.

Never in all the time gone by since then had Eldin suspected the weapon to be in any way different. He had of course noticed that it refused to notch, no matter how much

he used it, and that it would not rust, however ill he cared for
it, but that was all. Now, however, coming to him from nowhere, he felt suddenly sure that the sword was capable of
what he was about to demand of it. Later he would not even
remember the dawning of this awareness, but for now—

He gripped the hilt of the blade in both hands, sprang forward, used Hero's crouched, unsuspecting back as a spring-
board and hurled himself into the air over the flat, nodding
head of the wand-snake. Into the crack of the stalactite he
drove the point of that strangely-forged blade, using all the
great strength of his mighty arms and powerfully muscled
shoulders; and more than a third of the sword's length grated
deep into the heart of the shivery stone. Now, swinging forward as he hung from the hilt, he drew up his legs and aimed
a tremendous kick at the stalactite's thick wedge.

And with a loud crack the mighty tip of that depending
stone dagger broke off and fell like a plug into the hole, effectively cutting off the wand-snake's "head" where it pro-
truded into the cave. Thrown backward by the force of his
own kick, the Wanderer landed in a heap beside Hero, who
was still trying to draw air where he lay face-down in
moondust.

The two girls meanwhile had backed well away from the
shaft, and both were in a position to see quite clearly what
next happened. They uttered piercing little shrieks of horror
as the severed head of the wand-snake threshed for a
moment—as if in some sort of inorganic agony—before falling onto the sprawled questers and exploding into a gray-
glowing cloud which momentarily hid the two from view.
Then, in another second, the cloud had cleared and the pair
slowly, dazedly got to their feet, dusting themselves down,
apparently unaltered . . . Or were they?

Having "seen" all of this through the eyes of the four, Eeth
now spoke again in their minds, and her relief was a near-
physical thing as she said: *"You have saved me, both myself
and my unhatched sisters, for surely would the magic of the
moonbeasts have turned us all to stone! And you are lucky,*

*for in severing the head of the wand-snake you destroyed
much of the magic's potency—else you were now frozen gray
figures, lifeless as moon-rock."*

"Much of its potency?" queried Hero worriedly, bracing
his shoulders and stretching his back. He turned to the pulsing chrysalis. "All of it, I should hope . . ." Then, feeling an
unaccustomed stiffness in all his limbs, he looked at Eldin.
"Tell me, old lad," he said, his voice tight and nervy. "These
aches I feel: surely they simply result from that great kick in
the back you gave me?"

Eldin nodded. "And mine from my fall," he said . . . and
suddenly appalled they stared into each other's eyes. Then the
Wanderer gave a small groan as he deliberately set about to
bend arms and legs, testing them against the possibility of an
unimaginable horror. Not satisfied with the results of this
self-examination, he turned again to Hero and studied his face
minutely. "Of course," he said, "it could be the foul light in
here—and certainly I don't want to sound pessimistic—but
damn me, lad, I've never seen you looking so gray and—"

"And old?" asked Hero, as the Wanderer paused in
midsentence. "You too, Eldin. You're starting to look stony
old!"

Eldin groaned again. "Oh, no!" he said. "I mean, *you* can
stand a few years, but me? Who'll employ a quester who's
stiff as a board and looks old as Methuselah?"

"Methuselah?" Hero looked puzzled.

"A long-lived waking-worlder, I think . . ."

Ula and Una now approached the pair. "Are you all right?"
they wanted to know.

Eeth, slowly pulsing in her cocooned half-sleep, answered
for all. *"It is as I feared, and I have read my inherited mem-
ories and instincts aright. It seems that the partial wand-
snake retained a partial magic—which it expended upon
you,"* she said.

"You mean we've been partially petrified?" said Eldin.

"I mean," Eeth answered, *"that you are now feeling the
first effects of what must soon become a permanent—"* And

she too paused as she realized the awfulness of what she was saying. But the questers had received their tinkling message with crystal clarity.

"Permanent paralysis?" Hero was aghast.

"Petrification?" Eldin too.

"Eeth," Hero was filled with a sort of leaden urgency—a numbing need to get something finished—as finally he realized their predicament, "we have to get out of here."

The moonmoth-to-be shook her mental head. *"You'll never make it."* Her mind-voice was full of sorrow.

"And the girls?" Eldin wanted to know, fascinated by the numbness he could now feel coursing through his veins. "What of them?"

"They were not enveloped by the cloud," said Eeth. *"They are not the victims of moonbeast magic."*

"They can make it?" asked Hero.

"Yes, if they knew the way."

"Then you must guide us," said Eldin. "We'll take them as far . . . as far as we can."

"We're not going anywhere without you," Una sobbed unashamedly as she threw herself on his neck—only to draw back when she felt how cold he had grown.

Ula flew into Hero's less than usually responsive arms, kissed him on lips from which the color was gradually draining. Tears washed her face as she whispered, "Oh, Hero! Hero!"

But the questers thought only of the girls. "Which way, Eeth?" asked Hero.

"You are brave creatures," she answered, her thoughts awash with a strange mixture of pity and prescience of their terrible fate. *"You saved my life—the lives of my sisters, too— probably the entire moonmoth race. And now you have no thought for yourselves, only for your females. The least I can do is guide you out of here . . . With my mind, for of course I must remain until my change is complete."*

"Then let's be on our way," Eldin urged, "while we're still able."

Now there flashed into the minds of the questers and their women a picture of the cave in which they stood. So perfect, that picture, that they hardly realized it was there at all until the scene shifted to show the mouth of an upward sloping natural shaft hidden behind a cluster of tall, bulky stalagmites. *"Go then,"* said Eeth. *"Follow the shaft, and I shall guide you."*

The four crossed the floor of the cave and passed behind the stalagmite clump into the fissure, and as they went so the pictures changed in their minds, showing them every inch of the way they must go. Puzzled by something—even in the extremity of the knowledge that this most probably would be his last hour—still Eldin thought to ask:

"Eeth, how can you know the way so well?"

"My mother knew the way," came Eeth's crystal voice, a little fainter now, *"and her mother before her, and something of their knowledge came down to me. Also, I have been this way once before—as a caterpillar on my way to feed in the mushroom forest."*

"And yet your, er, sisters haven't hatched yet?" Eldin appeared to be trying to understand.

"I was deposited some little time before them," came the answer, with a hint of something like pride.

"D'you take me for a fool?" Hero suddenly asked the Wanderer for no apparent reason.

"Always," Eldin drily answered.

"Huh!" said Hero. "I know what you're up to. Taking my mind off things with your infernal moth-talk!"

"Taking my own mind off things, really," the Wanderer replied. "Hero, I'm stiff . . . and not with boredom."

"You're looking more than a bit gray, too," said the other. They paused for a moment where Eeth's mind-pictures said they must turn to the left and climb a steep incline. "Eldin, have you ever had that feeling you've been here before?"

"Deja vu?"

"No riddles, just answer my question."

"Aye," Eldin replied with a sigh as they climbed (but oh so

slowly now) the stony ramp. "Oh, we've been here before, all right, you and I. Staring into the teeth of the Old Boy himself. Death's grinned at us more than once."

"But this time he's in hysterics!" Hero answered without humor.

Now the way led straight up, an easy climb even for a pair of untried girls. Yellow moonlight showed high up at the top of a wide chimney full of ledges and cavelets and resting places. "There you . . . go," Eldin told the girls, and he rested his numb legs and aching back against a rocky wall. "Watch how you go . . . and you'll be . . . all right."

Hero came to a halt beside him. They looked layered with moon-dust, gray as pumice, but in fact it was the color of their skin, their flesh. "You've come . . . this far," said Hero, "and no harm done. With that . . . kind of luck . . . I believe you . . . should make it."

"No harm done!" cried Ula, clutching at him and weeping bitterly. She stood on tiptoe to kiss his mouth—and her hand flew to her lips in shock. Una, too, sobbed as she clung to Eldin's stony chest; sobbed all the louder when she no longer detected the beating of his heart. Then the girls stepped slowly away from the questers and stared at them with wide, tearful eyes.

Dust trickled down the wall behind the two when, with a scraping sound, they slowly settled and leaned together. And the last dim gleams of fire went out of their eyes.

For some little time Ham Gidduf's twin daughters hung in each other's arms and sobbed. Then, when it was done, they began to climb. Behind them a pair of statues became one with the shadowed, centuried stone, and from somewhere far below the merest tinkle of a tiny crystal chimed farewell in their minds . . .

The Return of Randolph Carter

Limnar Dass, where he stood on *Gnorri*'s bridge, simply could not believe his eyes. For long seconds he stared at the curving horizon of sharp-etched peaks, and at what rose above them, as a man might stare at some monster born of delirium tremens; except that this was no monster but the gladdest, maddest sight imaginable.

"Pinch me, Zura," Limnar said to the zombie Princess where she stood beside him. "Wake me up or relieve me of my command, one of the two, for I'm either asleep or insane!"

"Then we're both for the madhouse, Cap'n Dass," she answered. And under her breath she added, "Damn! Damn! *Damn!*"

"Damn?" Limnar faintly repeated her, slack-jawed and pop-eyed. Not really listening to her, his response was almost drugged, automatic. He could not take his eyes from that fantastic horizon.

"Limnar!" came Gytherik's ringing shout as he leapt up onto the bridge in a frenzy of excitement. "Do you see it? Do you see it?"

"We see it," Zura answered, "and I for one *know* I'm not dreaming. I've seen it before, and from much the same vantage point—and the last time it cost me my fleet!"

"Serannian!" gasped Gytherik.

"The sky-floating city!" sighed Limnar, almost sure now of his senses.

"Kuranes and Carter," moaned Zura. "I might as well jump overboard here and now!"

"No," Limnar caught her by the elbow—then quickly let go as he thought of all the poisons that she was. "You've played your part, Zura," he told her. "There'll be no punishment for you—not if I have a say in it."

"You're assuming, of course, that the dreamlands will win?" she said.

"Oh, they will!" cried Gytherik deliriously. "*We* will!"

"But Serannian!" said Limnar, still astounded and not quite accepting the evidence of his own five senses. "How can it possibly be?"

"I don't know," replied Zura, "and I care even less. If I survive—and if I'm not locked away—then it's back to the Charnel Gardens for me." There was no gladness in her tone, and suddenly the sky-Captain felt sorry for her.

"How can you take it so calmly?" Gytherik danced a jig on the bridge. "Look, it's Serannian. It *is* Serannian!"

And indeed it was Serannian, the sky-floating city, jewel of the dreamlands, fully emerged now from behind the mountains and approaching like some incredible stately behemoth of the sky. Beneath the aerial city a haze of warm, vented flotation essence, literally an ocean of that ethereal vapor, shimmered in sunlight from beyond the moon's rim; and on her flanks sailed the massed might of the dreamlands, Kuranes' and Randolph Carter's warship fleets. At the front, leading all into battle, came the Royal Yacht itself, whose colors told Limnar Dass a great deal.

"You see that flag?" he caught hold of Gytherik to keep him still.

"I can't quite make it out," answer the other, squinting his eyes.

"Here," said Limnar, "use my glass. Now tell me what you see . . ."

"A lantern, I think," the gaunt-master reported, "and what

looks like a great jaw—all set against a green and ancient hill."

"Aye," Limnar grinned, excitement flaring up in him until he trembled to contain it. "That's the King's standard, all right. Randolph Carter is back, Gytherik—and if you think you've seen it all, I've news for you. Do you see those bright-shining mirrors lining the decks of yon ships? They're ray-projectors, last used in the Bad Days. King Carter outlawed them for a time when the troubles were over, but now it seems he's had them installed in the ships of his fleet. You saw their like in Ilek-Vad, on the night of the mad moon's beam, and before that in the war with, er—"

"With me," Zura nodded. "And little use they were."

"Oh, I remember the ray-projectors well enough," Gytherik hastily replied. "Didn't you have a couple of them aboard *Skymaster* one time? I seem to remember that before we were friends, you shot down one of my gaunts with just such a weapon."

"Ah!" Limnar coughed. "Yes, that's right. I had forgotten. Actually, the projectors were undergoing trials at the time. They had been improved a little over models used in the Bad Days. And I think you'll find these even newer models are better still. They were originally designed for work against organic targets: to destroy evil beings and creatures," he glanced at Zura. "Living ones, that is. But I know for a fact that there were plans afoot to have them adapted for inorganic targets too. Then King Carter and Kuranes canceled the project, or perhaps they simply placed it under wraps? We shall see."

"I seem to remember," said Gytherik again, "that they were quite deadly enough in their old form!"

"Oh? Well, believe me," answered Limnar, "that if these really are the latest models, anything that passed for deadly before was merely a prelude. Now comes the concerto!"

High over the suddenly muted moonscape sailed the fleets of dreamland, and while they still could their mirrors gathered the rays from the sun beyond the rim and enhanced them in their batteries of projectors. Now the ships were descending, venting essence and spreading across the sky like a scarlet stain in the vastness of Serannian's shadow; and too late, the commanders of the Lengite fleet knew that they were doomed.

Pent fury—the furious power of the sun itself—was released then, to lash down from on high in the shape of dazzling-white pencil beams from the fleet's ray-projectors, and where those beams struck they brought death and destruction. They licked over sails and rigging and left them blazing; they lingered on wooden decks until timbers gouted fire and smoke; they penetrated deep to seek out and detonate magazines, filling the sky with falling debris and burning wreckage. And where a Lengite fleet had sailed, soon nothing remained but fire-tinged smoke and rolling thunder!

A dozen heavily armored escort vessels spiralled down, four to each of Limnar's three crippled ships, and put out grapples. Then, powerful engines pulsed; and they were lifted up, up and into the Bay of Serannian itself. This took some little time, during which the fleet had concentrated its ray bombardment upon Mnomquah and the cities of the moonbeasts. Where the former seemed amazingly invulnerable, the latter could not withstand the fleet's fiery fury.

How those windowless towers burned when the devastating power of the sun fell upon them, and how dreamland's gunners took revenge for the ravaged towns and hamlets of the land of Earth's dreams! Ah, but the moonbeasts were not helpless! They had their magic, and wizards who knew well how to use it. Up from the cities under attack sprang the weaving heads of wand-snakes, and wherever they struck ships turned to stone and fell out of the sky. For where the moonbeast wizards of Mnomquah's temple had merely played a cat-and-mouse game with Limnar's flotilla, now their brothers in the cities were in deadly earnest where the greater fleet was concerned. A full dozen of dreamland's ships were caught this way, for no sooner would the ray-projector gunners find and destroy one group of wizards than another would spring up somewhere else.

And yet the wizard-priests did not strike at Serannian itself, perhaps because they saw little profit in petrifying that which was already stone; so that high over the scene of battle Limnar, Gytherik and Zura, safe now behind Serannian's ramparts, could look down with bated breath and see how the fighting fared. And eventually, as exchanges between ships and cities grew more heated, there came that signal occurrence which put an end to the whole thing.

The flat nodding head of a wand-snake found its way into the bay of Serannian and hovered there over a half-dozen ships held in reserve. It was a large snake, this one, and the ships were sailing in close formation. Back went the cobra-like head of that magic-spawned smoke-snake, as if to strike, but before it could thrust forward and down upon the ships—

"Look!" cried Limnar, pointing out through an embrasure. "The promontory there—the Museum!"

Zura and Gytherik followed his pointing finger, saw the great circular building he indicated where it stood upon a jutting, fragile-looking promontory. Built on the very rim, beyond the Museum was—nothing! Beneath it, a thin-seeming fifty feet of rock overhung a mile of thin air. Between sky-island and Museum, a narrow, walled causeway was the only means of access. Now, clanking out from the shadow of the Museum and making his way to the center of the causeway, the Curator had come into view.

"Aye," said Zura sourly, "and I remember *him*, too! He was responsible for the destruction of many of my ships."

"Only because they threatened his Museum," answered Gytherik breathlessly, "as even now it might appear to be threatened."

Many-armed, built of metal, thin, tall, spiky, shiny and tough-looking, the Curator gazed at the nodding wand-snake through glittering crystal eyes. And as the vast flat head of the thing struck, so did the Curator. Out from his eyes shot pencil-slim beams of blue light which met the wand-snake's head in mid-thrust. The snake instantly stopped, as if time it-self had frozen for the semi-sentient thing, and began to glow with the same blue fire of the Curator's beams. The blue light raced down the body of the snake in a moment into the heart of a gray moonbeast city, to the top of a squat windowless tower—which also began to glow with that same blue energy.

Only then, when the source of the great wand-snake was discovered, did the fire behind Curator's eyes blink out. So did the wand-snake's head, its body, the squat building in the moonbeast city, and doubtless a large coven of moonbeast wizards!

Nor was Curator satisfied. If one such magical device could threaten his Museum—threaten to turn all of its aeon-gathered contents to worthless stone—then so could the oth-ers. He leaned over the causeway's wall, gazed down at the scene of battle below, and proceeded to destroy wand-snakes wherever he found them until none at all remained! Then, with the danger disposed of, he clanked back across the causeway and into his Museum.

For a long time now the ray-projector gunners had been bombarding Mnomquah where he still reared, half-in, half-out of his pit. As if contemptuous of them, more interested in the battle than annoyed by the puerile attempts of mere dreamlings, the moon-God had seemed to ignore them. By use of that power with which he had drawn the very moon down out of dreamland's sky, Mnomquah had surrounded himself with energies which all the ferocity of the sun itself could not penetrate. Even Curator's weapons would be use-less here.

Now it must seem to Mnomquah that he was invincible. Surely these invaders from the dreamlands had tried to de-stroy him—had employed their weapons to that end to such an extent that even now their batteries were failing and their beams losing their strength—and still he prevailed. They had done their worst, and he was unharmed. Very well, his moonbeast wizards and priests had failed him, and so he him-self must now take a greater hand in the battle. It would be a very simple matter, and after that he would make his mighty leap from moon to dreamland's Sarkomand.

As the last few beams from the now useless ray-projectors petered out, so Mnomquah reared up gigantically from his crater and reached a webbed forepaw into the sky. Fifty yards across, that paw, a great club which would cut a swath of destruction through a fleet of ships like a man swatting flies frozen in flight—and yet that swath was never cut!

Limnar Dass where he leaned out of an embrasure in Serannian's ramparts saw it all. His glass trembled in his hands at what he first took to be sheer lunacy as the Royal Yacht of Randolph Carter sailed down out of the moon's sky directly into Mnomquah's range, confronting that horror as a midge might confront some monstrous chameleon. And though Mnomquah could not truly "see" the King's ship, still he sensed its presence and paused before the sheer insolence of it.

Or perhaps that was not why he paused—perhaps he sensed something else . . .

For in the prow of the Royal Yacht stood Ilek-Vad's King in the red robes of a warrior, and his arms were raised on high as in invocation to Gods or Powers mightier by far than the moon-God. Still watching, hypnotized by the scene below, Limnar's flesh tingled and his hair began to stand on end as utterly alien energies awakened, took flight, and filled the air with their rushing. It was as if huge dark wings beat invisibly in the sky, as if they were shutting out all light, as if this might be the beginning of the End of the Universe.

Darkness descended like a candle snuffed out in a deep cave, until only Mnomquah and the Royal Yacht—aye, and the regal figure of Randolph Carter—were clearly visible in an otherwise universal gloom. And a SILENCE fell over the entire tableau like no silence before or since. Or perhaps there had once been just such a silence, in that far forgotten age when last this selfsame seal was set over the prisons of the Great Old Ones!

A seal, yes, in the form of awesome words of power which

even now Randolph Carter uttered, and which echoed up out of the silence like the booming of some great and alien gong. What those words meant no man would ever know, not even the King himself. Sufficient that he voiced them—and that Mnomquah recognized and was powerless before them!

For as the last WORD was spoken the monster's jaws snapped open in a vast rictus, his yellow tongue lolled out and writhed about the moon pit's rim, the pulsing beneath his membrane-covered sockets became a violent throbbing—as if his very brains were about to burst out—and he gave one huge and terrible cry before sliding backward into his pit and disappearing from view in a blinding blaze of light which sprang up on the instant all around his crater burrow.

And when next anyone dared look, all that remained of the moon pit was a vast flat expanse of bubbling, fuming lava . . .

The Survivors

It was a time of joy and celebration for some, and of sadness for a great many. So many proud ships were gone forever, their crews with them, and so many dear friends would never again raise their cups together in dreamland's wharfside taverns or sail the wide aerial oceans of her skies. Amongst those who would mourn most were Limnar Dass and Gytherik Imniss.

But first there had been the elation, the exhilaration of victory, of knowing that the battle was won, the enemy vanquished, the horror averted; and the fleets had gone down to sweep low over the moonscape, picking up survivors from wrecked ships and firing their more conventional weapons in broadsides upon the already devastated moonbeast cities. Survivors on the surface were few, for by far the vast majority of vessels had been destroyed by wand-snakes. There were some, however—a handful, from Limnar's flotilla—shot down more or less conventionally and hiding until the rescue ships came along.

Of the latter group: Sniffer and Biffer, Gytherik's last surviving gaunts, had once more proved themselves invaluable in tracking them down, and but for that fine pair of beasts many an injured or unconscious man would have been left behind to rot or fall prey to the moon's menaces. Gytherik had sent the gaunts down from Serannian, and tired as they were still they worked ceaselessly at the task he had given them until it was fairly reasoned that all survivors had been picked up. Even then, when Carter's and Kuranes' ships were called back into formation about the sky-island, still the gaunts searched on in a sort of frantic dismay. They had already discovered and rescued Ula and Una from where they had lain unconscious at the foot of the temple hill, and now they sought bigger game.

In fact they were after Hero and Eldin, which was the one task in which they were doomed to failure before ever they began. In the end they came to the now riven door in the hillside, from which there sporadically issued great black clouds of smoke and deep bass rumblings, and beyond which they were unable to proceed. And even as they pondered at that door in their strange gaunt fashion, so the entire hill settled down upon itself and diminished a little in height, belching fire and a vile-smelling steam which signalled an end to whichever moonbeast wizardries it had contained. So that in the end, defeated in the one goal they had set themselves above all others, the gaunts had only sufficient strength to carry their own weary bodies to the deck of the very last ship of the fleet where it climbed into the sky.

Later, their heads hanging in more than mere exhaustion, they reported to Gytherik; and that was when the gauntmaster and Limnar Dass—ever hopeful against all hope, even to this last minute—knew that indeed their sorrow was upon them . . .

Some ninety minutes later, when Serannian and its escort fleets had already commenced to spiral up and across the sky on that ethereal Gulf Stream which washed between worlds, the moon gave a shudder and a lurch and began almost visibly to recede. Mnomquah had released his spell upon the satellite, which would now wander back to its previous orbit. Perhaps the moon-God had considered it unwise to remain in close proximity to a land whose dwellers could wreak so much havoc and doom his Great Plan to failure. This time

they had been satisfied simply to replace the seal of the Elder
Gods on his immemorial prison, but what if they should later
decide that this was not punishment enough?

And so the moon gradually drew back, and Serannian and
her victorious fleets sailed for home; and much later Limnar
Dass and Gytherik Imniss were called to Kuranes' great
gothic manor-house to tell their tale and in return learn all
that had transpired in the time since they left Ilek-Vad to set
sail for Sarkomand. King Carter was there and Kuranes of
course, and many other Lords and Admirals, Governors and
Councillors and dignitaries; and when the pair had told their
story, every one in the great hall rose as a man to applaud. By
this time Ula and Una were revived if not consoled, and between bouts of uncontrollable sobbing Ham Gidduf's twin
daughters told their own tale of adventure and terrible loss on
the surface of the moon and beneath the domed hill-temple of
the moonbeast wizards.

When they were done there was a silence for a full three
minutes before Kuranes and King Carter related their parts of
the story; and while all of this proceeded chroniclers were
perched everywhere with their quills and parchments, scrib-
bling busily in the clean clear glyphs of dream.

Now Limnar and Gytherik learned of Kuranes' decision to
refit his and King Carter's fleets with ray-projectors against
whichever disasters loomed, and of how this work was completed with dispatch. And now it was explained how the inordinately bad weather which had covered the dreamlands,
obscuring Mnomquah's gold-oriented "view", had not been
accidental. The good priests of the Temple of the Elder Ones
in Ulthar had uttered their droning prayers incessantly to the
kinder gods of dream, asking and receiving their blessing and
assistance in the matter of the unseasonal weather.

And still the moon had sailed closer, causing earthquakes,
volcanoes and wildly exaggerated erratic tides, and eventually
threatening to pull Serannian herself away from the dreamlands and into an orbit of her own. That was when Kuranes
was smitten with his great idea, and in King Carter's absence

he had taken it upon himself to request Ilek-Vad's fleet accompany his own upon a fantastic, unheard-of expedition: an attack directed against the very seat of the problem, the mad moon itself!

The sky-island was after all maneuverable to a degree (her horizontal vents were often used to move her from the path of great storms), and her mighty flotation engines were in concert more than capable of providing the required buoyancy and lift. Once in the Gulf Stream, the magnified pull of the moon itself would do the rest.

As to why Kuranes had brought his beloved aerial city to the moon: there were several reasons. The very sight of that great mass in any sky would be sufficient to panic the direst enemy, and of course her bays would resupply and provide safe harbor for the warships. But over and above all of this Serannian was to be a symbol to any who would seek to threaten the peace and security of the dreamlands, a sign that her peoples would stand as one against any such aggressor.

Thus his decision could not be utterly arbitrary, for too much and too many lives were at risk: the sky-island itself and every man, woman and child of its citizens. And yet when it had been put to the vote, no single voice was found raised in dissent. And so Serannian had come to the moon, bringing dreamland's fleets with her, the results of which have been told.

And on the day prior to the commencement of that venture, then had Randolph Carter returned to the dreamlands from his Great Sleep and awakened in his palace in Ilek-Vad. He had sought for his friend Etienne-Laurent de Marigny in undreamed-of places, and had failed to find him. But he had found Elysia, the place of the Elder Gods themselves, and they had looked favorably upon his quest and had given him the great seal, those words of power which would return Mnomquah to the black lake at moon's core. So the King had sailed his Royal Yacht to Serannian in time to join the expedition, and thus the thing was done and finished with—with one exception. At his earliest opportunity Randolph Carter must sail to Sarkomand and set the seal of the Elder Gods over Oorn in her pit, and then at last the dreamlands might rest easy.

While the meeting in the manor-house was in progress, outside in the courtyard Kuranes' personal handpicked pike-men stood guard over Zura of Zura and Lathi of Thalarion. When all other business was attended to, then those fearsome females were brought in to hear Carter's and Kuranes' considered judgment on their crimes. Zura came first—alone, proud and haughty, dark and utterly alluring—and Lathi followed on behind, carried in her litter by eight hugely-muscled but otherwise vacant termen. There their sins were enumerated, and King Carter demanded to know their plea. Were they guilty or innocent of the charges brought against them?

"Guilt?" Lathi answered first. "My guilt is that of the hive-mother, who desires only that her children go forth and multiply and build their hives over all the land."

As for Zura, her plea was this:

"I am Zura, Princess of Death, and I do what my fate decrees. Without life there would be no death, and without death who would strive in life? Just as you must do your duties, O King, be sure that I must do mine."

"Such answers will not absolve you," the King told them then, "for you took sides with our enemies to destroy all the lands of Earth's dreams, above which no mortal sin could ever take precedence. You *are* abominations—!" And here he paused to seat himself once more beside Kuranes, for he had risen in momentary anger; and when finally he continued it was with a demeanour more fitting his high station.

"I have been informed, however, that in the end you repented and sided with the dreamlands, also that you fought bravely and without reckoning the cost. Very well, let us know pass sentence upon you. You are to be banished from the sane lands of dream forever, back to your own places of nightmare. And woe betide you if ever again you set foot outside those places, for then I shall see to it personally that you pay the ultimate penalty. There are places in the dreams of other worlds whose vileness even you could not imagine—to which I will gladly banish you if you break my ordinances! So be it ..."

Later still, after the return of Serannian to her customary place amongst rose-tipped cloudbanks in that ethereal ocean formed of the west wind's flowing into the sky, Limnar and Gytherik were on hand to say a final farewell to their old enemies. Lathi answered not at all, but merely sailed away with her termen in the tatty but still airworthy *Chyrsalis*. Zura, on the other hand, promised the two safe conduct if ever the winds of fate should once more blow them in the direction of the Charnel Gardens. And as she boarded that galley which would return her to Zura the land, so the pair saw in her eyes something which they had never thought to see there. A flood of glistening tears!

"Why do you cry?" Gytherik asked in amazement.

"For Hero and Eldin," she tearfully replied as the galley drew away from Serannian's vertiginous wharves. "For that pair of fool questers, so horribly dead and lost forever on the moon."

"You shed tears for them?" Limnar shook his head in disbelief. "Because they died?"

"Because they chose to do it on the moon, fool!" she answered with an angry toss of her head. "If they had done it here—*then they would soon be with me in the Charnel Gardens!*"

And leaving them speechless she sailed away.

Moontree

It had been a time of terror for Eeth in her half-sleep, a time of doubt and fear for her own future, that of her sisters and of the entire moonmoth race. For shortly after she had telepathically guided the questers and their females to that deep cleft from which the girls had climbed on alone, there had been such rumblings and growlings from the heart of the domed hill that Eeth had believed the entire mound must soon cave in and bury her forever. Indeed, the tremors—particularly that great final tremor—had brought dust and stalactites and all down from the ceiling, so that Eeth had been sure that this was the end; after which had come the relief of a deep, deep peace and quiet.

And some time later, with the splitting of her cocoon sheath, Eeth had emerged from her metamorphosis a moonmoth maid of exceeding beauty. It was the time, too, for the hatching of her sisters, whose protective shells had remained miraculously preserved through all of the tremors and quakes, and five fine grubs they proved to be. When all of them had broken free of their shells, then Eeth led them in the time-honored tradition of the moonmoth first-born, through the mazy subterranean ways of the hill and up to the surface, and from there the mushroom forest where they feasted and grew fat.

It was as she flitted on veined translucent wings at the foot of that final shaft which led to the surface, urging the crawl-

ing brood on, that she saw the gray stone statues of Hero and
Eldin and remembered them. They had been so full of life,
these two, and now . . .

But of course there was nothing Eeth could do, it was not
her problem. Indeed there was no problem, for they were lifeless now as the rock from which they seemed carved, and so
there could be no hope of restitution. But later, when the caterpillar brood was done with feasting and went down again
into the cave to fashion their cocoons, then Eeth alighted to
approach the petrified questers more closely and press an
elfin ear to the still chest of the once-handsome younger one.
But now, there was nothing there, no sign of—

—A heartbeat?

And after long minutes—another!

And now in the stony minds of the pair Eeth discerned the
feeblest mental stirring, thoughts that formed so slowly they
never quite managed to convey any message. The magic of
the moonbeasts had not been exerted to its full, so that not
even now were the questers fully transformed. They yet
lived—if such could be called life—but what could Eeth do
about it?

Disturbed and unhappy, she left the hill and went in search
of her life-mate, finding Aarl, a magnificent moonmoth youth
not long out of his cocoon, just beyond the moon's rim. And
as they idled the time of their courtship away in flights of
fancy across the canyons of the moon, often Eeth's thoughts
would turn to the questers where they lingered on in perpet-
ual horror and gloom at the bottom of their pit; until the time
came when Aarl read her thoughts and saw how they troubled
her.

"Of course," he said to her as they rested together in
the shade of a lofty crag, "we could always take them to the
moontree."

"The moontree?" Eeth repeated him. "Do you think he
could help?"

"He is a very old tree," said Aarl, "and very wise. Also,

he has great magic! Even the moonbeasts leave him in peace."

"What king of magic?" she wanted to know.

Aarl gave the equivalent of a mental shrug. *"My grandfather was a great friend of his. I can only tell you what he told me, that the moontree is a magic tree."*

"And you will help me take the dreamlings to him?"

Aarl was growing impatient with her. *"Of course! In fact, we'll do it now, if it will ease your mind. But I must protest that this is a strange sort of courtship, being bothered by matters such as these. Still, they did save your life, and so made mine worth living. This much we owe them."*

With that the two flew to the now silent domed hill beside the great lava lake, which still bubbled and vented steam in many places, entered into the half-hidden crevice in the hillside and fluttered down to the bottom of that shaft where the questers stood in stony silence, apparently lifeless. Not without a great deal of difficulty they lifted them, one at a time, out of their would-be tomb and over the moon's rim to the place of the moontree.

This was a journey of several sleeps' duration, of many halts and a great many hours of labored flight; but it was also Aarl's chance to show off his splendid moonmoth physique and great strength to Eeth, and so he grumbled very little. And sharing the burden and growing close in their task, so eventually they delivered the questers to the moontree and propped them upright between his great roots, which stuck up like grotesque hands and feet from the powdery pumice ground.

Now the moontree was, as Aarl had stated, very old and very wise, and there was indeed a great magic in him. Not a magic such as moonbeast wizards might devise or employ, but one born of his very ancientness and wisdom—and of his lineage. For amongst his ancestors were some of the greatest and strangest trees ever known in this or any other universe. Gnarled he was and squat, and gray as the crumbly soil in which he grew; with thoughts languid and slow, as befits the very old, and a great taproot many times his own length which quietly and unceasingly drew upon the moon's less loathsome juices. Gourds hung from his leafless branches, from which certain favored moonmoths might sip but which they must never steal, and his bark contained a poison fatal to all flesh except that of the gentle moonmoths.

He did not question the positioning of the petrified questers among his roots, nor even cause a twig to tremble in acknowledgment, but merely bade his visitors perch a while and talk of this and that and sip of his gourds; which offer, because they were tired and hungry, they gladly accepted. And so they chatted and kept company until all three dozed off. And because they knew he was a magic tree, Eeth and Aarl felt perfectly safe so to sleep amongst his gnarly branches . . .

Later, upon wakening, the moontree discovered his guests flown and remembered the stony figures between his roots. For a long time he simply pondered upon them and wondered who they had been. And, since the moonmoth pair had omitted to tell him, he wondered why he had been gifted such strange remnants in the first place. Tracing their contours with fibrous feeler roots, he asked them: *"What are you called?"* and translated their ponderously slow mental answers to read their names.

Now he pushed them down into soil at his feet and covered them with rootlets, trying his best to feel out something of their natures; and because he discovered them to be dreamlings and not of the moon, he sent a thought winging through the void to the heart of an enchanted wood in the Land of Earth's dreams, to inquire of a relative there:

"Do you know anything of the dreamlings David Hero and Eldin the Wanderer?" And while he waited for an answer he asked the same question of a Great Tree in Thalarion's hinterland, and of another which grew in the garden of one of dreamland's mightiest and gentlest wizards; and between times he developed feeder rootlets with which to break down the stony stuff of the questers into manageable nutrients,

which he then drank up into his gnarly trunk and branches until nothing at all was left of them. And in so doing he learned their innermost secrets, the very essence of their beings, and so fully discovered them.

Then the answers to his questions came winging back to his across the void, and in his slow methodical way he took note of the many legends engendered of these two. The Great Tree in Thalarion's hinterland had known them personally and loved them dearly; indeed, they had flown on his life-leaf to where it had taken root and was now a Great Tree in its own right in a certain wizard's extensive gardens. And the moontree in the enchanted wood had inquired of the wood's small brown zoogs, who knew tidbits of almost everything, and they too had had many favorable tales to tell of the questers.

And all in all it was just as the moon's most ancient and wise tree had expected: the dreamlings had been good men whose loss could not be borne by any sane or ordered dreamland. The cosmos may be blind and impersonal, but in cases such as this it must be made to see that certain laws are flexible and certain alterations imperative.

And if a tree can nod and smile, then, as the moontree made his very wisest decision, it may safely be supposed that he smiled and nodded . . .

Epilogue

There are places on the banks of the Skai where it flows down from Ulthar to Dylath-Leen, which are oases in an otherwise veritable desert. Birdsong is sweet there, and the water runs deep, cool and quiet. When travelers rest in these places, they sleep deeply and dream wonderful dreams within dreams; so that all such places have acquired something of reputations and are sacred. No towns or villages are built there; no rude dwellings spoil Nature's handiwork; only the songs of birds and crickets and the trickling of gentle waters break an ancient silence.

One night some months after the menace of the mad moon had been met and crushed, when the moon sailed in her old orbit, full and round and smiling as of old, a singularly strange thing came to pass. Down from the now tenuous aerial Gulf Stream dropped a pair of large, pitted seeds which, when they encountered the denser atmosphere of dreams, put out vanes that brought them spinning down like the airborne seeds of any simple plant or tree. Except that they were not.

They fell gently down through the foliage of just such a haven as previously mentioned, upon fertile ground by the edge of the Skai itself. There the next day, a pair of greeny-gray shoots were seen to grope upward toward the light; and as spring became summer so the shoots became saplings. Growing faster than mundane trees, and better nourished by far than any moontree before them (for of course, that is what they were), with one more turn of the seasons they reached maturity and put out gourds.

Now upon the strongest branch of each tree grew one gourd bigger than all the others put together, grotesquely huge and monstrously shaped; and these, when ripe, fell from the twin trees on the selfsame morning to shatter softly on the green banks of the Skai.

Within their sundered husks—unwrinkled, unmarked, naked and hairless as babes—the figures of two dreamlings lay curled in a sleep from which, with the fall, they slowly began to stir. Stretching out and drying in the warm sunlight, their at first shallow breathing grew stronger as their chests filled out with clean, sweet air. Then their fingernails hardened and hair grew on their heads and bodies; old scars appeared on skin which roughened momentarily, while worry lines etched themselves into faces full of character; yes, and there were laughter lines, too. A great many of the latter.

A fern, tickling the nose of the younger-looking of the two, caused him to start and sit up, shaking off sleep like an itchy blanket. Frowning, he stared at his nakedness, and that of his still slumbering companion. Then, pushing aside large fragments of gourd, he reached over to tug on the other's ear.

"Eh ... What? ... Who?" Eldin grumbled, coming yawningly awake. "Oh, it's you!"

"Eldin, old lad," said Hero, "I've just had the damndest ... dream." And again he stared all about him.

The Wanderer sat up, yawned again, said, "*You've* had the damndest dream? Well, let me tell you ..." And he too paused to stare all about.

Slowly they turned their heads to gaze wide-eyed and wonderingly at each other, and all about them the startled birds settled down again and returned to their singing.

BRIAN LUMLEY

☐	51199-9	DEMOGORGON	$4.99
☐	50832-7	THE HOUSE OF DOORS	$4.95
☐	52137-4	NECROSCOPE	$5.99
☐	52126-9	VAMPHYRI! Necroscope II	$4.95
☐	52127-7	THE SOURCE Necroscope III	$4.95
☐	50833-5	DEADSPEAK Necroscope IV	$4.95 Canada $5.95
☐	50835-1	DEADSPAWN	$4.99 Canada $5.99
☐	52032-7	PSYCHAMOK	$5.99
☐	52023-8	PSYCHOMECH	$5.99
☐	52030-0	PSYCHOSPHERE	$5.99

Buy them at your local bookstore or use this handy coupon:
Clip and mail this page with your order.

Publishers Book and Audio Mailing Service
P.O. Box 120159, Staten Island, NY 10312-0004

Please send me the book(s) I have checked above. I am enclosing $ _____
(Please add $1.25 for the first book, and $.25 for each additional book to cover postage and handling.
Send check or money order only—no CODs.)

Name _____

Address _____

City _____ State/Zip _____

Please allow six weeks for delivery. Prices subject to change without notice.

FANTASY BESTSELLERS
FROM TOR

☐	52261-3	BORDERLANDS *edited by Terri Windling & Lark Alan Arnold*	$4.99 Canada $5.99
☐	50943-9	THE DRAGON KNIGHT *Gordon R. Dickson*	$5.99 Canada $6.99
☐	51371-1	THE DRAGON REBORN *Robert Jordan*	$5.99 Canada $6.99
☐	52003-3	ELSEWHERE *Will Shetterly*	$3.99 Canada $4.99
☐	55409-4	THE GRAIL OF HEARTS *Susan Schwartz*	$4.99 Canada $5.99
☐	52114-5	JINX HIGH *Mercedes Lackey*	$4.99 Canada $5.99
☐	50896-3	MAIRELON THE MAGICIAN *Patricia C. Wrede*	$3.99 Canada $4.99
☐	50689-8	THE PHOENIX GUARDS *Steven Brust*	$4.99 Canada $5.99
☐	51373-8	THE SHADOW RISING *Robert Jordan (Coming in October '93)*	$5.99 Canada $6.99

SPINE-TINGLING
HORROR FROM TOR

☐	52061-0	BLOOD BROTHERS *Brian Lumley*	$5.99 Canada $6.99
☐	51970-1	BONEMAN *Lisa Cantrell*	$4.99 Canada $5.99
☐	51189-1	BRING ON THE NIGHT *Don & Jay Davis*	$4.99 Canada $5.99
☐	51512-9	CAFE PURGATORIUM *Dana Anderson, Charles de Lint & Ray Garton*	$3.99 Canada $4.99
☐	50552-2	THE HOWLING MAN *Charles Beaumont, edited by Roger Anker*	$4.99 Canada $5.99
☐	51638-9	THE INFLUENCE *Ramsey Campbell*	$4.50 Canada $5.50
☐	50591-3	LIZZIE BORDEN *Elizabeth Engstrom*	$4.99 Canada $5.99
☐	50294-9	THE PLACE *T.M. Wright*	$4.95 Canada $5.95
☐	50031-8	PSYCHO *Robert Bloch*	$3.95 Canada $4.95
☐	50300-7	SCARE TACTICS *John Farris*	$4.95 Canada $5.95
☐	51048-8	SEASON OF PASSAGE *Christopher Pike*	$4.50 Canada $5.50
☐	51303-7	SOMETHING STIRS *Charles Grant*	$4.99 Canada $5.99

Buy them at your local bookstore or use this handy coupon:
Clip and mail this page with your order.

Publishers Book and Audio Mailing Service
P.O. Box 120159, Staten Island, NY 10312-0004

Please send me the book(s) I have checked above. I am enclosing $ _____
(Please add $1.25 for the first book, and $.25 for each additional book to cover postage and handling.
Send check or money order only—no CODs.)

Name _____
Address _____
City _____ State/Zip _____
Please allow six weeks for delivery. Prices subject to change without notice.